THE FIXED STARS

THE FIXED STARS

Thirty-Seven Emblems for the Perilous Season

Brian Conn

FC2

TUSCALOOSA

The University of Alabama Press
Tuscaloosa, Alabama 35487-0380

Published by FC2, an imprint of the University of Alabama Press, with support provided by the Publications Unit of the Department of English at Illinois State University, and the School of Arts and Sciences, University of Houston–Victoria

Address all editorial inquiries to: Fiction Collective Two, University of Houston–Victoria, School of Arts and Sciences, Victoria, TX 77901-5731

⊗

The paper on which this book is printed meets the minimum requirements of American National Standard for Information Sciences—Permanence of Paper for Printed Library Materials, ANSI Z39.48–1984

Library of Congress Cataloging-in-Publication Data
Conn, Brian.
 The fixed stars : thirty-seven emblems for the perilous season / Brian Conn. — 1st ed.
     p. cm.
 ISBN-13: 978-1-57366-153-9 (pbk. : alk. paper)
 ISBN-13: 978-1-57366-816-3 (ebook)
 1. Plague—Fiction. 2. Social problems—Fiction. I. Title.
 PS3603.O5425F59 2010
 813'.6—dc22
                                        2009038689

Book Design: Quintus Havis and Tara Reeser
Cover Design: Lou Robinson
Typeface: Baskerville
Produced and printed in the United States of America

Contents

Long, long ago there lived an old queen who was a sorceress, and her daughter was the most beautiful maiden under the sun. The old woman, however, thought of nothing but how to lure people to their doom.

"The Six Servants"
Fairy Tales of the Brothers Grimm

CHAPTER 1

THE ROPEMAKER'S DAUGHTER

1.1 The Speech of the Old Man

I am a humble servant of people. In this world we work together. You are a woman of fierce intelligence and I can see that you have been thoroughly educated; I need hardly explain to you why we people can survive only together and never apart. There can be no more devouring of one another in those prisons which I shall forbear to name—you know the prisons of which I speak.

The race of people does not have it easy. There is not much luck for us. The race of people finds trouble where we ought to find trouble, for trouble purifies us: the philosopher reminds us that person is the animal that is purified by striving. But you distrust me, Molly, and not without reason; for have you not stumbled upon me sleeping beside this crossroads, with neither partner nor visible handiwork, with hair on my head and a velvet girdle round my body, and with the mien of one untutored in the love of people? And therefore perhaps you think that, disdaining the labors which civilization requires, I occupy myself instead with concealing my scalp under hair and my form under velvet. But discard the notion, Molly, even as we discard certain other notions which I shall forbear to mention; for enigmas of every description surround us, as fog surrounds the sea: even a head covered in hair may contemplate essential labors; even on the hearts of the garishly clad may be graven the image of darkness.

We people were born to strive, and there are none who strive more than I. Even when people lived in those deranged collectivities the name of which offends decency—even then they hardly strove more than I now strive. Just as the chemist compounds elixirs, just as the beekeeper nurtures bees, just as you weave these ropes which I see here in your wagon, so too do I strive on behalf of our civilization, with this difference: that my striving surpasses that of all others. For the charge laid on me brings me each day into the greatest imaginable peril.

You scoff and harden your heart against me—and rightly, Molly, rightly. "This old man," you say, "thinking himself what he no doubt calls an intellectual, will end by presenting to me a dream of those towers and homes of depraved design which for so many centuries held people bewitched"—I mean those rectilinear labyrinths of steel and despair which none would care to hear me describe, the towers and homes of late capitalism.

But I ask your pardon, Molly, for matters lie with me not precisely as you think. The dream that I will present to you is a different dream.

A group of travelers came near this road not long ago, as no doubt the carers for the land have told you: wise travelers from distant coasts, clad like myself in velvet, not because they cherished textiles but because they had traveled through a difficult region. And it was they who laid my charge upon me, on a hillock in the shape of a kidney near a region where the people suffer defects in their genome. We walk together in this world, Molly, and the civilization that binds us binds us not one atop the other, as we were bound when the idle throve; but it binds us side by side. Nevertheless do some of us by chance or blessing possess a peace more puissant and a love more loving than the peace and love of others, and the strength to stand against the oldest enemy of people. It is to me that such puissant peacefulness falls, and to me my ghastly task, the accomplishment of which, as you will presently hear, offends decency.

Know, then, Molly, that although you and I cherish between ourselves the things that people cherish, and rejoice in the love among people, there yet dwells in the land a monster who cherishes not those things, and whom it is my calling to bring to peace. I refer, Molly, to the vampire, or *wampyr*: that monster who, clinging to loathsome solitude, nourishes himself by means having to do with the genomes of people and with dreams of despair—means which strike at the very heart of our communities.

It is in the struggle against this monster that I find my calling. I see now that you have not been educated so thoroughly as I had thought, and that weakness tempts you to turn away from me and to think me an old braggart and a teller of tales. But I shall make it my duty to deliver you to peace. When I have completed my speech, at a time not far removed from now, then the two of us will be joined in a certain love, which, though it be not the ordinary love which joins people, will nevertheless accomplish the ends of love. Then, owing to the nature of my love, you will become aware of certain animalcules of the dark, and witness their acts and hear their voices; and even as my peculiar love together with all the other kinds of love form together the great spectrum of loves, so too does the manifest speech of our civilization, which is both like and unlike my speech, sound in harmony with the songs of the animalcules of the dark, which also is both like and unlike my speech, and make with it one utterance, the utterance of utterances, which is woven of the speeches of people and also of the songs of the animalcules of the dark.

To put the vampire to peace is no small work: we achieve it only by a terrible means. For darkness and solitude are his native elements, and the hanging rope which slays us people who live in community is to him as the sea is to the octopus, as the veld to the lion; and the means of bringing the vampire to peace is also the engine of delusion. I speak of a certain element, Molly, yellow and orange in color and rich in scent: that element which is the spirit of discord among people, and which was the fuel and fetish of an epoch which saw people bound not in love but in strangled networks of toxins and cravings: that element which makes man into meat, water into mist. Do you know the element of which I speak? I hope you will forgive my bringing up matters on which no friend of people will care to dwell; but what is required is precisely that the heart of the vampire be cast into that prickly and beguiling phenomenon with which the peaceful have no commerce.

You recoil strongly from me now, for to cultivate this element is a perversion. But I myself do not cultivate it; I wait, rather, for a certain season, that season which comes after spring, that season which dries the trees and brings the lightning, and makes of the forest an abomination; then I search out the vampire, and, coming upon him, cut out his heart and hurl it into the objectionable phenomenon from afar. Still you recoil, and I see that you hope I will leave you soon. For you suppose that, my duties being bound to a certain season, that season which comes before fall, I idle away the remaining seasons in low schemes, in accumulating commodities, in erecting structures. You dare! Let me assure you, friend of people, that I am no idler. Though we find ourselves now in the last days of spring, and the lightning not yet come, the matter of vampires requires my constant attention. For the vampire is not without cunning; our ways are transparent to him; when the season approaches during which that phenomenon which the peaceful abhor menaces the forest, he departs with his harem and household for other lands, where the people be fewer but the climate damper, as suits him. Therefore it is my duty to mark him with this chemical spray, which has been distilled and decanted using only the most universal technologies by the unambitious working in small groups. The advantages of this spray are fourfold—

1.2 Smoke

When Molly and her mother first arrived on that coast, they came to the bathhouse. There they met the matron, who wore a hairmold over her scalp the likes of which neither of them remembered having seen before. The bathhouse was neither large nor small, but was well placed among cool cedars, and overgrown with fragrant woodbine; and it overlooked a fertile valley, which many of the people called the finest valley in that half of the continent, although none could say which half of the continent that was. When Molly and her mother had put aside their things and taken the numbing drug, the matron looked them over. It was a fine spring day, and they went nude and unshod.

"Are you contagious?" the matron asked.

Molly looked at her mother and her mother looked at Molly.

"It is a simple examination, then," the matron said. She ushered them into a narrow wooden room lit from high above by six skylights. "Wait here," she said, and left.

Molly and her mother had just time to turn to each other and begin to ask what there was about them that had led the matron to think them contagious, when there burst in upon them a very small man wearing tight boots. This man lost no time, but, saying, "Hi, hi, hi," sprang onto the bench which ran the length of the room and began to examine them, first Molly, then her mother. In each case, his procedure was this: he first chafed vigorously his patient's face and all her limbs, and, producing a miniature color chart from a pocket in his boots, held it against her breast in order to measure the flush his chafing had raised; he entered this measurement on a yellow index card. He next addressed her heart and liver, listening to the first with bare ear to bare breast, not for long, and palpating the second with moist fingertips. Finally, he took down a small blowgun from a hook on the wall, discharged a cloud of choking powder in her face, and demanded to inspect her buttocks.

When he had satisfied himself, he sprang down from the bench and left the room, saying, "Aha, aha."

This procedure and protocol dismayed the two women. They opened their mouths, each about to suggest that they quit the bathhouse and resume the road; but before they could utter a word, the matron returned.

"It is only a precaution," she said, "because we once had a contagion here." With that she brought them into an antechamber scented with anise and citrus, in which a great number of people lay in hammocks, sipping cold infusions and recovering from their baths; and from that room she brought them into a long hallway. The far end of this hallway opened onto the cedar forest and the mild air of the afternoon, and along the two sides ran cedar doors, each decorated with a number carved of darker wood and all but the last standing open. From the bath-chambers within came the sounds of splashing and laughter and the mild scents of pine-soap. The matron led Molly and her mother the length of the hallway, counting all the while on her fingers. The planks of the floor cooled their bare feet, and the breezes of the bathhouse cooled their scalps, and as they passed the open doorways the people within left off looking at each other and peered instead at them, but continued their laughing without interruption. When they reached the end, the matron hesitated, saying: "I thought there had been more baths." They followed her back the length of the hallway, and back again a third time, she in growing confusion, and Molly's mother started to say, "If there is no room—" but the matron interrupted: "No! There is number twelve." She composed herself carefully. "Number twelve is perfectly pleasant."

At that moment a man, hairy all over like a bear, happened to enter from the end of the hallway that was open to the cedar forest, and to overhear what the matron said. His eyes grew wide, and he cast a darting glance at Molly and her mother; then he charged into a nearby bath-chamber—

it was number eleven—and they heard the sound of voices raised, and then splashing, and before they could contemplate the meaning of anything a group of four emerged and hurried past them.

"You might use number eleven," said the matron, adjusting her hairmold, "but it is not clean. And number twelve is perfectly pleasant." And, grasping in her horny grip an elbow of each of them, she brought them to number twelve.

It was a cozy chamber, higher than it was deep, and filled through a window on the opposite wall with light and birdsong and the dry smell of the forest. The tub was built into the floor and lined in pink tile; it occupied half the room. There was a chair and a scale. The matron preceded Molly and her mother, and stood in the doorway as though listening; then, turning with a sniff, "I will bring towels," she said, "because there are none."

Molly and her mother, left alone, selected fragrances from their bathkits. "What a strange woman," Molly's mother said. At the sound of her voice, cries of panic erupted to the right and to the left. A shattering crash and a cracking thump sounded nearby; somebody cursed. "That will be numbers ten and fourteen," Molly's mother said. "It may be they're not used to strangers." And, indeed, it was not long before a floor creaked on the left, and another on the right, and the slap of running feet faded up the hallway.

"I hope we will be welcome here," Molly said.

They opened the rubber seal and admitted the icy water of the creek into the tub. They had lost time in the examination room, and the numbing drug would soon run its course; they leaped into the bath and began scrubbing.

But Molly, whose senses were younger and sharper, soon

remarked on a peculiar quality of the water: "It is distinctly pink." The hue vanished against the tile of the bath below, but when she scooped up a soapdish-full and scrutinized the water against the white, there was no mistaking it: the water in that bath was pink and getting pinker. "Earth in the pipes," said Molly's mother; "it is a rustic place." "But it swirls," said Molly, "like smoke."

Molly's mother froze at the word. "We do not discuss—" she began. But Molly said, "I don't like it, Mother." Around them swirled eddies of pink, now of red, swirling indeed like smoke—precisely like smoke. "An animal has been killed upstream," said Molly, scrambling from the bath; "a large animal, or else—" "But perhaps it is something they do here," her mother said, "adding a red substance to the water; suppose it is a perfume or some other luxury. I ought to have brought you traveling earlier, Molly, and taught you to trust more in people; for to trust in people is the most important lesson a young woman can learn."

Nevertheless, Molly's mother stepped out of the water, which now ran crimson; and when she stood beside Molly she turned to look where Molly was looking, which was in the direction of the bath, and this is what the two women saw: black clouds, unseasonable, had passed over the sun; the sky was dark; the room drew its light from the air above the tub, which shone all through itself with a glassy texture and a pale blue light, and in which, in a gathering and refracting of this light as though it were passing through a lens of semi-fluid shape, the features of a man's face now began to form.

And who knows what might have come next? Except the floor creaked behind them then, and someone screamed: it was the matron, holding in her arms a thick stack of towels.

She hurled these without delay in the direction of the tub and the uncanny light, took hold of Molly and her mother, and, showing herself stronger than she looked, propelled them before her up the hallway.

They came into the antechamber and there was further screaming; everybody left the bathhouse.

The commotion lasted well into the evening. The matron became ill and was taken away. The man like a bear and his group of four gave new towels to Molly and her mother. "That old man who died of the cold," the man like a bear said—"it was not long ago." "I shall never recover," Molly's mother said, and told the story again.

The man like a bear said, "Certainly there was something detestable between that old man and the matron. She was only a girl then. She likely told you of a contagion, but there was never a contagion: that old man died of cold, the cold of the water and the cold of the matron. Now he is bound here," the man like a bear shook his beard sagely: "bound like a dweller in one of those long-ago concrete prisons of which it is impolite to speak."

1.3 Andrea and Thomas

In the wagon they found one hundred and forty lengths of rope.

"We will bring them to the crèche," said Thomas.

"We cannot carry them to the crèche," said Andrea. "They are too many."

"Someone else who finds them might become a victim of greed," said Thomas. "Look you on the smoothness and power of these ropes. It is better if we take them to the crèche. They are the work of a person and are to be respected. Together we shall find the strength to bring them, for together we are strong; and though we are not yet grown, yet already we bear responsibility for the community. I would like it if you held my hand."

They held hands and sat on the back of the wagon. Andrea had bathed the night before, and felt fresh; Thomas had bathed the night before that, and felt shame. They took out some dried fruit.

"We might drive the wagon to the crèche," said Andrea, "if that would not be making too much of ourselves."

"But where is the ox?" said Thomas.

"We might borrow an ox from the nurturers of oxen, downroad of the cairn," said Andrea. She jumped down from the wagon. Many hours remained in the day, and as far as the eye could see the road was empty. Some roads are like ribbons but this road was like rope.

"It is as you say," said Thomas.

"Andrea," said Thomas, "I would like it if you helped me with something." In his voice she heard the sound of strangulation.

"Thomas!" she said.

"I would like it if you tied me with this rope," said Thomas, "because that is what I desire."

1.4 Contagion

It was the year mosaicists became preoccupied with roads; I remember it because I remember that day, browsing the new work in the cedar arcade that runs the shady side of the proscenium meadow, and looking up from the new mosaics and seeing the woman who nurtured spiders approaching me, far off yet, from the upmountain forest. The year's collection was just beginning—the first of those road mosaics were out, plus work in spidersilks, breedwork of exotic cyclobacteria in several media, and a few masks of wood and rubbers, but not yet much metalwork—and so it must have been early in the season, coming up on the John's Day festival. It was bright out, I remember: I can see the mosaics in the bright.

The woman who nurtured spiders was flushed, I saw as she drew near, and even as she spoke to me her attention was fixed elsewhere. "Four taken sick near the apiary," she said. "Contagion."

Let me say at once: it was never shown to be contagious.

"No fever," she added. "Not yet."

I felt suddenly distant from her, as though she were speaking from the other end of the arcade and I listening through an ear-tube.

We don't often see disease; outside of that time, that contagion as they called it—as we called it—I've never known a case. Our community has more chemists than is usual, I think; they say a quality of the mountain brings them; and so the local probiotic wards excel even the common wards that the traveling chemists loose on the roads every half-moon, and the common wards are fearsome enough: I once watched them at work under the lens, and didn't feel right in my skin afterwards. And they work so well, they and the local wards, and have worked for so long, that we forget about them, and trust them, as we trust all the invisible world. But we no longer have immunity in our bodies, the way people did before community probiotics; so that if the wards do happen to fail, an incursion of influenza will reduce any of us to wrack. I've never seen it, but others have, others who came here from communities that no longer exist. Fever isn't anything to reason about. The blood...it heats up, frankly.

It wasn't influenza that time; it was unknown. The first sign was a blackening of the tongue, not painful; but soon thereafter the whole mouth swelled and stiffened, so that, pain or no, the victim could not eat. That struck four of us on the first day. Two were women who made surgical implements, and they self-quarantined in the structure where we make surgical implements, near the apiary; and the other two, having initially quarantined themselves behind stones, but being also at that time near the apiary, and discovering by shouts and go-betweens the situation of the first two, soon joined them there. The practitioner of medicine came, concluded nothing, instructed them how to put feeding tubes down their throats, and left them with canisters of nutritive liquids; and, she having been near them and the whole thing being a mystery, at once quarantined herself in a silk-curing shed.

The woman who nurtured spiders related all of this and then hurried away. There was no one else in the proscenium meadow. I was alone again with the yellow waving grasses, and it was easy to imagine that she had never come.

I don't mean to suggest that there was any connection between the contagion and the road mosaics. Only that I remember looking at all that pebble and tile and junk, and seeing the road in it, and feeling as though she had never come, as though I'd imagined her—I remember other times too, standing alone in the arcade on a bright empty day and thinking I'd imagined everything, I don't know how many times I remember it—but I remember that time that it was she in particular I felt I'd imagined, she and her contagion.

The first of the road mosaics could have been any white object with green and black objects around it: it could have been a shark among kelp, a mist in the forest. Somehow it was known in the community that it represented the road. No one knew who made it. It wasn't beautiful unless you knew it was the road, nor, we supposed, was it intended to be; but another mosaicist took such offense at it that she completed a series of very precise and realistic landscapes, or rather roadscapes, nothing like the first, in very small stone of the kind that comes from certain caverns. There was a menace in that series, growing as it went on, until soon she was rendering not only the road but the crossroads; and on that day, the first day of the contagion, she happened to have hung the last of the series, the crossroads with the gibbet: the gibbet just where the gibbet used to be, although there hasn't been a gibbet there since I can remember—that is to say, since I can remember remembering—not a trace of it.

I felt my tongue in my mouth. Was it swelling? Was it blackening? I wouldn't have said then that I was afraid; but the woman who nurtured spiders had planted a notion underneath the road-images on my mind's surface. We discussed it afterwards: the same notion got planted in all of us, we all felt our tongues in our mouths once we had heard the news; we couldn't help it. It's a silly thing to think of now, but we forget our tongues like we forget the probiotic wards, or the dead: forget them until one day we think there might be something about them—something about our eyes, our kidneys, our hands—and then it all comes in on us.

The next day there was another case of swollen tongue, also near the apiary, self-quarantined with the others. Meanwhile their pupils had dilated. The structure where we made surgical implements had shutters over unglazed windows, and even a curtain over the entrance, all to save the eyes of the Kloss-Ring spiders that were sometimes required there. The five quarantines had closed everything up, not for the spiders but for themselves, because the light hurt their eyes. Anyway we supposed that was the reason, because those who had glimpsed them had reported the dilated pupils, but of course they never told us themselves: the only sound they made was a kind of howling in the back of the throat. It's a sound made with minimal engagement of the tongue. Not the only such sound, and not a nice one, but it's the sound they did make, particularly when we let the light on them. We took turns bringing them canisters of nutritive liquid, and anything else we imagined they'd need. We would tap on the shutter, and when they howled we would set what we'd brought on the windowsill, and go away.

The chemists worked as much as people can work, and understood nothing; the news, from moment to moment, was *no fever.*

The wind blew downriver for a time, too strong for the messenger spores to travel against it, and so we hadn't any news from up. Finally the long-distance runner came back from delivering a parcel that way: no contagion, she said, farther up where the river still ran cold; but at the next community up the valley they had set a stake where the road turns off, and a green flag.

It was the nearest community to us, not actually very near, but the nearest. Our policy is and has been to trust our neighbors faithfully, but wisdom takes precautions: we had our five quarantines, and the practitioner of medicine showed no symptoms, and so for us the matter seemed to rest; and no one would break the green flag, the contagion flag; no one would enter that community while it flew, no one would run from it.

No one would run. But if anyone did run, they would run to us.

We posted a watch, just our side of the two cedars at the foot of the mountain. Pairs of us, changing six times in a day and a night; everybody took a turn.

I took turns myself, and don't remember them any longer, or rather can't distinguish them from other times I waited or watched in other places, or imagined waiting and watching; but, though I can't recall the images, I mean the specific images of those watches, I remember that a change came over us—over all of us, I think—or else over the road itself. It was a long straight stretch there, lined either side with river-stone. I had seen the prospect more times than I could think. But as I sat watch, I found myself looking at it, for the first time I suppose, without moving—it seems a small thing, to look awhile without moving—and I was reminded that a thing we see while we're moving looks different from a thing we see while we're still. One day I became aware that I was seeing a new road there, or a newness in the road, and had been seeing it for some time: something in the slope of the mountain, or the number of the dandelions, some new strangeness and bigness of a place I thought I'd known.

It wasn't only me: as the watches went on, this different

road, the road-from-stillness, began turning up in the mosaics. And although I'm calling it as a single thing with a single name, *the road,* I think it's wrong to do so. It gets harder, as I go on, to say what's right and not what's wrong. In fact no two mosaicists could agree what the new road looked like. Perhaps indeed it was many new roads, a different one for each of us. And there may be another thing here that I've said wrong, though it's hard to tell: because already there had been variation in the mosaics, from the beginning there had been, but it was a variation, if you understand me, in depiction, not in vision; that is, you could see the same road behind all those early mosaics, the same road, perhaps, in different lights; whereas now you saw as many different roads as there were mosaics—or more, even, because sometimes you saw many roads in a single mosaic, one above the other, one behind the other, or all somehow twined together—until it became frightening to look at them. I made up my mind not to go to the proscenium arcade any longer, because it gave me vertigo; but I went there anyway.

I called it the new road just now, and that was wrong too—it had been there all along, only you only saw it when you stood still.

I'm not a mosaicist myself, but a musician.

It happened only once during all that time that a person did try to pass into the community, I mean a person beyond the usual bearers of crates and so on. It was a woman. I happened to be on watch, a partner and I. We stopped her, or tried to, and whether it was right to do so we never learned; nothing came of it in the end, and now most everyone has forgotten. My partner has forgotten too: he never touched her.

It was evening, about the time one first begins not to see as far, and thinks for the first time of night. I'd settled down in a patch of fern. The air was full of frogsong, cricketsong, lilac. Soon my partner came down from the trail; it was the man who bred pleasing odors, and I asked him the news.

"Not yet," he said, meaning fever. "And for my part I say let them come out from that structure and take their places side by side with us."

It was what many people were saying then, though nobody ever developed it much farther; all it meant, all any of our talk meant, was only that maybe the thing wasn't contagious. And maybe, we thought already, it wasn't: true, all the cases were localized in the vicinity of the apiary, and that was like a contagion; but it could just as well have been some vulnerability in the air there, something in the ground, something nearby that bit them in their sleep. As for the people themselves, and whether in fact we would have liked them side by side with us, with their swollen black tongues and their swollen black pupils, I never heard that said; I never heard anybody wish for five black tongues to lie silently inside silent mouths side by side with us. Although perhaps that was precisely what my partner would have said; perhaps on that occasion he might have gone on. But we put it all aside at that moment, and turned to listen: we had heard footsteps on the road.

A voluptuous woman appeared, with a shape on top of her head; I couldn't make it out in the twilight. I asked her where she came from.

"The next thing I knew," she said, "I was in the river."

The man who bred pleasing odors donned his mask and gloves.

BRIAN CONN

"It's only that we've had contagion here," I said, "and they've had the same nearby. Have you seen any such thing? It will please you to have my partner inspect your mouth."

She swayed, and I stepped forward and caught her. She was wet, as though she had, as she said, been in the river. The thing on her head wavered and I worried that it would fall, and perhaps break. When it didn't, I concluded that it was a kind of hair. She sagged against my chest, and I lowered her to the ground.

She was nude and barefoot. She carried nothing. The man who bred pleasing odors inspected her tongue and pupils, which he found normal.

"We ought to quarantine her," I said, "and myself besides, for she fell on me when I was yet unmasked. Let me carry her to the canopy of the angelophytist"—which was the nearest to the road—"and let the angelophytist summon others to discuss the matter. I think you need not quarantine yourself; but you might walk ahead and warn the angelophytist of our approach."

But he protested, rightly I thought, that one of us must remain to watch; and so, after donning my own mask, I picked the woman up and carried her by myself. We were drawing near the angelophytist's canopy, so near that I began to see the dim shifting glow of the messenger spores in the dark, when she stirred in my arms. I set her on her feet; she swayed and seemed not to see me. Something in the scene made me uneasy. I couldn't guess what troubled her, even what manner of thing, a weakness in the flesh or a weakness in the mind. Her body had been hot, and by touching hers mine had become hot too. She crouched suddenly, or rather sank; and when I knelt to help her she flung a spray of dirt in my eyes. By the time I cleared them she was gone.

I was wet from carrying her. The forest was quiet. The angelophytist came out from under her canopy, and I called out to her to organize a search for the woman, but to keep away from me: I would have to quarantine myself.

I did so in a mushroom-cellar. People came all that night to ask me, from the darkness above, about the woman who had thus come into our community, and thus, it seemed, left it; and as they asked, the scent of her moisture on my skin seemed to linger, through question after question, until I began to fear that all my answers—it had been dark, it had happened too quickly, I couldn't guess where she had gone—were falsehoods, that I had brought her with me somehow, and that she even now shared with me the dark of the cellar; until, running my hands over my skin and finding it dry, I realized I had only been smelling the damp of the mushrooms.

I lived out the season in quarantine. My tongue never swelled, and my pupils never dilated, except so far as pupils ordinarily dilate in the dark; but nonetheless I stayed there until the first cool day came, and the first rain. Nobody blamed me for what had happened; nobody had expected any such thing, not really. But I don't recall sleeping, all that airless season, except in the stolen moments just before dawn; and when I did sleep I dreamed of fever, a fever come into the community through the woman I'd let pass, and the whole community overtaken with it: the hives empty, the webs empty, the meadows overgrown with thorns, the fever spread to other communities, in every direction, and all the communities of people liquidated. Awakening alone, I looked out into the early morning gloom: from the cellar

I could see the tip of a cedar and a small trapezoidal patch of sky, filling as I watched with a kind of luminous transparency, as though with albumen, which as it brightened seemed to me not the birth of possibility, as the day ought to seem, but the maturing, yet again, of some organic poison.

The people who came, sometimes, to bring me fruit and honey and news—when had they last come? I asked myself. How long had it been? Days. Days since I'd heard any human sound. Fever. That small patch of sky—and, in my solitude, a small chance, a dwindling chance, I thought, of any person's face left to pass across that patch, my patch, out of all the sky.

Of course they did come finally, they always did, with the fruit and the honey. They looked red in the face. They wouldn't approach closer than the stunted pine that splits the stone, some distance from the cellar mouth, and so all I ever saw of them was head and shoulders, and those usually in the pine's shadow. They maintained a blank expression, it seemed to me, and moved unsteadily on their feet; and as the season aged they began to curtail their visits, and the news, and to back away out of my sky-patch before I could ask more. I couldn't tell why. When I asked afterwards they all said it hadn't been so; but I remember it so, and I remember, all that season, knowing the community only in short fragments, disconnected, confused, contradictory, like histories of forgotten times.

They never found the woman—or rather, nobody remembers finding the woman. Of course that wasn't news anymore, not after a while, and they stopped telling it to me in the mushroom-cellar. But I asked them later, when I was out: I asked them all through the winter.

When the season aged and the leaves changed, they brought me curious news, which had come by angelophyte from the community upriver. The contagion they had suffered there was not our contagion, but something quite different: a whiteness in the eyes, not a blackness in the tongue; fainting spells, fever-dreams. It had indeed been contagious: one part in six of the community had died of it before their chemist bred a counterbiotic. Some had died and been sent off properly with sandals, others had died and been buried, with what sandals came to hand, by neighbors who later died themselves; some had gone into the forest to die, and at least one had thrown himself from a high place; and when everything was over, and the community much reduced, no one could say for certain whether everyone absent had died, or whether some—one woman, for instance—had not died, but broken quarantine and fled.

As for our contagion, it was never understood and never cured, and it has never reappeared. But it ended, as things so seldom do anymore, on a particular day. I was still confined to the mushroom-cellar. They came the next day to tell me; and it may be that I remember what they told me better than I would have remembered the event itself, for many of those who saw it have since forgotten.

The structure where the five victims had confined themselves was crescent-shaped, for reasons to do with the manufacture of surgical implements, and the habits and preferences of the spiders and the biotic colonies. In the bowl of the crescent there was a kind of balcony, with a short ramp running up to it from the ground, and the balcony gave onto the entrance: thick curtains of translucent cyclate, of a kind made, I think, from a cereal, and processed by a common cyclobacterium to about the consistency of horn. I've seen similar stuff elsewhere; it transmits light but not shapes, except roughly. So when one came to this structure at dark, and found it lit from within, the curtains would glow—sea-green, they glowed, when the beekeeper approached them that night—and if there was movement within, as, she said, there was, a darkness would undulate over the green, inarticulately, like an angelophyte colony at rest. It was brighter than an angelophyte colony that night, brighter than a phosphor-lamp, brighter indeed than any light-source the beekeeper knew. She set down the bags of nutritive liquid, put on her mask and gloves, and tapped at the window shutter.

She got no response—or rather, she heard a gurgling within, or something between a gurgling and a snore, and then silence again. She didn't count it a response. She went to the front curtain and pulled it aside. Inside, she saw—or said she saw, and no one has thought of any reason to doubt her—four pale forms, pale almost as chalkstone: four, she said; not five but four. The fifth may have been lying on the floor, for the others were stooping over something, or circling it, or even, she suggested, marching. The light came from a luminescent foam around their mouths. The shadows were thick, she had only a moment to see. One of the forms came toward her with outstretched hands, longer hands than are usual in people; it wrapped them around her throat and began to strangle her. There was a terrible strength in the fingers, she said, and as she struggled to pry them loose she succeeded only in gouging the flesh of her throat; and her throat, it was observed afterwards, was indeed covered with gouge-marks, and bleeding, and under her fingernails they found scraps of her own flesh. She stumbled back, and back again, dragging with her the hands and arms and body that held her, all of which weighed very little; and she cried out as best she could. She had just reached the edge of the balcony, and felt the railing against her spine, when she lost consciousness, and, as it seems, tipped backward, overbalanced the railing, and tumbled off the balcony through the air.

Her cry, muffled though it had been, brought the man who spun hemp. He saw no pale figure, though he reached the scene quickly; he remembers the curtain closed again but still glowing, sea-green, as the beekeeper had seen it. He worked to revive her; and, when finally she had opened her eyes and, saying, "Filled with teeth," closed them again, he performed the usual prophylaxis and carried her to the silk-curing shed where the practitioner of medicine was still under quarantine, and where the beekeeper was some time recovering.

By morning all the community knew the story of what the beekeeper had seen. They gathered around the structure: the glow of the curtain had faded before daybreak, at the very moment, perhaps, when I, waking, had begun my vigil of my patch of sky. Still no one dared open it, and no shouting elicited any reply from within.

Under the circumstances, the community behaved exactly as it ought: they sealed the building in spidersilk, the black, plaster-thick silk of the Nobuku spider—the Nobuku spider, whose web admits no air, and which the nurturer of spiders does not like to release; but on that occasion she released it. Afterward they left the structure, and the forest took it.

I came out of quarantine not long after that. They came one afternoon and told me I might, and then went away. I stepped out into the outer air, cool already with the fall, but bright, brighter than any air I've known before or since; so that now, though others say bright and think of a quality of the season of brightness, the season of the sun, I say bright and think of a burst of cool air, not cave-cool but wind-cool, and a pricking sensation all over my skin, and the scent of a dry dusk approaching. A fawn regarded me from the edge of the forest. A weakness in my limbs led me to sink down on the split stone, and she ran away.

Some days later I visited the proscenium arcade. The season was ending, and I wanted to look at the road mosaics that had been hung in my absence; and I had to do it before the snow pageant, when we would tear them all down and the proscenium arcade would stand empty again.

I wondered, as I crossed the meadow against the early morning bluster, whether the woman I had touched would appear in any of them. In fact she appeared in all. She looked different in each one, as she might, for she might have looked like anything. No one had agreed on the appearance of the road in its stillness, though all had seen it, and no one agreed on the appearance of the woman in her flight, for none had seen her. I have said I do not remember well, but perhaps I've said wrong again, because I remember, or seem to re-member, each of those mosaics very clearly, from first to last: I remember becoming disoriented; I remember feeling the images, not as idle artifacts, but as active incursions on my sight, a collective curtain or wall of false images drawn over my recollection of the true image, which obscured from me all those sensations of her which had remained, not only in my eyes but in my nose and on my skin, and which obscured the road too: as though it would no longer be possible to see it, it which was truly in the world, as anything more than an arbitrary vision, one more in a series, an artifice lasting at most until the snow pageant.

I must have turned away and left the arcade; but I don't remember.

Whether it was truly that day that the curtain was drawn, or whether it was only that I became aware then of a thing that had already happened, I don't know; but there isn't anything to see anymore, at that patch of road or any other, and if I go there I find nothing to do but go away. At times the light does strike it just so, or there is the shadow of a bat flitting by in the twilight; but then it recalls to me, not itself, but one of the mosaic-images of itself; and at those times, as I turn back and begin to feel, in my limbs' movement, the edge of an obstruction, I see or remember or imagine not the road before me, nor any longer the roads that appeared in the mosaics, nor anything else to do with roads, but the dim interior of a room cut off behind a web, and five people therein.

Five people I had known—were they doubly lost to me because doubly cut off, they by the silk and I by the quarantine? Or were we rather brought closer to each other in our solitudes?

I imagine the scene within their structure the more vividly, perhaps, because I never saw it from without: in the deepening gloom I hear the sounds outside fading, the gentle tread of the spiders over the walls, the world falling away. The black silk, the scent of the remaining air. I imagine the scene as something drawing away from me; yet it never entirely vanishes.

BRIAN CONN

1.5 Picture-Books of the Late Capitalists

"It is a pamphlet that came to the crèche," said Heather, "by some other road than the ordinary road, I suppose; for though it has not the letters in it of the late capitalists, those letters which they wrote now great and now small, but only images, it is a pamphlet of the kind we no longer meet on the road, not even we children; not even the eldest of us, who have delayed the maturing drug for seasons beyond counting, and attained wisdom beyond the reckoning of the grown—none have met such a pamphlet on the road, where, it is said, all things that exist do meet."

On the first page a man clad in varicolored textiles walks a white road beside a black road.

"In an earlier pamphlet the same man idled within a structure," Gretchen explained, "the home of a friend."

A summertime friend. The boundary between the white road and the black road wavers in the summer air.

"They had no contraceptives."

"The friend," Gretchen said, "was a woman."

He is walking in search of contraceptives. His friend has stayed behind. He desires to collect contraceptives and bring them to his friend's home. On the next page he stands inside a structure where there are no contraceptives. On the page after that he stands outside a different structure and cannot enter. He walks to further structures. The road brightens as does the sky. "And finally in this picture he is blind," said Sheila, "owing to the sun."

*

The trees blossom. Any day the progress of things may snap like strong silk overstretched.

A man speaks to a woman clad in textiles of a single color, asking a favor. There are six men, the man who has asked her a favor and five other men. The first man has asked her a favor on behalf of one of the five other men. Why on behalf of that one in particular? On the next page she performs the favor for all of them, all alike. But the one who asked her to begin with, she does not perform the favor for him. He did not ask for himself.

"Soon we will sleep when light remains in the sky," said Devon. "Is there not something staggering in it, that the light will surpass us in its wakefulness? So that the day will never be complete—that is, the day and we will never be complete together."

He remembered sweating in a hammock without blankets, uncertain whether he was dozing or feverish.

*

"Only in pamphlets wherein the light surpasses her in its wakefulness does the textile cling so closely to her body. She goes to a rectangular pool of refined water, and also to the seashore. The people in the pamphlets wherein light surpasses her in its wakefulness are different from the people in the other pamphlets."

She enters a harrow and remains there from dark to dark despite the long course of the day, and when she emerges a woman clad in a floral print proffers her a red liquid in a green vessel.

"Glass," said Heather.

"Though the people who greet her wear textiles of different colors in each pamphlet, the glass is always green; the liquid, we think, always the juice of the tomato. And perhaps all of these people are made of one substance, we think; that is, of one absence, like the absence which deceives us when the road is dry; for these pamphlets are filled with lines that rise from the earth and sky and the bodies of people, all depicting the shimmering air."

*

A man clad in garish textiles speaks on one page through a black horn to a friend on a different page. Afterwards he speaks through the same black horn to a different friend on a third page. But she laughs: the first friend is with her, their pages are the same page: they have each spoken to him via his black horn, but they have spoken to each other more simply, through the air. They are in the garden together.

His sink is full of water, old water, dirty water. Something got burned. Now he is on the porch. The hair on his head attains a great volume in a breeze from the window. The leaves are coming out in the rubbly lots, below and farther on, lime-green. A bag flutters in the branches of a tree.

"In this pamphlet the season waits outside," said Samantha, "but the garish textile man is inside."

"It was considered a great advantage," said Robert, "to inhabit a structure with many walls, so that there would always remain some region of the structure obscure to the capitalist, a region in which the season might dwell. Thus the season and the capitalist may inhabit the same structure, and the season, like the capitalist, be trapped forever in the next room."

In the next room the season transpires. He falls asleep in the sunshine.

"It seems to catch him by surprise," said Devon. "Here the textiles for which he cares have molded suddenly."

*

"And here they walk the seashore together," said Lincoln, "and on the next page he walks behind."

On the seashore the sand is the yellow of mustard. Summertime friends: the more of her skin shows the more his eye follows her.

"Yet, when we look closer, it may be that his gaze is not for her skin but for the sand. And neither looks at the sea, although there is an island there."

He wants to be the one to put the sand under her feet. If it is hot enough it may burn her. He will be the one to decide whether it burns her or not; and, if so, he will be the one to decide how much to burn her. On the next page he reclines in an empty room. There is a window here, looking on a roof.

"The calculus of escape," said Dorian. "He has left the door to this chamber open. Outside the door is a second window, overlooking lime-green trees. It is from that direction that the breeze blows."

"The door," Jeremiah explained: "they put them between rooms, as in the bathhouse, and kept them closed ordinarily."

"But he has left this one open in order to communicate with the second window, for in that direction lies his best escape."

"It is only a pamphlet that came to us," said Heather. "I feel dizzy."

"We haven't the earlier pamphlets anymore," said Malcolm. "After a season they come apart like a face in the leaves when the leaves fall."

*

The man clad in garish textiles returns to a place where he went in a previous pamphlet, a grassy spot on a hillside, above a road. That time the thick brown heat-lines of summer's end radiated from his body. Now it is a new summer and the fragile green heat-lines of summer's beginning. On the previous occasion he cut himself climbing over the hilltop fence, and bled. Now he looks through the fence down at the road and sees himself comfortable under a lime-green tree, bleeding once again. He walks the length of the fence and back. Would he cut himself again, should he climb the fence? And was it the road that comforted him that time or the blood?

He walks away from the fence and among women with covered heads. Some pages later we find him not far from where he started. A complex separates him from the fence which separated him from the hillside where he once sat bleeding.

"But all this time he has the same name."

"It was a red red red blood," said Barnabas. "I miss that pamphlet now."

A blood so red this pamphlet could not have come to them on the safe road. It came by a different road perhaps, a road where its red lingers in the air through which one gazes at the foliage.

1.6 Rope

"Now is the time when we are pure of heart," the old man said. "Here we make our peace with whatever befalls.

I shall enter the creature's dwelling and disturb his solitude. The danger is to me as the autumn rain. You must remain here by the door. Take you this sickle, which is of silver, and hold it ready: for when once he perceives the unwavering peace which is in my heart, he will not long remain within. He will flee, Molly, and you will see him; and although he will assume a form not his own, you will know him if your heart is pure. You must overcome him swiftly.

"But it may be that the condition of your heart is mixed. We may omit no contingency; we must destroy him regardless. Therefore take you also this gossamer dust, which is the corporeal residue of another such as he, and which has an odor pleasing to people but repugnant to monsters; and if you doubt your heart, cast it in the face of whatever creature emerges from this place. If he sneezes and grimaces, and you sense that this dust is repugnant to him, then overcome him without delay. But if he inhales deeply of it and you sense that it is pleasing to him, then embrace him, for he is I. I see that your flesh is young and strong. Make yourself ready. Darkness falls: the crepuscule holds court."

*

"Then he bade me wait there in the dell," said Molly, "while he dove into the fern brake."

"At least he instructed you how to distinguish a person from a monster," said the matron. They were sharing a glass of juice in the outer antechamber of the bathhouse. "Did you keep the powder?"

"I hid it in the mountains, along with the sickle. I did not like to have them, but I did not like to throw them away."

The matron swung a leg over the edge of her hammock,

and with a friendly push of her foot set Molly's swinging. "And did you await him in the dell?"

"I did not," said Molly. "I climbed a nearby tree, to look down unbeknownst on him and on the fern brake."

"And was there a dwelling in the fern brake?"

"No structure of any kind, but only the old man."

"And what did he do?"

Molly got up and refilled their juice from a red clay pitcher. It was early morning and they were alone. "He stood very still," she said, "until the last blush faded from the sky. Everything was silent in the forest: neither sound of animals nor breath of wind. No insects chirped. At last, when I could no longer see him well, he seemed to raise both his hands and remove his hair."

"His hair?" asked the matron. She rocked forward out of her hammock and raised the cushion of the large wooden bench that ran the perimeter of the room.

"He was wearing a wig," said Molly.

*

"But when she got up to refill our glasses of juice," said the matron, "I noticed a mound of flesh above her rump: a tail, no longer than my toe and red at the tip, which she had not had before."

"Certainly not," said the man like a bear; "I mistake me whether or not she had a tail before, but if she had one, it was never red."

"So I thought to myself what had happened," the matron went on. "I thought that it had been a falsehood, yet a falsehood partially true: for the cunningest falsehood is five parts truth. I thought to myself that she—our Molly, I mean, as she is and with no tail—had indeed joined with such an old man, for one does find these old men on the road, I have heard; and that perhaps they had approached the den of some spirit of darkness, she and he together; but that, contrary to the sequel she described—she the tailed Molly who spoke to me—contrary to her, the creature had overcome them both. And so it was the creature which now presented itself to me, in the disguise of Molly, and the entity which filled our juice glasses was not Molly but the creature, which, however, could not entirely disguise its tail."

The man like a bear looked sharply at her. "You are of suspicious mind. Why should such a creature come among us? And if it came among us, why should it recount this incident? Why should it speak to you, when speech is to its tongue as thorns to the tongues of people?"

"I suppose there was some reason," said the matron.

The man like a bear wiped away the gnats which had come to drink sweat from the hollows behind his knees. They stood near his canopy, the canopy of blue silk which for seasons innumerable he had kept pitched against the basalt of the mountainside. Under its shade his hammock still swung with the memory of the leap he had made when the matron had shaken him awake. "And why should the old man have worn a wig?"

"There was no wig," cried the matron. "It was false about the wig—the wig was among the false portion. Oh!" she buried her head in her hands. "I thought you might interest yourself in finding her remains."

"Let peace erupt within you." From a hemp pouch swinging at the hammock's head the man like a bear took a pot of strong balm, which he applied to her wrists and ankles. Soon her trembling ceased, and she stood breathing deeply with closed eyes.

"In what words did she continue?"

"In no words. As soon as I had understood the situation, I opened the compartment in the bench, and took therefrom the noose which hanged the child Caleb, whom I had hoped to make my own. Do you remember?"

"There are so many of these children."

"I have kept it since then, because it was on him when they cut him down, and, though I did not like to have it, I did not like to throw it away. I thought such a thing would captivate the creature that called itself Molly, and it did: it drew her on as the flower draws the bee. I led her into the upper antechamber," said the matron, "dangling it before her and promising to reveal to her further fetishes of death."

"The upper antechamber!"

*

"Naturally I did not believe the matron, for it seemed quite fantastical, the velvet and the wigs; and moreover what spirit of darkness sports such a tail? Nevertheless I accompanied her to the bathhouse. It may have escaped your notice," said the man like a bear, "but the interior of the bathhouse is in the shape of a spiral."

"I had thought it near-square inside," said Molly's mother. She cocked her head, remembering. "The façade of it appears flat from the bank of the creek, but the mass of it lies under deep shade. I have never asked myself the shape of its interior."

"It is in the shape of a spiral, like the shell of a rare aquatic creature: several chambers, their number uncertain, entwist each other like climbing vines."

"Or a length of rope."

"Just so," said the man like a bear. "But the chambers of the bathhouse climb so innocently, and curve so cunningly, that we misperceive them, and, stepping within, believe ourselves in a suite of ordinary rooms; but in fact we stand in a spiral chamber, and similar chambers lie above and below us; for in this shape each chamber lies at once above and below every other chamber."

He took a seat on a fallen tree. He had found Molly's mother watering cabbages, and had brought her to the edge of the field, near the hemp pavilion of those who watered cabbages. There the cabbage-watering song of the others reached them but faintly.

"I understand," said Molly's mother.

"The space in which we bathe occupies but one of the chambers. If you look you may discover trapdoors in the ceiling and floor, through which one might reach the others; but we cover over these passages with innocent ornaments, for those who pass through them often lose their way."

"Lose their way," said Molly's mother.

"Lose their way," the man like a bear affirmed. "I only report to you what the matron has done."

"She lured her into a labyrinth, you mean to say," said Molly's mother, "or a prison; or something worse."

"Now now," said the man like a bear, hastening to interpose the fallen tree between Molly's mother and himself.

Molly's mother beheld him glumly. "I took her from a community by a steppe," she said at last. "The people there found me too forward in my personality, and I heard of a child who taunted the other children to distraction, and I thought that we two might take to the road together. And she has been exceptionally slow as a daughter, but bold among the road's strange hazards, and she has learned well how to make rope."

"All is not lost," said the man like a bear.

"But is Molly lost?"

"Yes," the man like a bear admitted. "She is lost. Though it is sometimes possible to retrieve these people, if they remain near the aperture through which they disappeared."

Molly's mother swayed on her feet, and he climbed over the fallen tree and helped her to sit.

"We might make appeal to the crèche," he said. "The children find their way around those rooms better than most."

Molly's mother shuddered. They looked for a time on the watering of cabbages; then the waterers of cabbages moved on to squash, while Molly's mother mused visibly. "It is curious, though," she said at last, "that Molly should be led by a fetish of death."

"Now now—" the man like a bear began.

"For she was never easily led," Molly's mother went on, "being of a stubborn disposition. Moreover, the matron is of little intelligence."

It took him a moment to grasp her drift. "You doubt the matron's account?"

"Perhaps there is some false portion in it."

"But why should she choose a falsehood so damning?"

"Who can say?" Molly's mother sprang from the log and began pacing. "After all, perhaps she was correct. Perhaps the creature with which she spoke was not Molly, but some creature of even littler intelligence than the matron, and it followed the noose as she said. Or, again, it may be that she told partly the truth: it may be that there was such a creature in the shape of Molly, and that the matron spoke with it, but that it was in the end of greater intelligence than she, and, far from following her into the upper antechamber, it overcame her and presented itself to you in her guise—and so all that about the velvet and the wig and the tail were only its way of speaking.

"In any case there may be some false portion in it," she said, "and we must question the matron—supposing she is the matron—to find it out."

The man like a bear said nothing, and Molly's mother opened her mouth to speak further, but stopped; the man like a bear gazed mournfully on the waterers of squash.

"Where is the matron now?"

"I know you for a woman of wisdom and understanding," said the man like a bear. "I had omitted that part. When she brought me to the bathhouse, and opened the trapdoor, and bade me look in, the situation struck me forcibly. I was alone with a suspicious and morbid person who, as she herself said, had just come from luring another through the same trapdoor toward which she now ushered me. A strange light swam up from beneath. She moved toward me; it seemed to me then, and it does so still, that her fingers became elongated, as did her head and especially her jaw."

*

"And so, as though he had never seen a woman moving toward him before, he pushed her through the trapdoor." Molly's mother sipped nutritive broth on the veranda of the crèche. "I demanded him to show me to this antechamber, which he did by pointing at the threshold, for he was too fearful to enter there himself. I looked through and saw only darkness, not at all the light which he hallucinated; and only silence answered my calls. And now I fear they are lost, Molly and the matron both, just as he said—supposing that the matron was the matron, and Molly was Molly; though in fact either or both of them may have been something quite different."

The children, assembled before her, listened politely.

"If they were not something quite different before," said Ulrika, "then they very likely are now."

"Although," said Lemuel thoughtfully, "if they were indeed something quite different then, they may be Molly and the matron now."

"Or they may be entirely the same now—which is to say, something quite different."

"Or they may be a thing more different still."

"That seems most likely," Ulrika concluded: "a thing more different still."

"I said to him," said Molly's mother, "that the only sensible thing to do when a labyrinth is at hand is to equip yourself with a spool of thread. I had no thread, but I gave him a long coil of fine light paracyclate rope from the pavilion of those who water squash, no thicker than twine but stronger than the best spidersilk, and offered to tie it myself to some suitable anchor this side of the trapdoor, and even to watch over the end for him as he explored the labyrinth. And do you know what he did?"

"Did he flee?" Dean guessed.

"He fled!"

"But you ran after him," said Deirdre.

"I am faster and stronger than he," said Molly's mother. "I caught him up, threw the rope around him, and brought him back into the bathhouse."

The children stirred. "Before you continue," said Ute, "will it please you to bathe?"

"I?"

"It is at times such as these, when matters seem to press most urgently, that we are most in need of immersion in chilled water."

"Her blood rises," said Deirdre. "Even as we speak, it rises."

"These are the conditions for brain-fever."

"I assure you I am no more feverish than you are," said Molly's mother. "And it seems to me that the longer we delay here, the farther Molly and the matron—always supposing— may wander from the trapdoor in the upper antechamber, and the more difficult our search will be."

"You are partly correct," said Lemuel: "some people are soonest found if soonest sought. But others may only be found after a certain time has passed."

"Although if too long a time passes, they will never be found," said Seamus.

"Certainly," said Lemuel. "If too long a time passes."

Ulrika refilled the nutritive broth that Molly's mother had finished. "You mention Molly and the matron only. Then you did not cast the man like a bear through the trap-door as well?"

"Naturally I did in the end. His eyes rolled in his head and he foamed at the mouth." She pushed away the nutritive broth. "Have you no fruit juice?"

A silence fell on the veranda.

BRIAN CONN

*

"She is a mother herself, you understand," said Lemuel, "the mother of Molly. Thus she knows that fruit juice is not permitted to children."

"Indeed, the rules regarding children are well known throughout the community," said Ulrika. "And although Molly was older that we, and grown somewhat, she still bore a name, 'Molly,' as only those who are children may do, and so she was still a child. Thus she too was not permitted fruit juice, which she knew; and she could never have accepted it from the matron, as, we were told early in this tale, she did."

"As for the matron," said Liesel, "she is a hospitable woman. All of us visited her on occasion, although of course we are not permitted to bathe except during full dark. But without a doubt she knew that children are not permitted fruit juice."

"And she knew that Molly was yet a child," said Ulrika, "for she knew her name, 'Molly.'"

"Thus she would never have offered fruit juice to Molly," said Seamus, "as, we were told, she did."

"Furthermore," said Lemuel, "the man like a bear is an astute man, if morose on occasion, and would have detected all of these discrepancies at once."

"As would anyone, told that Molly had been served fruit juice."

"Therefore Molly cannot have been Molly, the matron cannot have been the matron, and the man like a bear was no more himself than I am; that is, very little of this is true."

"Though some of it may be," said Andrea, "some of it."

"The creature calling itself Molly's mother dissolved into a pool of odorless white liquid as soon as we brought ropes to bind her."

"It was not a large pool," said Thomas. "We cleaned it up."

The ropemaker looked out over the balcony of the observatory, down over the darkening valley. "But all these people have vanished from the community," she said; "and if very little of it is true, then at least the part of it is true that says they have vanished. Where is Molly? Where is Molly's mother?"

"You refer to her other mother," said Lemuel.

"Her other mother," said the ropemaker; "I know very well where I am." She loved best this time of day, when the sun had set and the moon not yet risen, and only a single star was visible: as though all the gentle shades of dusk were pouring into the sky through a pinprick in the vault of heaven.

"We had supposed," said Ulrika, "that none of them ever existed."

"And yet they seemed to exist," said the ropemaker. She sat down on the deck of the observatory and wrapped herself in a blanket against the night's cool; but, realizing as she did so that the nights would no longer be cool, she let it fall open around her breasts. "I bore a child by Molly's mother once," she said, "I mean in the natural way. We left it in a community of arborists, on a cape. I wonder whether it is there still, now that one of its mothers never existed?"

They sat for a time in silence. A patch of air yellowed below as the breeze puffed a cloud of pollen from a treetop. "When we twist rope," the ropemaker said, "we twist together strands made up of smaller strands, also twisted.

We begin by twisting together the smallest strands, in one direction or the other—for example, we twist them as the sun moves—and so make of them strands somewhat larger. And then, when we twist together the somewhat larger strands to make the rope, we twist them in the opposite direction—for example, we twist them opposite the movement of the sun."

"Perhaps the air throngs at all times with nonexistent creatures," said Deirdre, "twisted sunwise; yet when these creatures meet, and twist oppositely round one another, they begin to exist."

"And the fates of Molly and the matron, the man like a bear and Molly's mother—Molly's other mother—perhaps all were as an unbinding of rope."

"Might such a thing happen?" It seemed not impossible, in the hot and darkening dusk.

"We will incorporate into the history of the crèche the notion that it might; though we shall tell it provisionally, as a thing that was said and not as a thing that happened; that is, as a thing of which we have no knowledge. But that way we shall remind ourselves of it hereafter."

"After all," said Ulrika, "the aged spring sheds its mask: it is the season of unbinding."

They lay at ease on the deck of the observatory to watch the passage of the fixed stars.

CHAPTER 2

ABLUTION IN HELICAL STRUCTURE

2.1 Silence

We required someone to guide the building of the bath-house in silence.

"Though perhaps this person might speak," said the woman who grew nutritive moss, "if it be only in the way that other people speak."

The woman who brewed dyes grew disturbed. "I would like a person who does not speak in any way."

"It may be too much to ask."

"Yet perhaps there are those who devote themselves to the art of building structures in silence," said the woman who brewed dyes, "and it makes no difference to them whether they speak or not."

This state of affairs came about because of the woman in the well. It was the curer of silks who found her, but the finding of her surprised none of us. Already, several days before, she had screamed terribly in the night. That was the second full moon after Yule. Those of us who often dreamt of inhuman places woke thinking we heard one of the ancient mechanical sirens calling us to despair; those who had no such dreams woke into an inarticulate state. Many joined the screaming. These screams rent the community. Nobody knew how they carried so far. Nobody dared go out into the night. Even the nearest neighbors screamed alone. Finally we tired of it, and one by one we fell asleep. When day broke we knew that some tragedy had occurred, but we did not know its form. It was shortly thereafter that the curer of silks found the woman in the well—the small well, even then seldom used, where during the season the bees swarm in quest of bee-bread. We knew her: she was the woman who had cared for the apricot orchard, a beautiful woman. Her hands were bound together with rope, not rope of spidersilk, as we use most often in our community, nor of synthetics, but lank brown rope of the fibers of the horsetail moss, which grows in solitary places. We found no marks on her except those that might have been caused by her falling into the well. She smelled of ozone. While the maker of sandals labored she continued to smell of ozone, and the site of the manufacture of her sandals smelled of ozone for several days afterwards.

We trust each other well in our community; but somebody had bound the hands of this woman. After some discussion we concluded that it could not have been one of us. But who else was there? Perhaps there was some reason behind it; perhaps her story was in the end a loving story; the ways of people are not simple. Every day and every night we carried with us a vision of the well, of a tunnel of stone extending before us into darkness.

The community had long been of a size to be improved by a bathhouse. Now it was thought that by building this structure together we might begin to knit the community more closely; and once completed it might knit us closer still, for we would bathe together within its walls. At the same time, since the screaming in the night, it had become necessary to observe a certain silence, or rather a stillness: as though we were bruised interiorly; or as though we stood on the edge of a precipice, and even a stray ray of light, striking our shoulder, might topple us. We could not tolerate the heaving of bales and stones, certainly not the sawing of logs. If we wished to use wood we must split it bacteriochemically into shingles that fit simply into our hands, and bear them simply to the creek as people bear simple things in their hands, and afterwards bind them, likewise bacteriochemically and in stillness, into the form of a bathhouse; we must forbear visible violence and rely on the innumerable microscopic violences of bacteria. If not wood then there were cyclates, clays, and pastes, materials of malleable consistency or that might be made malleable. All of this was after all no impediment to us, but a guide and a comfort in a time whose meaning we could not easily understand. With a structure subtly erected we would substantiate our community not grossly but subtly—not as a thing cobbled from boards but as a thing recast, without the wounds of night's screaming, as though we were an impression in wax.

"There is the young builder who built the cairn of the androgyne," said the woman who nurtured camelids, and the triskele on her scalp seemed to deepen suddenly as a cloud passed over the sun, "no longer young. Although he did not build in silence then, he is said to build in silence now."

The woman who purified astringents said: "But his silence is unfathomable."

"His cunning is unlike peace."

"His arts are not the arts of people."

An expression came over the face of the woman who nurtured camelids, as though she were looking far off, although in fact she had fixed her gaze on the nearby compost. "He was here long ago, I remember, or else a child of his, or it may have been his mother. At that time he constructed a certain shed. It was long in use but it may be lost now; for so humbly and so harmoniously had he constructed it that it was often impossible for us to find, and when we did find it we found it most often occupied by animals, which were asleep there. And he said to me—my birth tree had fallen that season, because of its age, and I wept to see it helpless on the forest floor, it which had been planted at my birth and had outgrown me; and so I went with him and helped him to saw it, for he used saws of hard cyclate then, and we sawed very vigorously until I nearly fell from exhaustion, and afterwards I felt better, and the logs became part of numerous structures and some were made into masks—and he said to me that day that it was necessary, when building, to conceive of the community in a peculiar way. And he went on to speak of the community as a kind of soup."

At that she brought her gaze back to the stone circle where we sat, and squirmed against the hemp wrap she wore, for it was yet the cool part of the year. Then, all as one, we imagined her skin against the hemp wrap, and a sense of tragedy struck us; and we squirmed against our own wraps, hemp and silk and cotton, and longed to put them off, but said nothing.

"By a soup," said the chemist, "he meant…"

"A mixture no doubt," said the deliverer of infants, "or rather a composition."

After a time had passed, the man who distilled vinegar said, "I would like it if we had faith in people. This builder is a person whose heart beats as any other person's, and if he desires to speak of the community as a soup then I would like us to accept this as a way that a person may speak of us."

All agreed that we desired to have faith in people.

"Then I will send to him," said the angelophytist, "and desire him to come to us."

2.2 The Green Door

The builder was standing at the crossroads, doubtful which way to turn, when he perceived a child running toward him—running with incredible swiftness, and wearing a peaked green hat of special magnificence. It was the first warm day and neither of them wore clothing. The child drew up, beaming; the builder retreated one step and set his satchel between them.

The child doffed the green hat and made a sweeping bow. "The welcoming hat," he explained, and said that he was called Hector. "You were observed by Lemuel through the stationary lenses. And he spoke in the crèche, saying: 'A man elegant in gesture has arrived in order to perform prodigies.' For we suppose that you are the builder who built the cairn of the androgyne, and that you have come to guide us in the building of a bathhouse. But I spoke wonderfully, saying: 'At that crossroads the way is twisted, and even the wisest are deceived.' Thus I come to guide you, that you may guide us." He bowed once more. "Also to deliver glad news: the crèche thrives. The community doubts itself, and suffers under the specter of fear; but in the crèche we do not fear. Therefore we invite you to share with us the roof of the crèche, and to live free from fear. Already we love you joyfully."

The builder listened to this speech without expression. Hector bowed a third time, and this time remained bowed, waiting for the builder to answer. But the builder did not speak. They stood for several minutes at an impasse, the boy bent nearly double, his head collecting the dust of the crossroads, and the man observing him quietly.

At last the builder spoke, in a round reedy voice like the voice of a fish.

"Has the crèche women?" he asked.

"Boys and girls only," said Hector.

The builder nodded, but Hector, still bowed, failed to see it. "It is well," the builder said at last; and Hector straightened.

The builder followed him among thistle and tall grasses dotted with white butterflies. For some time they walked beside a row of cherry trees, planted straight but let to grow wild, and flush with white blossom in the early spring; and as they neared the end of the row a gust of wind stirred the boughs and shook loose a hail of blossoms, which covered grasses and thistle alike, and covered the builder too—a kind of autumn, he thought, the fleeting autumn of cherry trees, which comes in the spring but which marks, like the later and longer autumn, the beginning of a descent—and the butterflies played among the blossoms, and were indistinguishable from them, so that it was not possible to tell which things were alive and which were no longer.

Soon they passed between two towering cedars and in under the canopy of the forest. The path steepened as they began to climb the mountain. Hector spoke unceasingly. He named the trails they passed and enumerated the nutritive plants to be found in the vicinity; he pointed out the proscenium meadow, the great nut orchards; the apiary, the arachniary, the structure of the chemist. The mountain closed in on them with the smell of sun on stone. Hector led the builder roundabout through the pumpkin patch, speaking all the while while the other remained silent.

"And the well," Hector said, "the well where we found the woman—it lies not far ahead. Are you weary? The climb grows steep."

But still the builder said nothing.

Hector capered ahead up the path. "Yours is the silence of unpeopled places," he said. "They said it would be; and it is. Even now when you are weary, even when you have not yet begun to build, already it is the silence of death. And already we love you better and better, for in the crèche we adore all silent things."

The cedars gave way to a vista. Beyond a fern-shaggy meadow and the lumpen mossy stone that watched over it, the land fell down to the valley filled with shadows. They gazed down on the river and the road beside it, and the builder, musing on this prospect, began to speak.

"I keep silence for my own safety," he said, "and also because there is so little to remark upon. But I will speak to you now, and I will speak to you a second time at the crèche; and perhaps on another occasion I will speak to you a third time. But you must do me a service."

Hector placed himself at the builder's disposal.

"The creek lies ahead," said the builder, "and I desire to bathe. But even now the people of the community throng the bridge, awaiting us; for Lemuel, who saw me through the stationary lenses, has warned them of my coming, and taken them from their laboratories and looms, their animals and fields, and they have gathered to greet me—at the bridge, as I have said, because they tell themselves that we must cross it in order to reach the crèche. But I do not want to meet these people. Therefore you must precede me to the bridge, and speak captivatingly to them. Meanwhile, I will come to the creek at another point, by way of the forest, and begin my bathing. Speak to them on any topic you like, but see to it that none of them leaves, for anyone leaving may happen to walk up the creek and so disturb me; but I think none will leave so long as you speak, for though they be silent they value speech, and their silence is to them a penance. Having bathed, I will swim across the creek and make my way to the crèche, where they are not permitted to come, and where you may rejoin me."

"Then you know our community well," said Hector, crestfallen, "and you knew already everything I said to you on our climb. But how is it that you know of the movements of people, and the activities of Lemuel?"

"You ought not to interrupt," said the builder, "but because I am old now I will offer you advice, and perhaps therein you will have your answer. Do you understand?"

Hector said that he understood.

"And will you speak to the people at the bridge, as I have asked?"

Hector said that he would.

"Then my advice to you concerns doors, roads, staircases, ladders, windows, and all other ways people have devised of coming together and keeping apart. I advise you to mark them well. Mark their number, their location, and their characteristics, and the means of their opening and closing; and if they be windows, and if they be glazed, mark well whether they be operable windows or fixed windows, for the first permits passage without bloodshed, but the second does not. But most of all, learn to know ahead of time what obstructions await beyond."

The call of a dove brought a chill down on them. "Perhaps this is one of those things that you are alone in understanding," Hector said.

The builder looked hungrily down the path. "I have, as you suppose, been in this region once before. At that time, which was long ago, I came to a green door in the hillside. Far off there, across the valley. A woman lived there. But, passing her door as I came today, I sensed that she had died long ago, and therefore I did not enter."

Hector reached up to take his hand, but he clutched his satchel to his chest and retreated into the forest.

Hector continued to the bridge, where he found a multitude of people gathered, exactly as the builder had said. When they asked him where the guest had gone, he spoke to them at length of the doors, roads, and staircases of the community, their number, location, and characteristics, and of ladders and windows, and the bloodshed the windows of the community might bring, for there were some few of them glazed, and none of them operable. By means of this speech he lulled them into a torpor, and when the light failed he took his leave.

When he had gone, they complained bitterly.

"We shall have to trust even the children," said the man who made sandals for the dead.

In the great kitchen of the crèche, the phosphor lamps shone blue-green on a feast. The builder reclined on woolly cushions, and the children gathered around to rub with their burning hands his feet and calves and head, and to whisper unintelligibly in the stillness under the kitchen vault. Then the children fed each other tomatoes and avocados, honey and fresh cheese, oranges, grapes, and sweet lettuces; and they brought out strong herbs to chew, and caressed each other. After Hector had arrived, and had hung the welcoming hat beside the door, the builder said, "Because I am old, I will offer you advice."

He tore himself from the heat of their hands, and rose to tower above their tiny eyes and slick narrow faces. He began to speak, but choked, and fell. Only when he lay still on the floor was he able to breathe again. Ute and Ulrika stooped to soothe him, and Hector capered the length of the kitchen and back again. The builder asked for rest. They brought him into a long room where thick sleeping rugs lay scattered on the floor, chose him a rug and blankets, and lay him down.

He woke knowing that someone had called out to greet him. The sound still echoed in his ears. The children lay in pairs and triples naked on their rugs. The room was longer than he had thought; along the long windowed walls crouched cedar chests, wicker chests, winter wardrobes, blankets, cushions tossed carelessly in heaps; at the far end someone had called to greet him from the threshold. But the threshold was empty. There was the smell of snow in the room, although the air was not cool. He started toward the door, but after a step, seeing Hector smiling in his sleep, returned to his rug and lay supine. He thought he would not sleep again, but soon he dreamed of a bathhouse, cold in the shadow of the forest.

2.3 Shapes of the Bathhouse
Transcribed by the eidetic

All gathered where the creek overruns the shoulder of the valley, descending thence to join the river. The guest said: "Many desire to overlook the valley while bathing." Several inquired into the guest's health, but he said nothing more. We made known to him our policy of faith. All agreed to place the bathhouse on this spot.

Suggestions were entertained concerning the shape of the bathhouse.

> **Woodbine.** Many felt that a bathhouse in the shape of a woodbine would fit easily into the community, as a woodbine fits easily among the trees of the forest, as though to bind them together. But the question was asked whether we desire to exist in the way of a woodbine. The woodbine stands motionless: at peace or imprisoned? The woodbine competes for light. Certain vines are to be feared, and certain berries are toxic in the mouths of people; also certain men. The chemist hastened to add that she did not refer to the guest. A bathhouse which mimics a multiplicity of vines must separate the bathers. The suggestion was set aside.

> **The Well.** In order to aid in the transfiguration of our specific fear. But the guest does not share this fear: he did not know the woman who perished in the

well; he was not here on that night. Shall we then ask him to build this shape? Better to accomplish this transfiguration invisibly: for the shape of the bathhouse may be the shape which precipitates our transfiguration, but it need not be the shape of our transfiguration itself. Already we have filled in the well with earth. We resolved to fill its memory too, with the new images the seasons shall bring, and erect no monuments.

A Snowfall. A thing perpetually falling yet also still. As our community remains a unity though individuals come and go. The idea was fanciful, but all desired very much a bathhouse in the shape of a snowfall. It was suggested that the name of the bathhouse be Snowfall. All fell silent. The name was found unsuitable.

The Polk-Ring Spider. As we harvest metals from her web, as our ancestors built on her back a new civilization of peace, so too shall our community harvest a new peace from the bathhouse. But the analogy struck many as strained. With what do we equate the community as it stands today, that the spider might transform it peacefully into metal? With the ore-flies which she traps and consumes? Better suggest the Kloss-Ring Spider, which shapes metals already refined. It was decided that metals are not germane to the bathhouse.

A Crystal Lattice. Hexagonal, as cinnabar. Or else another geometry. By thinking in this way, we think on the ways in which people fit together. But not all are moved by archaeocrystallurgy. Many were uncomfortable with the implied comparison between people and cyclosilicate. Two present were taken ill and a third complained of a sensation of being swallowed by the earth.

A Bridge. Joining the two banks of the creek: as each person to each other person, as the present to the past. The baths to lie in its midst, directly over the water. In a moving speech, the man who arranges lilacs extended this metaphor to the relation between the guest and the community. The guest did not speak. We reiterated our policy of faith. Building to commence after a day of rest.

We entrust these notes to the repository in the bole of the cedar.

2.4 The Crèche

He is oppressed by a slight stifling fullness at the base of the skull. He wishes for one of the others to ask him about the painting which hangs above the mantle. In the painting a bear sleeps in a forest glade. Just now his blinking left a speck in his eye and the bear was distorted. A speck through which the posture of the bear appeared to shift. The bear appeared more hideous. But it became the old bear again. He wishes to discuss this event with the others. He will not say anything himself. Several days pass. There is a cheese on the table. He descends into the cellar and relieves himself. A ray falling from the phosphor lamp at the head of the staircase blues the steam which rises from his urine. He wonders does the splash disturb those who sleep above. The dark of the cellar facilitates the senses, the better to scent the mineral content of the urine. Yet those above, their senses too are sharp. They may discover that his diet is too rich. He leaves the cellar. They are seated around the table. The cheese is plump and white. They accompany it with chemical bouillon. The crèche is in the shape of a T: the great larder is the cross of the T, the sleeping hall the column of the T; the great table lies at their junction; the great vault rises crushingly above them. The sleeping hall is in the shape of a tunnel. Wishing to sleep, he rises. The crèche rotates thirty-one degrees around the wheel of the great table. He falls. Often the crèche has rotated in this way. Sometimes thirty-one degrees, sometimes another number. They pick him up and carry him to a pallet nearby. Some of them coming in from the sleeping hall seat themselves around the cheese. He studies the black vault. Under the ribs runs a papery residue: the waste product of the beneficial animal which nests in the vault. He goes into the sleeping hall. Children are sleeping here. Windows line the walls. He goes to the basin and arches over it making pillars of his arms. Some children enter and sleep. The moon is a green sliver between the cedars. A substance overflows his mouth and falls into the basin. He cleans his teeth. He wonders is the steam which rises from his urine the same as the fog which suffuses the crèche. Or else is it his breath. He lies on a woolly mat. The weight of his body rests on his neck. He wakes having heard a voice call out to him. The sleeping hall has lengthened infelicitously. The sleeping hall is in the shape of the skeleton of a cylindrical creature. The children are asleep.

2.5 The Speech of the Young Woman

They worked in teams of twelve, each day a different team, plus auxiliary teams of different numbers: in the forest to see to the bacteriochemical splitting of shingles, on the riverbank to see to the curing of clays, in the fields gathering dyes; three and four and five teams at once, all according to a schedule kept by the angelophytist.

A low arch of cedar, the bridge, soon spanned the creek; bath-huts sprang up, nine along each side, first in frame, then clad in rough yellow cedarwood, and soon afterwards polished and polished again to shine glossy and cool in the summer sun. Between the two rows of bath-huts, a canopy of cured spidersilk in green and brown rippled in the treetop breeze, casting the walkway in autumnal shade. Walking the bridge in the evening, marveling at the day's work, they heard the creak of wood below and the shudder of silk above.

They worked in stillness. They bred carpenter cultures to shape and bind the wood in undetectable violences, they cast the plumbing in cyclates, and they kneaded the river's clay, slowly and coolly, into tubs, to be fixed by lab-bred lithotroph colonies whose action filled the quiet air with the scent of lettuce fields after rain.

They rose every day at dawn and worked until sundown under the direction of the builder, who circulated mutely among them. Silent as they were themselves, still they never trusted his silence, but they came to trust his measured motion; and in future seasons, when they chewed strong herbs at dusk and recollected him to one another, they recollected him neither as a voice nor as an utterance, but as a body—a body passing quietly, in the gathering creekside heat, among the casks, crates, tiles, shingles, retorts, and stills. At sundown he returned at once to the crèche; he never visited any other place, and he attended neither artistic performances nor any other assembly of the community. Then they would gather again around the bathhouse, without him, to marvel by phosphor-light at those of its artifices which he had revealed to them.

"For myself, I find it provocative," said the woman who spun hemp, "exceedingly so; and I desire to please him in whatever way he desires."

"But perhaps the children please him well enough," said the woman who constructed stringed instruments; for the children praised him without fail.

"But the children are uneasy," the woman who brewed dyes observed. "They seldom leave the gardens and pastures of the crèche, more seldom even than they were accustomed to do; and when they do leave, they walk with anxious glances over their shoulders."

"And Hector insists that he is a wolf," said the man who nurtured caterpillars.

They contemplated the children.

"But perhaps it is in the nature of children," said the beekeeper doubtfully, "to call themselves wolves."

*

Before dawn, unobserved by the community or even, at first, by the children, the builder walked a circuit of the crèche and its appurtenances. Singly at first: the structure itself, the pasture, the hanging field, and finally the garden, where even in the cool half-light the scent of tomatoes spoke to him of the heat of afternoon; then in combinations: garden and field, pasture and structure and the small copse in which the hive was kept; and finally all together, all the territories of the children. He made this walk every morning, looking sometimes at the ground and sometimes toward the structure, but always as though searching for something; and finally Ingrid, rising early in preparation for shearing the sheep, spotted him out the window, and thereafter the children watched him every morning from the darkness of the crèche, but without telling him. As the bathhouse progressed, day by day, so did his circuits lengthen, until the day's teams arrived at the site before him, and waited, and he arrived shuffling somewhat, and seeming not to see them.

"The eldest one of you," he said in the evening to the gathered children; they looked toward Ute, and he addressed himself to her: "Do you recall my coming here, long ago? For I seem to forget whether it was I who built this structure or whether it was another." And when Ute told him that, though she was likely the oldest living creature on the mountain, she was not so old as that, for the crèche had been old even when she was young, he murmured to himself that perhaps it had been another.

"But I too am very old," he said.

He asked a skein of silk from the spinner of silk, and the next morning he measured with it all the perimeters he had been walking for so many days; then, as the children watched and wondered, he measured the thicknesses of the walls, the depth of the cellar staircase, the angles and arcs of the vault, and the spaces between the shutterless windows through which seed-pods blew. That day two women who had gone to gather citruses with which to cure the indigo tiles discovered him crouched beside a little-used trail, tapping his fingers one against the next, and manipulating piles of tiny stones with the nervous twitch of a squirrel gathering nuts.

"Figuring, no doubt," the man who made sandals for the dead said afterwards: "it is the way of builders."

Sensing the two women, the builder swept the stones aside and rose. That evening, and at other times thereafter, he entered the crèche through windows; but, no matter his point of entry, he found that it remained the same crèche.

He had felt it before: some difference in the structures he had built, or thought he had built, in the days when he spoke: some vanished or else inaccessible part of them, like a phantom limb he had forgotten he ever possessed, that made them alien—as though (he thought, probing with his tongue the underside of the moldings) the words he had uttered while building had seeped invisibly into the joints, and, now that he no longer claimed them, had absconded from the subtle part of his sensorium, taking with them from each structure some unspecifiable quality or space, and preventing him from knowing whether it was his own structure or the structure of another.

*

A bellowing erupted as the community slept, everywhere at once it seemed, as though a steam-driven brass bull rampaged in the heart of the mountain. Those who often dreamt of inhuman places woke thinking they heard the onset of cataclysm; there were none now who had no such dreams, and they all joined together in screaming.

When day broke, and they emerged blinking and shaking from their canopies, the day's building teams made their way to the creek; and others made their way there too, not all, but those whose hearts were strongest. The bathhouse had fallen in: all the debris had washed away; only gouges in the earth remained, and the splintered ends of six beams.

They stood in the brittle brown grass in the naked heat of the sun, saying little; and when they did speak it was only to say, as though it meant anything, that there had been some accident.

Finally the deliverer of infants went to toll the bell, and then they all came. They blamed nobody in particular. Nobody spoke of the screaming. The children came from the crèche to trail behind the builder as he inspected the beam ends, the soil, and the gouges.

"A subterranean fault line," said the bacteriologist.

"A person may curse the earth," said Hector, "commanding it to reject us."

All morning they sat in silence looking down at the valley, where the white road and the blue river followed each other side by side away from the mountain. Then, as the day warmed and the shade diminished, they began slowly to go away, one by one, and return to their laboratories and looms, their animals and fields, until by the time orange touched the horizon none of them remained. When dusk fell for certain, the children returned to the crèche; and finally the builder sat alone under the stars, studying the creek under the aspect of night.

He had not seen night since he had arrived. Every evening he had gone at once to the crèche. He found it pleasant to discover once more how far one could see in the dark: all the way across the mountains, and all the way, if one knew the shape of its shadow, to the hollow where lay the cairn of the androgyne.

He got to his feet, as though without meaning to, or as though having expected to do something quite different; and, although he continued to feel in his mind the feeling of looking out over the creek toward the scarcely visible or else invisible cairn, in fact he walked into the forest, and wandered there. Having only starlight to find his way, he cut his feet on stones, and became covered with burrs and the oils of nocturnal weeds; and gradually it was borne in on him that he was no longer on the bank of the creek, and moreover that he was dirty.

He became aware of a feverish moaning. Following it, he found himself in a dell, deep in the forest, which lay on no path or trail. Two elephantine oak-roots thrust out like gnarled elbows from the far slope; they held a drift of earth between them, worn down into a deep sunken ledge, like a root-and-earth throne. A slender woman was seated there, painted from head to toe with phosphor. She held to her lips a curious instrument: she blew over a bridge between twin parallel flanges of bone, causing a ghostly spark to leap to and fro between them, and it was from this spark that the ululation emanated. When she spied the builder she lowered her instrument, and the noise ceased. She observed him with impatience.

*

In the end, it was she who spoke.

"You needn't look at me that way," she said; "I am only playing a haunting melody in this dell, in order to frighten the children. And had you not interrupted me, I would presently have put away my flute and gone to hover in the forest nearby, within view of the crèche, and at a distance from it which I have calculated to produce an effect of great mystery—for I have painted myself with phosphor, as you can see, and my body glows with a spectral light."

The builder looked about him. The dark of the forest overlaid the dark of the night and it was impossible to know where he was; but his legs ached, as though from climbing up and up, beyond the community and up into the lonely places of the mountain.

"The crèche is nowhere near," he said. "We are in a hollow deep in the forest."

She looked at him crossly. "There is no such place. We are in the forest behind the crèche, on the spot where the children are hanged—a melancholy spot enough, but I see no reason to pretend that we have met each other in a wonderland of your own imagining. I believe you are unbearably stupid."

The builder sat down beside her on the ledge, observing as he did so her feet, which, like his own, were unshod, and their soles cut and abraded by stones; but unlike his own they appeared quite clean, and the light which spilled from them was fresh as the dawn.

"I have been sitting here some time," she said, "I scarcely remember how long, desiring only a moment's peace in which to play haunting melodies and hover mysteriously within view of the crèche; and yet you people will forever come, you and others, importuning me for I know not what, and I must put aside my flute and speak to you, though you be unbearably stupid."

She began to weep. "Quite recently a woman came this way," she said between tears; "we ended by coupling here on the forest floor, to our mutual satisfaction, and afterwards

I bound her lovingly with the hanging rope, and she fell a great distance; and I thought I should have my peace finally, but now you have come too."

The builder pulled up a clump of dry grasses which grew near at hand, shook the earth from their roots, and set to work braiding them together by the light of her body. As he worked, she gradually left off weeping and watched him, and soon began to play again on her flute, though without taking her eyes from his fingers.

"A pair of sandals," she said, putting her flute aside. "Are you making me a pair of sandals? It is most kind of you, though I say so only as a matter of form—but perhaps you are making them for yourself. Why do you not speak to me?" When he did not answer, she snorted and turned away from him, saying, "I see well the insufficiency of your heart."

*

"When I was born," she went on, "I was born under a dark sign, and the air in the room held the sound of thunder, although the sky was clear. All but me were deafened. But because it was this noise that welcomed me into the world, I have never yet been at peace, as children are at peace who are born into stillness, but I have always heard the echo in my memory of this sound, and the echo in my body of the way I trembled in its belly—in its belly, I say: for so unexpectedly was I torn from the body of my mother, where I had enjoyed a measure of peace, and so violently was I thrust into the clamor of the night, that all memory of my mother's peace fled from me, and in its place the rumble of thunder took root, so that my memory of the time preceding my birth is no longer a memory of peace but a memory of thunder—

which is to say, I have always felt myself to be pressing, and pressed against, and perpetually at the threshold of calamity. And at the time I was born, my mother's heart stopped. Therefore our hearts were never together in the world as two separate hearts, but only as one heart and then another, with a rupture between; for indeed my heart stopped too for a short while at the time when my mother's stopped, but the doctors caused mine to start again. And my heart never learned from my mother's the way of being at peace in the world, but strains within me like a bird imprisoned within a structure of late capitalism.

"Despite this discomfort I made my way in the world, as we people make our ways. And it seemed to me that some seed of that peace which I lacked, that peace by the grace of which people enjoy the world's fruits and find repose in each other's company, must yet lie hidden in some portion of my heart that I could not make my own—as though in a sealed and forgotten chamber of not-heart or near-heart which the heart I called my own never compassed, or in some slight variation of my heart which, as it happened, I had never realized; and I thought that it was this seed in a hidden or unreal chamber of my heart that agitated me so, and that I must either cause it to grow and constitute itself together with my single and simple heart as it beats in the world, or else expunge it entirely, becoming as though made of clay. Therefore I took to the road, and walked there for many seasons, studying all the communities and all the people I came across. And in particular I endeavored to perform alongside them all their rites of peace, I mean caring for apricot orchards, sitting on hillsides at the cusps of the day, chewing strong herbs, sexual congress, and the like, in order to discover whether any of these activities spoke to the seed in my heart; but I failed at all of them, and on those few occasions when I felt myself on the threshold of understanding, I felt at the same moment my body become paralyzed, and the earth tremble beneath me as though shaken by thunder. And others also felt the trembling of the earth, and became frightened, and always I resumed the road for their sake.

"But as I went on the people became fewer and fewer, and the communities too; and even the sky's light diminished. And although my unease grew ever greater, there was a love for people born within me; but it was a dark love, and contrary to that love which grows in the hearts of people at peace: a love for people under the aspect of darkness.

"I frequented certain deserted places, where the people look neither like us nor like each other, and where they perish swiftly: those places of fallen concrete, and of ancient metals made and shaped by other metals, and of bound masses of space which the sun does not touch—all of them overtaken, now, by the devouring mosses and creepers we have bred to overtake them, yet present still in the gently regular shapes and forms of our mosses; and there in those spaces long unlit I felt that there were more people, not the people unlike each other who perish swiftly, nor yet any kind of people I know, but a subtle people whom I sensed subtly, and who lived so timidly that I could not sense them otherwise than subtly. It was those people in particular whom I came to love, for they dwelt, I thought, in the same rarefied and imperceptible place as my heart's deficiency. But as I came to sense their gentleness and timidity in other people, first in the people unlike each other who perish swiftly, and then in all people— as I came to sense in people those qualities of absence which balmed the absence in my heart, I came to love them all.

"But I love by different rites than those by which ordinary people love, for the rites of peace elude me still. It is for this reason that I frighten the children: for although the heart is the organ of love, yet fear also is a function of the heart. And by frightening the children I exercise their hearts, not those knowable and conspicuous chambers with which they perform their everyday rites of love, but rather the subtle chambers; and it is not known, I think, what parts of our civilization may depend on those chambers.

"All that time I walked the road, I walked unshod; and although I see that you have nearly finished weaving a pair of sandals out of grass, and that you have sized them small as though for me, I hope that you will not attach too much importance to them, for they will not suit."

*

As she said this, the builder became aroused, which she sensed easily enough; for it was summer, and neither of them wore clothing. At the same time, the glow of her phosphor deepened, and the smell of ozone filled the air.

"How long have you been here, frightening the children?" the builder asked.

"I am glad to hear that you speak to me now."

"It occurred to me to do so," said the builder, "though I may stop at any moment." But, kneeling on the friable loam and beginning to fit the grass sandals to her feet, he added: "It is a matter of caution for me: for each utterance has weight, even as our bodies have weight; and because I am so old, and the weight of my body so small, there are few utterances left to me."

A look of sorrow overtook her face then, and she opened her mouth and might have made some remark of understanding; but at that moment something, either a sandal or his fingers, happened to tickle her foot, so that she cried out and flung herself off the ledge and lay writhing in the grass. She went on laughing for some time, and he knelt watching her. He had tied one sandal on one foot, and he held the other in his hand. Suddenly she snatched her bone flute from where it had fallen and rose solemnly to her feet.

"I do feel that laughing corrodes me somewhat," she said, "and I always have. Perhaps, of all the substances of which I am composed, the scarcest is some substance which commutes with laughing; and, of all the substances of which you are composed, the scarcest is some different substance which commutes with speech; for we are all composed of numerous substances, and who knows with what other substances they may commute? And in you the substance which commutes with sandals is not at all scarce, for I see that you have made these without any suffering to speak of, whereas with me that substance which commutes with the wearing of sandals is quite vanished, or has donned its sandals and gone off so that it is no longer part of me, and now all that is left of me are many many words, and a little laughing, and the glow of the phosphor with which I have painted my body, and also this flute. But you are yet filled with blood, for I smell it; and I wonder what will be left to you when it is gone."

So saying, she tucked the flute under her arm and disappeared. Both sandals remained, although one had been on her foot and she had not removed it.

The builder sought for a solitary seat in the mountain's rock in which to think further. Instead he found, near the top of the ridge, a cavern, which narrowed as he followed it into a winding passage. No light penetrated there; navigating by touch, he lost his bearings; and, some time later, when he no longer knew what part of the mountain lay above him, the passage opened, the darkness eased, and he found himself enclosed in a gentle starlight gloom: he had reached a deep grotto, dry and silent, overhung high above by six cedar boughs in the shape of a spiral.

He lay down on a bed of fern and moss, and looked the length of the stone chimney to the circle of sky at its top. There, darker against the sky's darkness, which after all is not darkness but an emptiness which permits people to move together, he saw silhouetted the six cedar boughs; and it seemed to him, as he lay exhausted, that their spiral lengthened, and descended into the chimney at whose bottom he lay, so that he lay at the bottom of a spiral which came from the sky through the cedar boughs and down through the stone, and which, continuing into the mountain beneath him, enfolded him in its coils. He desired, by traversing this spiral in one direction or else the other, to find the woman from the hollow, and to compose their two substances into a new substance; but at the same time, he reminded himself, he might encounter persons of a substance alien to their two substances, whom he must work to avoid—"Although perhaps these people populate a different spiral," he said to her in his thoughts, "perhaps the spiral which forms in the day, while only some few of us populate that which forms by night." Then, seeing the day's spiral approach the night's spiral in order to ram it, and seeing swarms of squat persons hurl themselves onto the night's spiral and clamber over its delicate flesh like so many monkeys, he felt it tremble beneath him; and he hoped (for he feared that he would not reach her at once) that she might find, elsewhere in the spiral, some shelter for the subtle parts of her.

2.6 Residues

The woman who had cared for the apricot orchard celebrated beneath the earth. A cake, iced pink, rested on a slender pedestal before her. Equidistant around the chamber's circumference, in lieu of exits, rose three lit candelabra, each as slender as the cake-pedestal. She was accompanied by a wolf and a bear. The wolf and the bear contended over a green hat. She did not like to cut the cake until they had settled the question of the hat. But it seemed that each had as strong a claim as the other. Whichever won the hat would have the privilege of greeting her. Could they not greet her together? Beneath the earth, she thought, it must always be one before the other: just as the chambers beneath the earth lay one atop the other, communicating by ladders. This, the topmost, was hung with red velvet of inferior quality. There was no ceiling. The argument stretched interminably. Already it had been a season or more. The bear argued cogently but the wolf mounted vigorous rebuttal.

It struck her that she might cut the cake but not yet eat it, in order to hurry them. She sought beneath the pedestal for a knife. Their arguing voices cradled her warmly. An oak grew beneath the pedestal. She plucked one leaf and pressed it onto the icing, which gave way. The cake revealed itself deep red within. The argument of the wolf and the bear grew heated. Inside the cake she discovered a staircase winding up the chamber wall. She ascended toward a region black as midnight, intending presently to return to the wolf and the bear.

Passing through the midnight region, she attained a region of indigo. Here the scent of sulfur set her heart steady: she was passing near a hot spring. From above came a muffled clamor of people making merry. The staircase flattened, widened, whitened into a broad spiral ramp of cedarwood with walls gleaming white. Light steady from above yellowed the molding. Soon yellow light streamed from all sides along with joyous singing. She stopped and listened but could no longer hear the argument of the wolf and the bear.

Flattening and widening as she climbed, the staircase came to resemble a broad hallway curving away forever toward windows from which yellow light poured—and toward baths: lemon and lavender wafted from beyond the curve, and the people splashed so near that she flinched from phantom droplets. She came to twin trapdoors, ceiling and floor, each with handle and hinge of wrought iron, and built-in folding ladders. Heaving on the upper in the hope of encountering the bath, she climbed into a hallway identical with that she had left, and after that passed through further trapdoors, portals, and hatches, but found herself still, as it seemed, in the same hallway. But which direction was up and which back down? For so subtle was the winding of the way that both directions now appeared flat and straight. She resolved to find the bathers and ask them to direct her back toward the wolf and the bear, those rascals—had they only put aside their differences and welcomed her properly, she might even now be plummeting with them toward the formless depths. Instead she wandered a system of spirals, each above and below every other, coiled like concentric corkscrews within a cylindrical structure of vast dimensions.

The songs of the bathers swelled and dwindled and swelled. Did they hear when she called? It seemed sometimes that they did; and sometimes she heard a rapping on the other side of a wall, and once the murmur of another who wandered like her in an adjoining spiral, above or below; but she never met anyone—quite as though the spirals were built, she thought, to keep certain people together and others apart. She soon forgot about the well. Stopping one day at a narrow embrasure which appeared in the passage, she looked out on the mid-day sky and the road below.

CHAPTER 3

THE GREEN DOOR

3.1 Mercury

The man who bore crates was thinking of the meal in the spidersilk pouch that hung from the hook beside his head and swung with the sway of the wagon—thinking of it only obliquely and with strict casualness, so as not to exhaust it, it being the only thought available to him on this stretch of road—and meanwhile watching the moonshadow at play on the mountainside, and listening with one ear to the carbon-rubber groan of the harness; when suddenly he became aware of a very small man sitting beside him. He startled, like an ox, and moved to beat the man away, as during the day he beat away flies. But the small man laughed, and the man who bore crates withheld his blow.

The stranger was foxlike in appearance, with tiny sunken eyes and a muzzle of olive complexion, and very small pores, or none.

"Practitioner of medicine," he said, by way of introduction—and then, with a wink, "fertility doctor."

The man who bore crates returned his attention to the

road. The oxen trod with unvarying tread. He looked out over the river for a time, and when he looked again at the seat beside him, the small man winked twice, one eye and then the other. The man who bore crates seized him in both hands, stood on the step, and raised him over his head in order to dash him to the ground.

The laughter of the small man accelerated, and he squirmed as though his bones were made of shivering-rubber. "Ticklish!" he cried. "Oh! Oh! Oh!"

The man who bore crates set him down. "Apologies. I had thought you a spirit of darkness," he said, "possibly contagious."

"No," said the small man. "Practitioner of medicine." With good humor he tossed away two tomatoes that had fallen from the spidersilk pouch and been crushed beneath him when the man who bore crates set him down.

"But you neither bit nor stung me."

"Well noted: it is for all people to know what harmeth and what harmeth not."

"You failed also to transform yourself into a noxious animal, to vanish in a stroke of lightning, and to shroud yourself in toxic vapor. Therefore I set you down again."

"Practitioner of medicine," the small man repeated.

"Were there two tomatoes?"

"Two," the doctor affirmed.

"Then both are gone. The soil on this mountain is the best soil for tomatoes," the man who bore crates brooded, "and I had but two. How came you onto my wagon?"

"Clambered up the wooden rungs."

As he thought it over, the expression of the man who bore crates grew stern. "And how came you onto this dark road, far from any community, with no company but the night?"

The doctor wore an innocent expression; the man who bore crates glared down at him, and the doctor watched him from the corner of his eye. All at once he burst out laughing. "Harmed, my friend!" he laughed. "I did harm!"

They had come to a crossroads beside a fork in the river. The oxen stopped; four roads, a ford, and a narrow bridge led in six different directions. The man who bore crates peered down one road and then the next, this one black under cover of trees, that one white under the moon; the river murmured audibly over the stones of the ford. "An obscure road," he said. "It puzzles even the oxen, wisest of animals."

He took down a second pouch of spidersilk, which hung beside the first—then, thinking of it and being in no hurry, took down the first pouch too and peered within.

"No tomatoes."

With a solemn expression, he replaced the food pouch and took from the other a scroll of translucent film one handspan square. As he unrolled it, the angelophytes within, scenting the musk of others of their kind on and about the road, luminesced in the shape of a sickle in melon green. The man who bore crates pored over this; after a moment he turned it upside-down and pored further.

"Rarely have I come this way, and never at night. The spores suggest the bridge." He let the film snap back into a roll and stowed it in the pouch. "But the spores are often mistaken: more than once they have shown me mountains where in fact there was the sea. It seems to me that this way may be better."

So saying, he spoke the word to the oxen and pointed

them toward a path that descended into a spinney; but they set off down a third way, neither the way the spores suggested nor the way the driver suggested: they took the way along the riverside.

"Though perhaps harm is too strong a word," the doctor said, "for I harmed only the crust of people, which is to say the dry and dead portion."

The other made no response, nor did he correct the oxen; he was preoccupied with other thoughts. They drove in silence awhile, and then, "I do not blame you," he said, "about the tomatoes. Only there are few comforts in this region. There may be comforts in the crates, but I must not open those even when I am hungry."

"And why not?" said the doctor, "for are they not a type of crust? Open them and ask yourself whether you might go on to open what lies inside. Perhaps the two of us might be joined in love."

The bearer of crates looked down at the scalp of the doctor, which bore, it seemed in the strange light of the moon, a series of small indentations, as though meant to be picked up in one hand. He said nothing.

"I mean a kind of love which has to do with the opening of crates."

"Salt may form a crust," said the man who bore crates, "as might snow; but as for person I think she forms no crust."

"My dear bearer of crates," said the doctor, throwing an arm around his waist, "the night ahead of us is long, and the road longer still; yet even they are not long enough for me to instruct you in the history of person's crust. Why, certain ancient capitalists, desiring to transform that which was base in themselves into that which was glorious, expressed the desire in this way: dross into gold. But gold is neither more nor less than the sun within a crust. And they found themselves willing to part with many objects necessary to their peace, in order to obtain gold."

"Oxen," said the man who bore crates, and the oxen hesitated and turned toward him, but he was not speaking to them.

"Oxen," said the small doctor, "and fruits and more, but most often, as it happens, crates—so long as the crates were not filled with gold. For the crust may be taken off a crate, but the crust of gold lies within the gold; and their desire was to see crust and substance made one."

"As at times a quantity of salt may become entirely crust," said the man who bore crates.

"And was it not these same capitalists," the doctor went on, "who ended by covering the earth in concrete and cinder?—a crust which began by accreting on their hearts, until it overflowed and manifested on the surface of the earth."

"Most suggestive," said the bearer of crates; and, when he sensed that the doctor had concluded his disquisition, added: "Then you damaged a supply of gold in your community, and they cast you out?"

The doctor burst out laughing again, so vigorously that the oxen grumbled. "What community requires sun-with-a-crust? There is quite enough sun, it seems, without the crust. And after all I am no mineralogist, but a fertility doctor."

Ahead, among the irregular moonshadows that stretched like nightmares down the mountainside, a more regular shadow stood out, head-high at its top and abutting the ground on its bottom. They drew up alongside a closed door of painted wooden panels, green-black in the night. A citron grew nearby, and there was a melon patch, and on the other side of the road three stone steps descended to the river. The oxen stopped at the driver's word. He slid down from his seat and lumbered toward the back of the wagon, where the crates soon thudded and scraped.

The doctor lost no time, but began rummaging through the spidersilk food pouch. Within, he found a clay tub of lemon-olive-bean paste and four wafers of sprouted barley impregnated with proteid algae. He devoured all of this and hurled the clay tub into the river.

By means of grunts, then cries, the driver communicated dissatisfaction with the crates. Finally the thudding and scraping abated; he emerged bent under a crate the size and shape of a child's bed, which he bore across his shoulders. When he had staggered to a position in front of the green door, he straightened, and let it fall. The doctor braced himself for a crash. But there was only a whisper, and the crate lay sound and straight on the doorstep.

The bearer of crates regained his seat and spoke the word, and the oxen strained at the harness. Soon they began rolling again.

"The philosopher too spoke concerning the transmutation of metals."

"You recall your history well, friend of oxen."

"When I tire of imagining the contents of the crates, which I must not open, I find little else to do on these roads but recall the stories told me as a child. But the condition to which the philosopher would have us aspire is not that of gold."

"It was in a community downriver where I did harm most recently," the small doctor said. "They engineered exotic clays there, and sometimes made paper."

"Mercury, rather. Dross and gold alike, saith the philosopher, into mercury."

A red bird flicked past, pursued by an owl.

"Perhaps you taught the childbearers of the community to nourish mercury in their wombs," the bearer of crates hazarded, "instead of living children, and it was for this that they cast you out?"

This time the doctor's laughter awoke a flock of waterfowl that had been sleeping in the river; they took to the air in a commotion of feather and water, and continued their migration.

"It was a small thing that I did," he said when he had recovered, "smaller than that, and I did it out of love. Shall I tell you?"

"You may if you like; and then if you try to harm me in the same way, I will have the advantage of you."

"In that community I tended the contraceptive moss."

"Were they wise to trust you so well?"

"Wiser than they knew: for, when it seemed to me that the condition of the community approached that of gold, I tore up the contraceptive moss, all out of love, and put in its place a mild hallucinogenic moss of like appearance, which I bred myself."

The man who bore crates appeared to digest the notion. By day he might have rejected it; but the night was deepening now, and the solitude of the road too, and he found himself saying: "So long as it was out of love."

"After that many were with child, though some knew it

and others did not; and some thought they were with child, though they were not; and many, both of those who were with child and of those who were not, believed that a child had been planted within them by a creature of darkness, which lay with them late at night on occasions when they found themselves unable to move."

So intent was the man who bore crates on the harms of the small doctor that he forgot to restrain himself from hungering. Absently, he reached behind him and took down the spidersilk pouch. Finding it empty, he continued to look into it for a time, and then looked at his passenger.

"There followed a swift movement of people in all directions," said the small doctor, "which I hold to my credit. Nevertheless, it was as you said: they cast me out." He had once again adopted the innocent expression, but soon saw that the gaze of the bearer of crates was fixed not on his features, but on the grains of sprouted barley littering the bench on either side of him.

"Did you take from me the clay tub of lemon-olive-bean paste and the four wafers of sprouted barley?"

The doctor tittered, then hiccuped. "It was out of love for you, my friend," he said. "For think of the night ahead: the moonlit road, none abroad but yourself; and the scent, as you pass it, of spring's wisteria, now hidden in the dark and strange in the moon's strange light: a night for meditations. And you have made a wrong turning I think, and an unexpected crossroads may lie ahead. But the night, like the river, wears a mask of silver and black: allow the hunger with which I have gifted you to focus your meditations and reveal to you the subtleties of the dark."

The man who bore crates clapped his hands over the

doctor's ears, and, lifting him by his head into the air, shook him like a dirty saddle-blanket.

"Out of love!" the doctor cried.

"Liar!"

The doctor squealed and screamed; but his screams, even as his bones rattled in his skin, were of laughter. "True!" he laughed, "True!"

The man who bore crates cast him onto the embankment, whence he tumbled with a splash into the river.

The oxen, the wagon, and the man who bore crates soon vanished around a bend of the road. The small doctor climbed out of the river and started on foot back in the direction of the most recent habitation, the green door in the mountainside.

3.2 The Speech of the Young Woman

afterward they brought me to a valley where there was healing, they said, in the air and water. whether it was the same valley as this or whether it was a different valley i don't know, only that they said there was healing, as though it were a thing, like gelatin. i did not find it so and i had very many dreams then. the women told me that the ancients had come to that valley as pilgrims for its healing properties, and then my dreams began to be of the ancients; but perhaps they were so already before the women told me. it turns my stomach to think of it now because i have it very peaceful here without anybody.

i have never been able to discover whether we have enough valleys or whether we must always use the same valley over again as though it were a cyclate. in the old world they had not enough valleys, though they had more valleys than we. when i had use of walking, the community thought me sound enough and sent me to purify the land where the ancient citadels were, and i went to far regions in order to sow the mosses and mycoids that digest structures. there i recognized the signs of a cramped people with an insufficiency of valleys. in the end they slept hardly at all and were only silent after a tragedy.

i had a thought today of something that i might say should the young builder return, or should someone else return, and should i find as before that i desire to express a thought. i mean a thought beyond the recollection he would have from me, of the time that i woke in the dark and found myself unable to move. that recollection is only one thing and i have quite forgotten it. and today i had a different thought, but i no longer remember what it was.

indeed, it turns my stomach to think of anything at all, even of the times when i walked, which i ought to think of with pleasure, for people have pleasure in walking and in recalling it.

for several days a black-winged bird has been building her nest under a certain eave. morning and evening i watch her carrying twigs and grasses. she alights every time on the same branch—and then up into the eave with her. then i see the sunlight from the river on the roof and walls. it was the same sunlight in the healing place, i think, but if that was a different valley then it was not the same water. and they are not the same roof and walls here as there, for these are the roof and walls of the burrow and those were the roof and walls of the healing place, and the builder dug the burrow but i do not think the same builder built the healing place unless he is very old. the sunlight is only light and dark. here i have the nutritive moss and the citron and the melon patch, and also the laboratory and my work, whereas there i had none of those things and the women demanded only that i take my ease. naturally i had my canes. for that was after the time when i woke in the dark, and since that time i have had my canes, though perhaps i had them also before that time.

i measure what i eat, but more and more all i can bear is the simplest of mosses. in my dreams there are feet in rainbow-colored stockings, the feet of healing persons. i am frightened. when the bee pauses, see how he hangs between invisible wings as though draped over a line. i sense too many days ahead.

but perhaps it was after all the same builder who made the healing place, for i know that it was he who made the terraced garden there. it was after the terraced garden was made that i became able to walk a little, with canes. the builder made a spigot in the garden, and i walked to the spigot. afterwards i told him of my recollection of the dark, and then he brought me to this place. the corridors of the burrow join as cleverly as did the paths of the garden, and he put a door on the burrow as he had put a gate on the garden, but in the garden they left the gate open, because they said it ought not to be closed; but i close the door of the burrow.

i worried how i would carry the melons and the citrons into the burrow, but the builder brought beryl-rubber and sewed me a pack; and he made me a spigot here in the burrow like the spigot in the garden, so that when i pull the rope a sweet water flows from the mouth of a flower. after he had demonstrated the spigot and i too had pulled the rope and caused the water to flow, then he asked me to recollect to him again the occasion i had often before recollected to him. perhaps i tell it differently every time. i don't remember any pain i said, and he asked me in particular to remember pain but i did not remember it. the voices of people disturbed me i said, and the cries of larger birds, for i prefer the smaller. and i never bore a child from it, for they were careful of that; but he knows well that i never bore a child. and the ring around the rim of the phosphor jar was the only light. and when the women told me of the damage i thought, "there then," as though i had always known that just such a thing would happen, though i think i could not have known it.

in this place a group of women come once in a season to perform on wind instruments, which the women in the healing place did not do. then they help me walk out from the burrow, and we four sit in chairs beside the citron, near the road, and it is all acceptable a little. and if there is something they need, a moss or some culture easily bred, then they remain while i breed it for them. i think they no longer come. but perhaps after all the season has not yet changed since last they came, and they will come again when it changes. though the time passes slowly here it never returns, that much i have discovered.

today i have ample work, not difficult; and perhaps at length i will recall a thing that i have not yet said to the builder. perhaps i have not told him that there was the smell of the sea. i will ask him whether i have told him, for perhaps i have not. when they took me away i was wet from seawater.

the ancients called this sea somnolent. i mean the nearest sea. it is some distance from here, not a great distance but too great for me. i imagine that if the women should come again, or if the builder should come—if anyone comes i shall ask them to take me there to the somnolent sea. i do not know what resources are required. can a wagon drive to the edge of the sea? i shall ask them to set me on the sand and leave me there forever, though they will understand that i mean only for a certain time. i will think how large is the sea, and yet with what contrition it comes to me there, as well as to others elsewhere. but it may be that all these things have already occurred. the burrow is white primarily. my bed is cotton-bat bound in white spidersilk, my linens dry, my chair woven of cane and covered too in spidersilk, white or else yellow, it is impossible to tell, some color of healing.

3.3 The Snow Pageant

It was Lammas. The end of summer. Time to prepare for the snow pageant.

"The community grows apace," said Ute. "We have received the crate."

But Hector said: "It is not the right crate. This crate belongs with a woman who is unknown to us; moreover it is neither the size nor the shape to hold a child."

Deirdre said, "Then will there be no new child this season?"

All the children sat very still around the table. Three days' fasting before discussion of the snow pageant. No light but the portrait of the bear, which cast the children in deep rose.

Already in the crèche they were aware of the scent of Yule, day of darkest night. During the hottest days of the year, the six spare days of summer, when the creek dried and the river ran sluggish and stagnant, and the sheep sickened, and none dared drink the water—already, then, one or another of them would think of rope. Then they would go into the cabinet of ropes, where the summer did not enter, and, smelling the ropes in the dark, think of Yule.

"How I hate this," said Ulrika.

"Perhaps the thing in the crate will do in place of a child," said Andrea.

"I dislike the crate," said Ute. "It is Lammas day; we prepare for dark times, contemplating snow; without reason there arrives not our crate but a different crate, which trembles with its own life and smells of apricots beginning to rotten. Where is the woman with whom this crate belongs? Where is the new child? Moreover the ungainly bird has lit recently on the roof of the crèche. I fear lest by opening this crate we invite an unwelcome thing."

"Yet we may not reject it," said Andrea, "for all things must be welcome somewhere. And it trembles, as you say: there is likely a creature within, child or not. To reject it will teach our hearts to harden."

"Might the correct crate yet arrive? The person to whom it came may bring it to us."

"The child within has surely been defiled," said Liesel.

Hector capered up the great hall and back. He alone of them was not weakened by fasting. "A sharp turning. Unbinding of cords. The wolf cometh."

The crate lay beside the great table. It weighed little. With strong fingernails they pried it open in the dark. The scent of apricot escaped, well rotten, and something ascending brushed their faces. They listened: a rustling, then crack of skull on table as hunger took the senses of Andrea. A drumming above as of gentle feet on the vault.

"It is a creature with feet."

"It is well," said Ute, and lay her head too on the table. "Unbinding of cords. Hector must instruct the creature in the meaning of the snow pageant."

3.4 The Love Story of the Young Woman and the Small Doctor

At first it was not easy between them. She awoke to find the floors of the burrow strewn with melon rinds. He liked nothing better than a melon, and for melon-eating he liked no hours better than the hours between midnight and dawn. She, awkward on her canes, could not easily tidy the rinds; he, cackling, retired at first light to the high shelf in the larder, and could not be coaxed thence until again midnight fell.

She sprayed him one day with vitriol, and he sprang at her and bit her right ear. The vitriol went high; the whitewash of the burrow blistered behind his head. The bite festered. It took her four days to design and breed the biotic to set it right: four days lost from her work, four days during which the half-wild spores in the laboratory reproduced idly.

After that she abandoned the larder during daylight hours, forsaking even the spigot of the young builder. But, between the hours of midnight and dawn, when the doctor had departed for the melon patch, she crept in among the rinds, and filled as many rubber-cyclate bottles as her pack would carry, and crept away again to stow them throughout the burrow before he returned. She ate citrons and nutritive moss in the laboratory, or sitting on the stoop in front of the green door—the latter particularly after evening rains, when the road's dust had been washed from the air, and the mountain shone green through the fog. Coming across melon rinds in the burrow, she cane-swatted them in the direction of the larder; and soon, by ricochet, could knock one across the threshold from anywhere in the burrow in three swats.

One night, entering the empty larder as usual, her cane slipped in melon pulp and she fell. The room reeked of rotting melon. Her elbow had been bruised, not seriously; the empty bottles in her pack were unbroken. On hands and knees she cleared a path to the spigot around the larder's perimeter. The next day she bred and loosed a deodorant colony with a cedar scent which recalled to her mind the young builder and his sawn planks; but, although the rooms smelled of cedar thereafter, it was over and alongside the scent of rotting melon, which remained, deep in the texture of the walls. She swatted new rinds out the green door, out onto the walk, and thence, at her leisure, into a mound aside the melon patch, where they returned to earth.

In the white haze of dawn, as she turned past the larder toward a breakfast of citron and nutritive moss on the dew-damp stoop, the small doctor called out to her, offering to inspect her womb.

*

She picked all the melons from the melon patch and concealed them in a shallow pool a short distance downriver. She worked all day. When at last she returned to the burrow, it was by phosphor-light that she moved her bedding into a large closet, doorless, bringing with her several bottles of water and a cake of nutritive moss. She cleaned her catheter. She took the ring-iron blade and the two Morris darning spiders from the laboratory, made herself comfortable in the closet, and allowed the spiders to seal the doorway. She slept soundly after her long labors.

Daylight, fighting through the pink striated strands of morris silk, dyed the closet crimson, and she within it, as though she had hidden herself within a monstrous misshapen heart. A wind blowing through the open door of the burrow whipped the silk aflutter: the walls of the heart jumped and snapped, but never regularly, never rightly.

Waking, she pressed against the silk, first her palm and then her shoulder; and though it gave with the elasticity of flesh, and filled the closet with the scent of vinegar and cloves, it sprang back undeformed when she released it, to resume quaking in the wind. She made sure of the blade, safe and sharp, wrapped in muslin at the bottom of the basket. Into the jar of the two spiders, the larger as large as a plum, its partner small as a fleck of blood, she dropped a pinch of nutritive moss.

At midmorning she heard the sound of voices, cut by the snapping of the silk—women's voices, first from afar, then from within the burrow: the three women from the mountain, come to sing to her. Shortly the braying laughter of the small doctor joined them. They moved off deeper into the burrow, the women and the doctor too; and then it seemed to her that both voices and braying laughter stopped, and a piping began; at least perhaps it was a piping—the music of the women, she thought—but after all the sound that reached her was no more than a murmur mutilated by silk: murmur of piping, or of piping and braying together, or braying and piping; and now and again a rhythmic thumping, as of dance. All of these sounds persisted through the night.

When she woke, the wind had subsided. The burrow was silent. She ate two citrons, drank water, and slept again.

When next she woke, it was to a tight murderous pain in her head. It was not possible to tell the time; the light was dim, but not very dim. The larger of the two spiders had died, and its partner had begun to eat it. She listened, but heard only her own breathing, which had grown loud— louder, it seemed, than ever before. The light did not change. She neither ate nor drank. Her skin was sweat-sticky, and had been so when she woke.

She rummaged in the basket for the iron blade, and thought, for a terrible instant, that she had not taken it after all—that she had misthought, misremembered, trapped herself behind head-throbbing and silk in the most foolish possible way. Then she nicked her thumb, too shallowly to bleed. She cut a long flap in the silk and gathered her canes.

The green door was closed, the burrow silent; the high shelf in the larder soiled but bare. Her deodorant colony had died, some time ago it must have been. She fled the stench. Outside, the fog had descended into the valley. The road was a paleness against the gray, the river an unseen whispering; on her head the sweat cooled to something like dew.

The fog fooled with voices: scarcely had she heard them, coming fast from the road, when they were upon her, the three women and the small doctor. Walking for pleasure: she had forgotten that people did so.

Seeing her astonished, they laughed; she laughed too. The five of them embraced one another. Then she fell, and they carried her to the stoop and helped her sit. The doctor picked up her canes from the ground and carried them to her. She began to cry and the women went away. Taking the canes she lurched away downriver. The small doctor did not follow, and she soon lost herself in the fog.

She went later to reclaim the melons, but found them covered in snails.

*

The doctor, it transpired, preferred snails even to melons, and preferred them in the heat of the afternoon. He fished them tirelessly from the shallow melon-baited pool, and, crouching, cracked their shells between his thumbs. When it was not afternoon, he again occupied the high shelf in the larder.

In a cleft in the rock she discovered the grave of a child, and also the remains of a crate. Atop the grave, in white river-pebble, had been laid the sign of mercury.

She had three dreams about this grave. The first, that she came upon it in a very deep darkness, and, patting the soil with her hands, found it open and empty, and knew that the child corpse had emerged and now shared the darkness with her. The second, that she came upon it and found the small doctor emerging, and frightened him back in, and spread the soil over him; but she knew afterwards that the small doctor who occupied the high shelf in her larder was not the real small doctor, who was in the grave, but the child corpse.

And the third dream, that she came upon the grave and found the child corpse emerging, and frightened it back in, but found the small doctor there in the grave already, and knew that the small doctor who occupied the high shelf in her larder was neither the real small doctor nor the child corpse, but a different thing altogether.

When she awoke, he was filing down her toenails with the filing stone. He gripped her feet and swept his arm down and down again in long arcs. She dared not move. When he had finished, he collected the toenail dust in a cotton envelope and replaced the filing stone in the fourth hanging basket from the threshold. She heard him scrambling back up to the larder shelf.

She devoted the day to work, but felt more and more the need of the new creature, the buoyant creature yet unnamed, which ought to have come to her long ago by crate. She cleaned the burrow, bred a frail thing with the odor of lavender, and thought with inarticulate worry of the child's grave under the sign of mercury.

In the afternoon she observed the doctor to sprinkle the dust from the cotton envelope onto his snails before he ate them. He stared across the river as he munched, bearded in snail slime: sprinkled and munched, sprinkled and munched.

The snails alone are not sufficient nutrition, she thought.

*

"Angelophytes," said the man who bore crates: "the messenger spores. The work that you perform in this area inspires in me a boundless love for you. These spores, which are grotesque in their ignorance, caprice, and utter futility, disturb the tranquility of my journeys and even threaten my existence; for it is scarcely a season since those I carry, which purport to guide my way, directed me instead into a vast crater belching smoke and fumes, in the very rock of which inhered so horribly that quality which the joyous shun, that it flowed as liquid across my path. I barely escaped with my life. Therefore in the name of all people I welcome what wisdom you can teach to these spores."

He had agreed to carry her up the mountain in his wagon for the John's Day celebration. Before dawn, worrying lest the small doctor accompany her, she had released a mild nerve agent; and had listened outside the green door, until, by a thunk, she knew that he had fallen senseless from his shelf. She left the door open to air the place.

"Alas," she said, "my spore-gift is not wisdom but flight. Already there flourish among the messengers a strain of anemotrophs, which take their nourishment from the wind; but even these linger near to the earth, for their weight confines them there; and should the wind fail, they fall to ground, though they be not yet where they may best deliver their news. But the messengers that soon mature in my laboratory will rise, as ice in water, to the limit of the sky, and there multiply, and, hearkening the instincts common to all messengers, dispose themselves, over the course of seasons, into an olfactive network vast in extent yet minuscule in figure, under which shall be bound together all people, on this and other coasts."

They passed between the two great cedars and under the canopy of the forest.

"And will there be no region hidden from their intelligence?" said the man who bore crates.

"The bowels of the earth," she said; "the depths of the sea; the interiors of people."

The man who bore crates spoke uneasily to the oxen.

Although she looked for the young builder at the John's Day celebration, she did not see him. Some said he had gone away, others that he had remained, but none could direct her where to find him.

She stayed one night with each of the three women who played wind instruments; all were with child. On the fourth day a man passed through bearing chocolate, and she rode with him back to the valley.

"Do you ever go to the sea?" she asked him.

"Never," he said. "They eat shellfish there and the land reeks of brine."

As she caned up her walk, she asked herself without hope whether the blessing of the John's Day bell might have freed her from the presence of the small doctor. But perhaps she should have brought him after all, she thought—that he too might be freed.

The green door stood open, as she had left it, but the doorway was stopped now by a snail-studded mountain of ruin. At its base, under layers of shells, web, and wicker, lay her laboratory tables: one atop the other, spiked together with shards of cyclate, shards of bottles and beakers, shards of dishes still dripping with the remains of the cultures that had made their homes there. The legs of the lower table were spiked to the floor and yoked tight to the door-frame with the boughs of the citron tree, which, a look told her, had no boughs remaining. The ring-iron blade was embedded in the tabletop. There could be no passing without climbing— and she of all people could never climb.

Surprising her with a merry whoop from behind, the small doctor leaped past her onto the top of the highest table, and with screams of laughter pelted away down the hall, keeping in the main to the walls and ceiling, where he clung with appalling agility.

*

At the end of a trail of snail shells she discovered her bedding, laid winningly in a small grassy plot by the river, underneath a sycamore. He had left her a quarter-cake of nutritive moss, some netting to keep off insects, and a single rotten melon, like a gift.

The sight of this arrangement robbed her of her wits. She set off down the road. It was late in the afternoon. There were a few dwellings ahead, but it was after all an obscure road, and though she had lived a long time in the burrow she had seldom left it; her neighbors were strangers to her. So perfect was her fury that she had left behind even the nutritive moss, and now went unladen; and so violent her progress that the canes tore open even the oldest calluses on her hands. Nevertheless the small doctor soon overtook her.

He was prepared, she saw, for a journey: pack—her pack—bulging, straw hat yellow in the sun. "Carboniferous obstruction of the oviduct," he sang; "I have seen it often: a lump of bitumen, roosting deep within your feminine parts, bears down upon the cruentous canal and deprives your thigh of quiver. To remove it is a simple procedure; I have brought my instruments." She slowed and swayed, feigning weakness; and, when he approached too close, lashed out with a cane and struck him on the temple. He staggered but did not fall. Eleven drops of his blood dotted the road around them, like lichens under the whitening sky.

An elderly man on a donkey, happening to turn a corner of the road ahead of them, witnessed this exchange. He and the donkey alike turned rebuking expressions on her, and he even began to speak, but she struck the donkey twice and it hurried away.

The small doctor wiped blood from where it had pooled in his ear and flicked her with a twelfth idle drop. "Constriction of the womanpiece," he said.

She lunged at him, and although he was keeping his distance now, and leapt away nimbly as a hare, struck him again. He fell this time, and she too: they tumbled briefly in the dust, she seeking any soft part of him to tear at with her hands, and then he rolled clear of her. The pack had torn in the scuffle, and snails, its only contents, spilled across the road: no instruments, but only snails. He sprang to his feet, and after a moment's thought abandoned snails and pack alike, and left her there.

She recovered her canes, but, instead of taking her feet, elbow-walked the short distance to the mound of snails. Tearing up one of the flat stones that edged the road, she ground each of the snails into paste. It was near dusk when she turned her attention to the pack: one by one, digging with her fingernails in the fading light, she picked out the tiny shell fragments that had entered into the weave of its silk. A layer of slime coated the interior, and soon coated her hands too; the bits of shell stuck to her; gripping the pack in her teeth, she pushed herself to the riverbank, found a shallow patch, and tumbled in to wash.

Presently she heard the clump of hooves on the road behind her. The small doctor had returned, leading the donkey on which the elderly man had passed them. "She will speed us on our way," he said. "Observe her eyelashes, long and black."

She regarded him from the water.

"As for the old man," he said, "I discussed with him the state of his reproductive organs, and he is now with child."

She looked away from him; and soon, having nowhere else to look, she looked in what she took for the direction of the sea. "In time," she said, "even if it is many years from now, I will surely kill you."

*

Some nurturers of oxen, the first dwelling they came to in the dark, kept a pair of darning spiders—common darning spiders, but sufficient to repair the pack. They loaded her with blankets, bottles, and nutritive moss, and she slept under their canopy. The small doctor slept in a tree nearby. At dawn she rode the donkey back to the burrow, where the green door tapped fretfully at the wreckage on the threshold, and, over the course of the long morning, she pried the ring-iron blade from the tabletop. Its edge was dull, its surface scratched, its handle cracked; but the blade still ran straight.

She directed the donkey toward the sea. The small doctor followed behind, out of reach; and when she stopped—to eat, to rest, or only to gaze from some high place out at the hills and mountains and valleys, range after range, all alike but each dimmer than the last until distance bleached them finally out of existence—then he stopped too, climbed a nearby tree, and waited for her to go on. Maybe he slept and maybe he didn't. She threw stones at him, but he threw them back. Finally, picking up a last long, flat stone, she made no move to throw it, but sat down by the roadside and began sharpening the blade. After that she carried the stone in her pack and sharpened nightly. She tore off one strip of blanket to wrap around the blade for safety, and another to tie it to her body every night before she went to sleep: cracked handle on her palm, guard across her wrist, blanket-sheathed iron down her forearm.

The small doctor seemed not to eat, but as he followed her she heard him smacking his lips; perhaps, she thought, he eats the dust of the road.

She took her time, stopped to rest. If she was slow to start in the morning, he laughed at her from his tree, but it seemed to her a peevish impatient laughter: so long had she heard his laughter that she heard through it now. She delayed, spending several days in a spot she found pleasant.

She taught herself to remain awake while lying still as though sleeping. In the middle of the night she opened her eyes quietly and studied his silhouette against the sky. Twice she saw the gleam of his own eyes looking back; at other times she could not tell.

After many days, finding no sign of the sea, she asked a man tending herbs how much farther it was. "The sea!" he cried. He looked quickly around as though it might have crept up on him. "It was near here recently, I think. And will be again? For now perhaps it lies in the other direction."

At that the small doctor began laughing, the honest merry laugh of his melon-eating days. The tender of herbs laughed at the small doctor's laughing, and the small doctor laughed harder at the laughing of the tender of herbs, and finally she laughed too. She laughed until she fell off the donkey. After all, the situation had become ridiculous. The small doctor fell over laughing. She lunged at him and caught his foot, and, flicking the blade free of its wrapper, severed the tendon behind his heel; then, as he thrashed like a fish on the riverbank, the other heel too. He made no sound, but sat in the road with a bewildered expression while the tender of herbs bound the wounds with strips cut from his seed-pouch. Together they lifted him onto the donkey, and she turned it back in the new direction of the sea.

They came near the canopy of the tender of herbs; he fetched them food and bandages from within, and accompanied them some distance farther.

"The late capitalists named that sea the Sea of Giants," the tender of herbs said: "the Giants' Sea. Why did they name it thus? They named it thus because those who inhabited this coast were giants: not that they were larger in their bodies than you or I, but that they kept a boundless faith in their hearts, even as they doubted all things; and therefore their hearts were thought to be large, ineffably so, in order to accommodate the immiscible and indissoluble multitude of their visions, as well as the other phantasms which forgathered there. In our civilization, we too must become giants, and admit all things into the ever-expanding chambers of our hearts."

3.5 The Means of Reproduction

"Naturally it makes no difference," said the deliverer of infants. "We send them tomorrow with the long-distance runner and they will have no more knowledge of their biological mothers than do you or I. But it is a prodigy in its way; and you children, whose burden it is to reckon the world's prodigies, perhaps you will value to know it."

"It is not altogether the first such we have known," said Hector.

The three infants lay side by side in a sunflower-embroidered silk sling under the canopy of infants. Two slept while the third looked sidelong over them.

The deliverer of infants recollected no diverser crop of infants. They had sprung from the wombs of the three women who played on wind instruments, all on the same day and all quite alike; but contact with the air had thickened the skin of the first, so that its eyes peered out as from under a mask of rubber; the skin of the second had fallen slack, leaving bulbous eyes thrust into space; and the third had broken out in a spiral seam from crown of head to soles of feet.

At first there had been four of them: one of the three women had borne twins. "The fourth was as other infants," said the deliverer of infants, "and continued so even in contact with the air; and it was that one, the infant which continued as other infants, which was devoured."

"One of the twins?" said Hector. "Or one of those not twins?"

"It is difficult to know," said the deliverer of infants, "for I stowed the four of them together in the sunflower silk, as is best for infants, before any distinction might be drawn among them; and afterward I went away for a time, that they might contemplate the winds and sky. And so perhaps it was a twin which did the devouring, and perhaps a twin which was devoured; perhaps one twin devoured the other, and perhaps one not a twin devoured the other not a twin; and so on."

Hector drew himself up and performed a march, not around the canopy but through it, to and fro, until he had awakened all the infants. They watched him attentively as though learning the march. "The march of the games of logic," he explained, "a not unpleasant pastime for allaying fears; study with me"—here he cut short his march and laid a hand on the buttock of the deliverer of infants—"and shortly this prodigy will fly from our thoughts, leaving wisdom in its wake. We must know, first, how many were twins and how many not twins; second, how many are twins and how many not twins; then how many will be twins and how many not; and how many had and will have been and so forth; and after that whether it be twins or those not twins which devour other infants. The arguments are many. Twins cleave to a solitary road, for never again will they enjoy the womb-community which once they shared, and naturally it drives them to bite. At the same time it may happen that the twinless infant, witnessing twin-affinity or what he takes for it, enacts incontinently the unsocial fantasies of a jealous heart. One of these will be a builder, I think."

The deliverer of infants started, flinging the goat-hair infant-brush into a shrub.

"For did the builder not come among us during the time before these infants?" said Hector. "And though he is no longer among us, did he not commune sexually during that time with the three women? We in the crèche remember it well. And that is how builders reproduce I think: by such communing."

Hector turned away to inspect the packs that the long-distance runners would wear, three runners to three distant communities; and he inspected the straps that would hold the infants in the packs. But all of that had been inspected before. Meanwhile he observed the deliverer of infants. "Come away," he said at last. "Come into the sun." He himself took one step and then another until he stood in the open air. The deliverer of infants followed him out into the heat, first of the year, and into the aroma of summer sap.

"Come away from them." Hector crouched at the head of the scree, and, when the deliverer of infants hesitated, went on: "Fear not the sensation of the sun, nor yet the visions it brings, for in the next season it will bring new visions; and fear not the other thing, I mean the devouring. For we in the crèche, who know all prodigies, know better than to remark the immeasurable matrix of prodigies in which we people dwell, I mean scent and articulation and the movement of fluids and the like, which, should we fear them, we should fear at every moment. Fear neither the season nor the infants, for I will oversee them."

By way of conclusion he bounded down the slope, one sun-dry stone to the next, away from the canopy of infants and on toward the richer scent and shadow of the cedars lining the creek. "Come away and give them a chance at each other," he called back. "We will return later and assess."

The deliverer of infants slid and stumbled to join him at the treeline. Hector clapped his hands twice in delight. "And what then?" said the deliverer of infants. "Should we see marks of devouring, further marks, marks on the body of one and the stains of the fluid of devouring on the mouth of another: what then? And should we see marks on the bodies of two, or all? Stains on the mouths of all? Tell me what then."

"Then they are solitary in their hearts," said Hector, "one or more of them. For this is how solitary creatures reproduce, I think: by devouring."

The deliverer of infants grew solemn. It was as he had thought but not liked to say. He stooped to pick up a stone, red and rectilinear, one of the stones of the late capitalists which the earth spat up. He swung it once and twice against the air, not yet violently. "Even as contagion reproduces."

"Even as contagion." Hector clapped his hands a third time in delight. "Do you know the history of the four children who were companions?"

The deliverer of infants sat in half-lotus position on a boulder half under the cedars and half out, and, laying the rectilinear stone near at hand, listened with one ear to Hector and with one ear for the cry of an infant bitten by another.

"It was the season when two were hanged. These two had agreed to go under one name, in imitation of a ceremony current among the late capitalists; thereafter we could not tell them apart, and so when it came time to hang one we hanged both. Then the crèche waned. Four children agreed to journey through the earth in order to seek out the whale. These four loved each other without fault, and relied on each other too—perhaps as twins in the womb and perhaps not— but on the high mountain where children go to learn burglary they had learned to rely on each other, and therein lay their strength."

"The whale," said the deliverer of infants.

"A fish," Hector said, "larger than most, which they sought for this reason: that the whale swims not in a sea of water but in a sea of images, that is to say, a reproductive sea: for within its nose, which in its girth outstrips the nose of all other creatures, it carries a quantity of oil; which is to say, a quantity of sperm. As the girth of its nose outstrips that of all other creatures', so too does the quantity of its sperm. And this sperm bears images invisibly in its structure, I mean images of whales; but owing to its waxy consistency the whale's particular sperm also bears images visibly: images I mean of those objects which impress it, for example the hands of children. Moreover, though the whale swims blindly, just as our civilization and the crèche which is an element thereof move blindly through the world, and just as we people move blindly amongst each other, the whale knows a song for repeating to itself when it loses its way, and the song returns to tell the whale messages from the deep; and the part of the whale which hears the song's return, and conveys it to the inner ear of the whale—that part is none other than the reservoir of sperm.

"All of this was the reason for the children to burgle the whale. By burglary I mean to take from by stealth. Not knowing what conditions to expect in the interior of the whale, they wove cloaks out of the wool of ewes, one for each child: red, blue, umber, and pink. Pink as of pink borage. Umber as of the last spadeful of earth dug during the digging of a well. Blue as of blue borage. Red not the red of the fox, nor of any flower nor any tree which grows its bark red, nor yet of any species of autumn leaf, nor like any other red thing which occurs to my imagination.

"But I might add that, although the sperm fills its nose, the whale has no sense of smell. The whale is a musician.

"When they emerged from the earth, the children found themselves in the labyrinth of the whale. In the whale's nose the sperm awaited them. They groped hither and thither in search of some hatch through which to decant the sperm from the head. Meanwhile they left impressions of themselves in the matrix of waxy sperm—that is, impressions of their bodies; and, each child recrossing her own path in growing bewilderment, and the paths of others, they found themselves coerced by sperm-paths into ways not of their choosing, and, although the sperm-paths sometimes fit them perfectly, they fit them at other times imperfectly, for the children, although similar, were not the same. This is what it is in the belly of a whale: impressions all around. The whale dived and the pressure grew; the children were impeded by the mass of sperm. Here a bluff of sperm, impassible, complete with miniature goat-track too tiny for the feet of children; there a ceiling of sperm crisscrossed with sperm-rafters from which depended a field of sperm-corn; an outcropping of sperm nearby in the shape of a window, but the window looked out only on more sperm. A history current among children held that a scent emanates from the head of the whale, attracting fish for it to consume. The children began to fear that they had made a mistake: that the entire whale was nothing but a glutinous mass, a trap, not a labyrinth precisely but a morass. The suffocating depths. Look where they might they could no longer pick out any cloak of red. Amidst the white of sperm they picked out blue of blue borage, pink of pink borage, umber of the well's deeps; but however their eyes thirsted for it they sighted no red in the whale.

"Only three children returned.

"And after that it was the time of the wolf," said Hector, "as you know."

The deliverer of infants plucked borage flowers, pink and blue, from a nearby patch of borage; and, as Hector looked on, inhaled deeply of their bouquet.

"Was there any scent in the whale?" said the deliverer of infants, "a scent as of red?"

Hector did not answer. The deliverer of infants arranged the borage around Hector's head. Even from afar, from beyond the cedar forest and the crèche and the river mad with thaw, from across all the long slopes of brown summer nettles, the scent of the road impinged on them, the scent of earth at once trodden and new. The deliverer of infants stood to face the canopy of infants, where a wind chattered.

"Perhaps one of the three who returned was no friend of people."

"Perhaps," said Hector; "perhaps one was as one of those three under the canopy. I mention the incident only to recall to you one in the web of fearful prodigies which are our fore-bears."

"We have let them alone too long," said the deliverer of infants. "It is to be hoped that they are not devoured." He took up the rectilinear stone and scrambled up the hillside. Through the dust of his climb they made out a cord above the treetops, and a kite shuddering in breezes which never touched the earth.

"It may have been a different species of whale," said Hector, following, "for a certain species of whale keeps im-ages not in the sperm but in the lungs. There are two lungs of the whale: one holds images of dead things, and the oth-er of things yet to come, here or elsewhere; but should the whale turn around, the lungs change places. Perhaps it was that kind of whale, and the images they sought lay not in the sperm but in one or another of the lungs."

They gained the top of the bluff; and in the shadow of the sapling which supported the canopy the deliverer of in-fants stopped to confer once more with Hector:

"Shall we destroy it? If we should see by the mouth of one that it has bitten another—shall we destroy it?"

Hector reached up and tugged the dangling cord to

loose the knot; the velvet blind, embroidered not with sunflowers but with stars, tumbled open from canopy to earth, separating with black of night the infants from the deliverer of them.

"They hear, you know," Hector said, "better than we."

3.6 The Heart

They are on a raft. The sun strikes the river. It is early fall now. The raft is made of ice. The sun has shone warmly for many days. Wendy's eyes are a mask as she crouches over Fabienne, who is sleeping.

The raft rocks under her heels. It has rocked that way before; it is in no danger of capsizing. The ice is clad in insulating cyclate, then in beeswax-impregnated burlap for comfort against the body. There is a damp smell, the smell of the river. The burlap warms Wendy's feet. She crouches over Fabienne. She has laid the pole across Fabienne's throat. They cut the pole from a birch when first they took to the raft. The pole is of little use for propelling the raft. It is flexible and not strong. It still feels young in her hands. They know very little about rafting.

They had agreed to sleep side by side in the afternoon. Fabienne had wanted it that way. When the sun lay on her eyes from a point nearer the horizon—not yet near the horizon, but nearer than the mid-day point—then, she said, it brought her a certain kind of dream. Should Wendy dream the same dream alongside her, they would be bound together in the best of ways. It was a dream about yellow she said. Wendy thought Fabienne fanciful, but she agreed to sleep in the afternoon for the sake of Fabienne. But when the time came she could not sleep. Her consciousness of Fabienne beside her prevented it.

Their skin touched at the shoulders; the hot dry touch of Fabienne's shoulder gave her confidence in Fabienne's continuing presence, but it also aroused her senses. Their contact was like the contact between two motes of dust. She feared Fabienne would fall off the raft. The river carried the raft all on its own. It was a clear dry day. Something as hot and as dry as Fabienne could end up anywhere.

Soon their shoulders sweat where they touched. Then Wendy became groggy. Wendy and Fabienne stewed together in the damp smell of the river. Together they made a moist clot in the dry day. The river carried them swiftly as ever but time slowed to sludge. Still Wendy neither slept nor dreamt; but certain of her impressions became heightened. Giants walked the earth, and her impression of them was heightened. Her eyes were closed and would not open. She felt Fabienne breathing beside her, and the pulse in Fabienne's skin. Fabienne had never been farther away. Even now a giant looked down on the two of them. She had one foot in the next valley over and the other foot in the next valley the other way; no feet at all in the middle valley. She bent over to peer at the women on the raft on the river which flowed between her legs. It was her breath, tepid and wet, which moistened their shoulders. A shadow passed across the sun.

The pole is warm against Fabienne's throat. It is warm in Wendy's hands. Fabienne is still asleep. Her throat appears cool and smooth, not at all sticky with sweat. Yellow pollen has collected in a sparse streak running from the throat's hollow out along the collarbone—the collarbone more distant from the mountain. A hot dry breeze full of pollen is blowing down from the mountain. Wendy may bear down on the pole or she may not. The pole will not break. It is strong enough. Wendy may choke Fabienne under the pole. She has arranged her hands close on either side of Fabienne's neck, to reduce the stress on the pole. That is, the stress she may put on the pole by bearing down on it. There is something wrong with the river; the raft pitches suddenly in a gust of wind; Fabienne stirs with it and then starts in her sleep. Her hand gropes for her throat and finds the pole there. She wakes.

Wendy lays the pole aside. It has given Fabienne a wood splinter in her throat. The length of the wood splinter lies snug under a translucent layer of Fabienne's skin. Fabienne's skin appears thick. Soon it will be time for bathing in the river. Wendy watches Fabienne but prevents herself from touching. Fabienne's eyes are brown.

"Unaccustomed impressions and sensations," says Wendy. "I began to feel different, particularly with regard to your throat."

*

"It is a surgery for expressing the love between people."

"A surgery by knife?" Fabienne has kept the wood splinter in her throat.

"By knife. But not a loathsome thing: those very surgeries by knife, with which once they transformed people into metal and wrought them ill, we now impress into the service of our hearts. It is a surgery that will place us inside one another, so they say."

It is a day in early fall, a day on the raft. They are eating onions. The valley is verdant; a mild onion grows there; it is this onion they are eating. They have also apples, lemons, and cabbages. All of these articles lie in conglomeration on the raft. The sunlight pearls the onions in their hands. White onion-milk dribbles onto the burlap. The burlap is hot under the thighs of the women. The women are hot near each other. But at night the air will freeze. Then they will open the cyclate vents of the raft, to maintain the ice. They will wear their hoods. They have been four days on the raft. Before that they did not know each other.

"Is it the river which sustains us?" Fabienne wonders, "or the ice?"

"The one who will perform it lives I am told by the seashore." Wendy takes the onion from Fabienne's hand and replaces it with a different onion. All day she has been replacing Fabienne's onion in this way. Fabienne does not mind. Wendy finishes the onion that had been Fabienne's.

"I only wondered what phase of matter sustains us," says Fabienne. "What is wrong with the river?"

The raft is spinning on the rivertop, as though they were nearing the edge of a whirlpool. But there is no whirlpool. The current is even. The air is still. The raft spins slowly atop the current. One apple rolls off into the river, making no sound.

"That mountain is under enchantment."

They look at the mountain. It is swathed in gray gloom although the day is bright. In their bellies Wendy and Fabienne feel an oily drizzle under choking clouds. They turn away from the wave of heat that washes over them.

"The river likewise then."

"A surgery," says Wendy. "Before we are both too much enchanted I would like us to mark each other."

BRIAN CONN

Fabienne, taking up Wendy's hand from where it lies atop a cabbage, bites playfully at the webbing between thumb and first finger.

"A mark that will not fade," Wendy says. "We have been four days on this raft and seen nobody, neither on the river nor on the road. Not since the community of ice-cutters have we seen any person. The waterfowl have migrated. The valley is under enchantment. I fear things will not long remain as they are. The road brought us together by chance. It was laid by the wise. There is a woman accomplished in the art of surgery who lives by the seashore."

The woman accomplished in the art of surgery appears between them. She is very old. Her head is made of stone. She carries a knife in one hand and a rag in the other. Her spine, after so many seasons under the weight of her head, has attained the shape of a hook. Wendy and Fabienne each see her, and each sees that the other has seen her. They laugh at themselves.

"I too am afraid." Fabienne sits near Wendy on the raft. Wendy puts an onion in Fabienne's hands but Fabienne gives it back. Wendy casts it into the river. They hold hands. They gaze on each other. The air dims. Thunder slumbers atop the mountain. The mountain is under enchantment. The sea is a long way off. Nobody has ever found it. The community of ice-cutters kept obsidian blades, flint blades, serrated cyclate blades, and metal blades. Wendy and Fabienne did not take any blades.

"A secret mark, but deep."

"So exceeding deep that it will astonish any who know of it."

They desire the same mark. They whisper together before sleeping.

*

Soon the valley will be under snow. What will happen when the valley is under snow? Nobody knows what will happen then. Finally it will emerge from the snow. Already there is snow upriver. There is ice. In the ice field at the top of the valley a woman instructed Fabienne and Wendy how to cut ice. Wendy and Fabienne happened to arrive on the same morning at the community of ice-cutters and raft-builders. The road brought them there separately, but the river and the raft carried them away together. Today the air is warm, but tonight the frost will not fail to come. They have blankets aboard the raft with which to wrap themselves together and enjoy each other's warmth. They have hoods of lambswool. The sun is shining. They sit naked on the raft eating onions. They pole now and then down the river. They have cut a new pole. The new pole is stronger than the old. Fabienne has kept the splinter in her throat in lieu of a deeper mark. Her hand shakes. Wendy's wrist is bandaged in white silk. Fabienne is looking up at the mountain. She sets the pole aside and returns to her onion. It is midafternoon: a day neither in midsummer nor in midautumn, but between them; perhaps the middle of some other way of reckoning seasons.

"I feel too easy in my stomach," Fabienne says, wiping her lips. All day she has been wiping her lips. Her lips are chafed red. Fabienne is not wearing a bandage. Only Wendy is wearing a bandage. They had only enough silk for one bandage. "Had it sickened me I believe I would feel closer to you; but it has left me quite as I was before."

The burlap has collected a black dust from the air. The beeswax has grown dirty and friable under the mountain's enchantment. Pellets of dirty beeswax collect in the crevices

BRIAN CONN

of their bodies, lending them the appearance of molting.

"Did I frighten you?" Fabienne asks.

Wendy takes up the pole. Its end drops thoughtfully into the river.

"Not enough," says Fabienne with regret. "My mark did not go deep."

Fabienne takes the pole from Wendy. The slightest of incidents ensues: Wendy's fingers draw away from Fabienne's when Fabienne's brush them in the course of taking the pole. It is the least notable of motions. Nevertheless Fabienne has noted it. Her feet and hands flush scarlet. Her face remains impassive. She snaps the pole across her knee. Now they will have to cut a third pole. For a long time they drift down the river in silence. Fabienne bears half of the pole in each hand.

"It is some peculiarity of my own skin I think," says Wendy at last, "that it feels as though everything I touch were wrapped in gauze. Do you recollect how things look through your eyes when they grow old, before the optic has made you a new pair? Just so do the surfaces of the world feel to me through my skin. Sometimes it is difficult to bear. Would that a new kind of doctor might make me a new skin, and I feel the world anew; but people have not that wisdom, not yet."

Fabienne throws the halves of the pole into the river, where they drift away, each toward a different bank. "I had thought it a pleasure to both of us, to be touched by each other."

"Would that we might share a skin," says Wendy, "by surgery."

"Surgery!" Fabienne spits. "Never in the history of people has it sufficed."

The road runs beside the river, spangled with early fall leaves. The wind whisks up the leaves and the rushes catch them at the riverside. In the distance, tiny as a toy, the crossroads approaches. The women see it there. One of the great gate-cedars has fallen across the path where it starts up the mountain. The river churns sluggishly. The crossroads remain in the distance. Fabienne seizes Wendy's wrist and draws her near. Wendy pushes her into the river. When Fabienne climbs back onto the raft her skin is pale and goose-pimpled. It no longer appears thick, but thin as the new fall sky. It hangs loose on her bones. Fabienne is disappearing. Onions, apples, and cabbages are not enough for Fabienne.

"It grows worse every year," says Wendy. "When I touch you I imagine the living feel of your skin; but I sense only a fine greasy powder. Moreover I know this powder: it is that powder which is all that remains of those prisons of late capitalism, those we scarcely recall. I held that powder in my hand, being in a place better forgotten, and it too is a fine greasy stuff."

"Then that is the reason for the condition of your skin." The day is warm but Fabienne is wet. She is shivering. The day is not entirely warm but partly cold. "An organism makes its home in that powder, one not beneficial to people."

Wendy inspects her own skin.

"Did the wind blow that day?"

"It blew so that the powder covered me," Wendy says. "And it blew the powder into great drifts and dunes among the fallen idols and other cultural materials of that place where I ought not to have gone. Is it contagious?"

"I do not know its life cycle."

Wendy sits on the corner of the raft. She urinates into the river. There is a wagon on the riverbank, beside the road at the foot of the mountain, attended neither by oxen nor by people.

"It is too much," says Fabienne, "this being felt as a greasy residue."

Wendy agrees that it is too much. They understand each other. They weep. Afterwards they catalog the occasions on which they risk touching each other. They agree that, once they have cut another pole, their fingertips will no longer touch when they pass each other the pole. They agree that they will sleep each wrapped in her own blanket and the two of them wrapped together in further blankets, that each may continue to enjoy the form and mass of the other's body, though not the texture of the other's skin. It will not be as warm that way. The night air will cut their faces under their hoods. But that is not all: should they be obliged to pass by each other on the narrow raft, they must take care not to touch. In particular they must take care lest the raft rock under their feet, pitching Wendy into the arms of Fabienne. It has happened before. They agree that when they must exchange places one of them will dive into the river. They will take turns diving. It is not dangerous. The current keeps raft and woman together. She who has dived off the raft must swim to the other end, back to front or front to back, according to which end she began at. Meanwhile she who has remained on the raft may walk unimpeded to the other end. Then she who dived may climb back up. She has had a bath out of it as well. The skin of one is dry and the skin of the other is damp. River water collects in the hollow of her throat. Things are altogether colder.

*

The water of the river is not visible. Only the sunlight on the river's surface is visible. It seems they are floating on sunlight. They sing together, but they can only think of melancholy songs. The beeswax is gone and the burlap abrades them. They are more content with singing together than they were with touching. They are content to gaze on each other. Their eyes are young. Each has had her eyes replaced twice. The two sets of eyes in their heads are young. The four sets of eyes that have been removed are old. Wendy begins to take the hand of Fabienne but Fabienne withdraws it.

Wendy proposes that they sleep face to face. By drawing their blankets around their necks and pulling their hoods over their eyes they will prevent their skins from touching but approach close enough to breathe each other's breath. The arrangement appeals to Fabienne, as Wendy knew it would.

Drifting near the riverbank they pass under a sycamore tree. One leaf falls between them. It interrupts their singing. They gaze on it, both of them, as though wishing to make something of the event; but a gust of wind blows the leaf into the river. Then they remember ballads about silk that are not entirely melancholy. The air cools. They discontinue singing and think about their breath. Tonight it will be cold.

In the early morning Wendy wakes to the sound of Fabienne choking. The sun has not yet risen. Wendy does not understand the sound. She imagines that an animal has found its way onto the raft. A contagious animal, she imagines. She rolls off the raft, away from the animal, but thoughts of Fabienne cause her to twist round as she enters the river. She is both on the raft and in the river. Her position is awkward. The river chills that part of her that is in its grasp. Fabienne is folded in two on the raft. She convulses without a sound. Her hood falls back to reveal her face. It is livid in the pre-dawn. Her eyes are sunk into her head. She does not see Wendy. Her gaze is far away and without intelligence. Wendy concludes that the animal is among Fabienne's blankets. She begins to climb back onto the raft. But the cyclate vents are open: the women opened them, the night being cold, to restore the ice. Wendy's foot meets ice instead of burlap. She falls into the river. She is underwater. She swims to the surface and wipes her eyes: Fabienne is no longer on the raft. Fabienne too has fallen into the river.

Wendy dives. Deeper in the river it seems to her the water is warmer. But certainly it is not brighter: in the river she is blind. She does not know where to find Fabienne. Moreover she has forgotten which direction is upriver and which down. She did not breathe deeply before she dove. She rushed herself. She rushes herself still. She swims deeper, with wild strokes in all directions, in the hope of striking Fabienne with her limbs. Although she did not breathe deeply she feels full of breath. It is easy to swim. Her limbs fail to strike Fabienne. Her foot strikes something but it is a fish. She has forgotten the position of the raft above. She swims deeper. At last she locates the body of Fabienne. It is colder than anything else. It is on the bottom of the river. Taking it under the arms, she pushes off from the spot where it lay. The mud there sucks at her. It relinquishes her feet unwillingly, leaving her motion-less near the bottom of the river, holding the body of Fabienne. Her breath is stale now. She kicks with her legs. She must save Fabienne. She thinks she and Fabienne have risen in the water on account of her kicking. They have gained distance she thinks. Fish swarm around her. They can see well underwater. She feels their gaze though they keep away from her. They are waiting for her to drown. But she must not drown. There is no more breath in her. Suddenly they break the surface. Wendy breathes. Fabienne is heavy in her arms. The raft is nearby. Wendy's limbs are numb. Fabienne does not move. It is a great effort to heave her onto the raft. Then Wendy looks her over. Her skin is blue. Her eyes stare. Wendy blows breath into her mouth.

Fabienne gasps, a long gasp which increases in volume. It would be a scream, but the air is flowing into her and not out. It is a sound not named precisely by people. Her eyes find Wendy's face. When Wendy wraps her in blankets she throws them off. She thrusts her head over the edge of the raft and retches into the river. But nothing comes. There is neither onion nor river-water in her. She curls into a limp heap and falls asleep.

The sun rises. Wendy closes the vents.

*

One moment it's there and the next moment nothing. There is a structure in the air, Wendy is afraid to say, there opposite the mountain: far away above the gold-trimmed treetops and beyond the rocky knoll.

"...stole my breath," Fabienne is saying. She has been saying it since morning. She is unhealthy. Wendy is unhealthy too. They are both chilled. Wendy's bandaged wrist throbs with her heartbeat. The wound there has become infected, she fears. She has treated it with probiotic yeasts. Nevertheless she fears infection.

"I felt the nearness of your lips," Fabienne says, "and a suction deep within me like a cough unextinguished; and then I felt as though a clinging mucus flowed from me in my sleep—as though my chest had been filled all my life with a bland fluid, so that I knew nothing different, until you drew it out with your mouth."

Fabienne believes that Wendy stole her breath in the night but afterwards returned it. Now she admires Wendy more than ever. Wendy's power to suck the breath from living things, killing them, arouses her deep affection. She does not take her eyes from Wendy as Wendy moves about the raft. She proposes that Wendy steal her breath again but keep it this time. Then Fabienne will die but her breath will persist in Wendy. That will satisfy Fabienne, Fabienne says. Soon, she says, she will die anyway. She believed she was healthy when she came to the community of the ice-cutters, but now she knows that she was never healthy. She knows that her body was only waiting to betray her by losing weight and letting her breath slip away. It waited until she was on a raft. But it did not know that Wendy, who loves her, would be on hand to take her breath and keep it. It will represent a victory over her treacherous body, she says, should Wendy consume her breath and not allow it to expire.

Wendy massages Fabienne's limbs. They are no longer cold, not on their surface; but they are bluer than Wendy would like. They are robin's-egg blue. They are not the blue of human limbs. Wendy can think of no remedy but to rub the blue out of them while Fabienne entreats her to steal her breath.

Through the birch trunks they glimpse a black stone blasted by lightning. It would be possible to walk between the halves, were they on foot; were they on foot perhaps they would do so.

Wendy leaves aside Fabienne's limbs and stands on the raft to look out at the structure in the air, up past the stone. She points out the structure to Fabienne. "I do not know what sustains it there." Her finger directs Fabienne's eyes over the horizon, but Fabienne's eyes settle on nothing.

"What structure?"

"It is both symmetrical and rectilinear."

"An ancient fortification," Fabienne suggests.

"I suppose it is sustained by some vapor."

They look together, but the structure will not reveal itself to Fabienne. She sees only the sky. It is not fall, but the sky is no longer the color it was. It is a paler color. Fabienne collapses onto the raft. Wendy feels dizzy. The pale sky spins around her. She seats herself beside the form of Fabienne. Her wrist no longer throbs. When she draws the silk aside the wound there gapes red as though new musculature had developed to pull its edges apart. Within it the probiotic yeast has faded to shimmering copper scale. She takes an onion. Fabienne wipes her lips. She has revived but continues to lie on the raft.

"All wonders are sustained by our hearts," Fabienne says, "not by vapors and other natural resources. But this is a singular structure, which portends something for us. Had you seen it without me near, you would have thought it a curiosity of the valley, and soon forgotten it; and had I passed this way alone I would have thought it nothing at all, for it escapes my senses. But because we pass this way together we understand it differently: it astonishes us by its simultaneous presence and absence, unusual in structures. And so this wonder, among all others, is sustained neither by my heart alone nor by yours, but by the conjunction of our two hearts."

Rushes flourish by the riverside. They stink of mud or of the organisms therein. There is something wrong with the river. They are spinning again on the rivertop. The water here lies close under the wash of the sun. Wendy watches Fabienne lying still. Would that she could glimpse the pulse in Fabienne's throat. The sun is too bright for that.

"Do you understand me, Wendy? For I am no longer talking about the structure in air, but about you and me."

At that Wendy looks away. She sets down her onion. A stillness settles on her body and indeed over all the raft. Fabienne too is still.

"When you fall still in that way," says Fabienne, "I feel you slipping under the shadow of death. Would that I had your heart in my keeping, by surgery or otherwise: for I would keep it better than my own.

"Tell me again about the structure," Fabienne says. "Describe its every right angle to me, first one side, and afterwards, in identical terms, the other, symmetrical, side; and let me assure you again that I see none of it; and perhaps this fey and uncertain thing may mark us in a way that surgery will not."

But Wendy will not say anything further. She is silent now.

*

"It is as well," says Fabienne; "after all, you would only say words; and when, long ago, they took down on paper the words of the androgyne, who was then a woman, she changed her sex in order to disavow the words they had taken down, and spoke thereafter only through violence. And when they chronicled his adventures, in tomes which they set children to read, then he changed his sex a second time, to that sex which is no sex, in order to disavow their chronicles; and thereafter the androgyne was never more seen on earth, but speaks to us only through those things for which we find no name.

"So you are right to think words no adequate token for human intercourse; but I am attached to them, in my way, for as long as I utter them I know that I yet live in some sense, and that I have not yet failed utterly to bring our two hearts together.

"There is something like a question I would put to you, Wendy. Even when first we met, in the community of the ice-cutters—even when I saw you from far off, trekking parallel to my own trek over the snowbound lake—even then a question came into my heart; or rather, my heart began to shape itself as though some question incubated there. I thought then that you walked as I myself should have walked, were I walking that side of the lake and not my own. We were at a great altitude, where, though the sun ventured nearer to us than it ventures in other places, that quality of it which melts snow seemed scarcely to penetrate the air—and perhaps it is that same quality that melts and hence disfigures the questions that would crystallize in the most delicate reaches of our hearts; for I have noted that it is in regions of the greatest cold that I most clearly comprehend those desires of my heart which shape themselves like questions, and in other places they flee from me, like snow from the sun.

"As cold as it was in the community of the ice-cutters, I despaired of putting words to the impulse which stirred within me. Only, as I have said, my heart seemed to promise that the words presently would emerge, to convey to you that desire I wished to convey, and afterwards to convey from you back to me that sentiment or promise or other pattern of mind which would fulfill my desire. The distance between us was greater then, and the road before us longer; and I thought it sufficient, for the time, that my heart should assume a questioning shape. I supposed that the words would come. Now the regions through which we pass are no longer uniformly cold, but warm by day, notwithstanding the fall; the distance between us seems less, or it ought to; enchantments fall thick around us, the road ahead fills with shadows, the waterfowl have migrated and the people, it seems, have fled; and still some confection of words by which you might know my desires seems, during the cold nights, almost to reach my lips. But in the end it shies away, and turns back finally to the inarticulate and inchoate reaches; that is to say, my heart finds no expression.

"Indeed, the closer I approach this question of mine, the more certainly it vanishes—not even like snow rendered into water, as I carelessly described it earlier, but like snow rendered by some violent upheaval directly into mist; and the more I fear that there is no such question as that I would put to you, but only the shape of a question, a nameless void which I desire you to fill, I know not how; and the edges of it crumble even as I would mark them, and the floor of it pulls back even as I would sound it. The cold deludes me, perhaps—perhaps in truth it brings me no closer to uttering the dimensions of the void, but only, by slowing all the processes of my existence and alienating me from the most vital of my own desires, lends that impossible utterance the mask of possibility. When the night is coldest you turn to me in your sleep, Wendy; and I wake in the dark knowing the dismal extent of my failure.

"It is no special thing, that failure, as we know who walk the road; for every morning we wake to an unfamiliar place, ignorant of what steps to take, and every day we fail to sustain our lives in any place, and we move on. It is no special thing, I say, yet dismal nevertheless.

"This valley will sustain us for some time, insofar as it has the power to do so. The air is sweet and we are as free as people can be. But our hearts we must sustain for ourselves— and in our hearts the dark spots withstand our every assault, while the bright spots fade every day. Unexpectedly and irrevocably they do fade. The same dark spots always, and the bright spots fading every day to be polished afresh.

"Let us make a compromise, Wendy. I will take up your silence to a certain degree; for, though I yet relish the sound of my voice, and the motion of my body, and the belief withal that we have time, you and I, to come together, I think it will please me no longer to refer to our hearts. It is a word I no longer wish to say—and in time other words may come to my mind that I no longer wish to say. And perhaps indeed over time my speech will lose the form of words and acquire instead a melody, and then you may understand me better. And then perhaps the melody too will wear thin—I know not whether it will or not, but perhaps—until there will be nothing left of it, and then you will understand me best of all, for we will gaze on each other in perfect ignorance. But because this is a compromise, Wendy, and we must concede equally, and neither of us stand triumphant over the other, I hope you will agree to take my breath again each night as I sleep—only so little, night to night, as to be imperceptible to me, yet enough that, as the nights accumulate and my body slows, I might find myself breathless, and know that it is not to age that I lose my breath, but to your depredations; I will know this because of our compromise. Likewise you will scarcely perceive, at first, that my speech lacks certain words on which it once relied; and only in the aggregation of silences over many years will you know our compromise fulfilled. But I hope that, as more words fall out of my speech, and I begin to speak as a flute speaks, and then as a bird speaks, and finally as a stone speaks, you might take more of my breath each night, and we might arrange matters together, through that silent communion which shall work unmediated between us, so that on a certain day neither words nor breath remain to me. We must arrange this conjunction carefully, this failure of words and breath together: for had I words and no breath it would torment me I think, as a worm which gnaws my gut; and had I breath and no words I should feel a stranger on earth, and a lost spirit. So you must do your part, Wendy, and I must do mine: we must work together. And I will suppose that you agree with me, and take your silent promise as a stronger promise than any other; and, as I set my words aside, I will always suppose the silence that you and I exchange to be, of all possible silences, the correct and proper silence."

CHAPTER 4

JOHN'S DAY

4.1 The Lemon Peel Woman

The young builder is there on John's Day. He sees the sweet plum woman. He was uncertain whether to come. The sweet plum woman is wearing paper wings. Come, they all said. You are not a child. You are permitted to come. The builder moves from one community to another, and his difficulty is to know whether he is permitted, or rather desired, to take part in the John's Day festivity. He wasn't here last John's Day and he won't be here next John's Day. He arrives and leaves midyear like a vagabond. Are any of them taking him by the hand? Take one by the hand, says the almond blossom man. That's what we're here for, to take each other by the hand.

The builder fills his mug with salted pecans.

Salt is a symbol of John's Day. The salt and the bell. The canopies over the proscenium meadow are woven of fresh river-rushes hung with silks, sky-blue and sea-green, and strings of rock salt beads like smoketrails. The grass is burnt gold and everywhere is a layer of dust. Lids of barrels clatter against sides of barrels and hands reach for peaches. Peaches, people say. Rapini marinade. Cashews.

The builder goes to the well and sees the lemon peel woman. She has painted lemon-yellow spirals on her shoulders and thighs, and on her scalp is a cap of plaited lemon peel. The builder and the lemon peel woman drink water together in silence. Something falls on the lemon peel woman and she screams. The thing falls off. It is lost. What was it? she says. I couldn't see, says the builder. The lemon peel woman leaves the well.

The pomegranate woman takes the brine moss man by the hand. They walk past the builder into the forest.

The pickled squash woman puts her arm in the builder's arm. They sit side by side on the well. She is a dark freckled woman wearing a spherical calligraphied silkpaper hat. She says, fathers mothers? He says, natural child: born on the road. She stands in front of him and puts her palm on his chest. What you need is a garland of ivy. She goes to the blue ivy woman. They speak at length and then go into the forest together. The builder is alone. He takes pickled cabbage from a barrel. The pickled cabbage man is at the salted plum barrel. The salted plum man is talking to the raisin woman. The raisin woman bites a pear. Apples smooth as marble, pears soft as down. I wasn't sure whether I should come, says the builder. Come, says the pine resin woman. Do you want to go into the forest with me? I'm only asking. It's kind of you to ask, he says. Not at all. She eats half of an orange. The white pineapple woman takes her by the hand and the two of them go into the forest.

The cranberry mash woman upends the empty pomegranate barrel. Pomegranates are often the first to go. The

BRIAN CONN

cranberry mash woman stands on the pomegranate barrel and plays a bassoon. It is the first music of the day.

The milk thistle woman is digging with a spade. The spade is hard black cyclate like the mud when the river recedes. She unearths three clay jars, sealed with beeswax since the last John's Day. She breaks the seals. The jars are filled with pungent fermented radish. She pours the contents of all three jars into the fermented radish barrel.

On John's Day the barrels are hexagonal, straight-sided, made of new yellow pine polished smooth; they are as high as a woman's thighs. The mugs are black outside and white inside and hang around people's necks on blue sashes. The chopsticks are chopsticks. The milk thistle woman pushes the fermented radish barrel between the salted almond barrel and the persimmon barrel. The avocado man scoops some fermented radish in his mug and eats it with his chopsticks.

Prepare for John's Day with pleasing scents and deodorant colonies. In the morning the air smells of grapefruit. There is no soap on John's Day.

The cranberry mash woman is a woman with a sharp face and long thin lips. She is the type to play a trick and expect a trick in return. The rosemary man rubs his knees. On the bassoon the cranberry mash woman plays a dirge. People laugh. The pleaching trees on the edge of the forest are hung with paper animals with feather eyes.

The beet green woman takes the last cantaloupe and upends the cantaloupe barrel. She mounts the cantaloupe barrel and says, shouting to be heard over the bassoon: "The sour acorn woman spurns my love." The brush thistle woman fetches the sour acorn woman and binds her to the beet green woman with two armlengths of blue and green thread around their wrists. All spurned loves will be bound with blue and green thread until the bell rings. The beet green woman tries to bring the sour acorn woman into the forest, but the sour acorn woman refuses. They agree to share fermented gourd.

Will you help make me a hat? says the sunflower woman. The builder agrees to help her make a hat. She has a freckled bottom but no freckles anywhere else. A leaf hat, she says. What kind of leaves? Maple leaves are too big, linden leaves too small, oak leaves too prickly. Elm leaves? They shake the branch of an elm, but no leaves fall. The sunflower woman collapses against him and then walks away, head heavy with melancholy.

The apple core woman trades hats with the honeydew man. Now the honeydew man has the black silk tricornered hat with white stones depicting a whale, and the apple core woman has the garland of orchids.

The cranberry mash woman finishes playing the bassoon and the lemon peel woman stands on the barrel and begins speaking.

There are speeches on John's Day. People air grievances. This woman eats all the figs and I had none at all this year. That man judges harshly my flute playing. Has not repaired the stair in the arachniary and it is difficult for the elderly. Lives in a remote place and judges harshly the community. Does too little work or too much. Does not tend the carrots. Spent many days straightening the rocks along the path, working into the night, in order to think well of herself. Copulated too vigorously in the oak I liked, and the branch broke. Lost two sheep through not properly shoring the unstable cliff. Will not eat my walnuts.

The lemon peel woman says:

"This is my fourth set of eyes. Four sets of eyes! The first two were green, the third was hazel; the fourth I told the optic I don't care anymore, and he gave me these yellow ones like a goat's. I don't care. But they're wearing out. Already they're wearing out. In the forest just now a caterpillar fell on me and I felt as though I were lost: in a place I hadn't noticed I didn't recognize, and at the mercy of things. I don't see clearly. I will have to get a fifth set of eyes and a sixth. I am tired of everything fading away."

The builder fills his cup with honey lemonade. There is honey on John's Day. Honey apples, sesame honey candies. There are bees everywhere.

Prepare by locating the medical canopy, with treatments for bee stings.

The string bean man and the green olive woman walk the arcade looking at sculpture together. The string bean man prefers wood sculpture, the green olive woman prefers it clay. He says, "Clay eater." She shoves him down into the dirt and sits on him. He laughs and laughs. She has wide hips, bright eyes, lofty buttocks.

The lemon peel woman steps down from the pomegranate barrel.

The cranberry mash woman says, "What we need here is a fish pond." The nasturtium man tells her there are no fish. The oak woman mounts the pomegranate barrel and makes a speech against the nasturtium man. The vine of heaven man brings the cranberry mash woman a spade. The milk thistle woman fills the fermented radish jars with fresh radish and buries them in the fermented radish hole.

The carob pod man asks the builder will he help him

make a doll out of banana leaves. He doesn't want to be bothered with spurned loves, in particular the love of the celery head man, and desires to bind himself pre-emptively to the banana leaf doll in order to put off the celery head man's advances. He has two bone needles, an armful of banana leaves, and pistachio hulls for stuffing the dolls. He doesn't yet have thread. But there is plenty of thread, for binding spurned loves.

The green olive woman is still sitting on the string bean man. She asks and asks whether he spurns her love, but he is laughing too hard to reply. Tears stream down his cheeks. Finally he nods. Triumphantly the green olive woman mounts the pomegranate barrel. She says: the string bean man spurns my love. The nasturtium man binds them with blue and green thread. They go into the forest, tripping each other.

The green tangerine man is chewing sage. He is wearing a bonnet of green lace. Would you like any sage? he asks the builder. He takes up a rubber-paper drum and sits on the cantaloupe barrel. There is a bashful music in the rubber-paper drum.

The vine of heaven man brings a second spade and the milk thistle woman gives her spade to the taro root woman. Together, the taro root woman, the vine of heaven man, and the cranberry mash woman begin digging a fish pond at the edge of the forest.

The coconut milk man gives some thread to the builder, and he sits in the shade with the carob pod man. The builder sews the head of the banana leaf doll and the carob pod man sews the body. The cranberry mash woman is a jaunty digger. Squat and shovel, straighten and fling. Her earth lands at the builder's feet. He sneezes.

The grapefruit woman takes the last grapefruit. The grapefruit barrel is overturned. The cucumber juice man climbs on the grapefruit barrel and juggles ceramic skulls, blue, green, and gray.

The carob pod man sews one arm of the banana leaf doll and the builder sews the other.

The nasturtium man goes into the woods with the rosemary man.

The almond blossom man mounts the pomegranate barrel. He says: "The pickled squash woman spurns my love." The celery head man binds them with string. The carob pod man sees the celery head man and runs to the other side of the meadow. The builder follows him and they sit behind the salt turnip barrel. The carob pod man sews one leg of the banana leaf doll and the builder sews the other. The sweet plum woman is sitting on the green mango barrel, which is overturned. Her wings never quite touch the top of the barrel. The builder says, "I wasn't sure whether I should come or not." The sweet plum woman says, "Of course you should come." She dips a cherry tomato in olive oil. "What do you think of my wings?" She wiggles her wings. "They are the most wonderful wings I have ever seen." "Thank you," she says. He says, "Because I am bound to the road, I never know where I stand. I wasn't here last John's Day and I won't be here next John's Day. Am I really here this John's Day? The years are like beads on a string: I have just one bead, and an unknotted string. My bead will fall off at any moment." The sweet plum woman says, "You should make a speech."

The carob pod man says, "Now you be the doll, and ask me to go into the forest with you so I can spurn you. Just on

behalf of the doll. I'm not asking you to say it for yourself."
The builder takes the doll and looks at it. The carob pod
man rolls his eyes. "You road folk are all alike."

The sweet plum woman has gone to the pickled cabbage
barrel to talk to the kumquat man. The builder sneezes.

The vine of heaven man hands his spade to the mani-
oc man. The pomegranate barrel and the grapefruit barrel
have been pushed together. The cherry pit man is standing
on the pomegranate barrel and the lavender man is standing
on the grapefruit barrel. They are arguing about the location
of the steps on the bank of the stream, which have not yet
been built.

The yam man trades hats with the beanpaste woman.
Now the yam man has the broad-brimmed waxpaper hat
with tiny blue bells, and the beanpaste woman has the skull-
cap of apple-green moss.

The builder taps the lemon peel woman on the shoulder.
She turns to look at him. He indicates the forest. "Oh," she
says. They go into the forest, under the pleaching trees and
among the pots of contraceptive moss. Her small buttocks
are like lemons. Two strips of lemon peel have popped loose
on her cap. She smiles at him over her shoulder. On a blanket
just inside the perimeter of the forest, the blackthorn woman
is crouched over the brine moss man. The soles of his feet
wink at the builder like the full moon, side by side round
the neck of the blackthorn woman. "Do you like it here?"
says the lemon peel woman. "Farther in," says the builder.
"It's in as far as I can!" says the blackthorn woman. The
brine moss man laughs and laughs. He moves his right foot
down and flattens his calf against her back. "I mean do you
like our community," says the lemon peel woman. She takes

the builder's hand and they move deeper into the forest. He says, "I may make a speech." She says, "Do. It helps at first." There is a blanket against the edge of a pine, sloped up over the roots. The lemon peel woman kneels and brushes off the pine needles. She has always liked this pine, she says. This has long been her favorite pine. She lies back on the blanket and stretches in a straight line, hands up toward the pine and feet away. "What do you like me to do?" he asks. "Do what you like," she says. She drapes her arms over his shoulder and plays with the large vertebra at the top of his spine. He presses her ankles together with the soles of his feet, takes her wrists in his hands, and pulls her straight again. Holding her in this position he brings his genitals near hers. "Hold very still," he says. "Lie straight and don't move. Would you like a blindfold?" She giggles. "I don't mind looking." "It's for your own safety," he says. She grabs his shoulders and rolls on top of him. "Lie very still yourself," she says. He closes his eyes. He lies very still. Presently she is through. "Now you lie still too," he says. "Lie still." She stops bouncing. "Lie straight." They lie straight, arms at their sides, eyes closed, like figurines placed face to face. She wiggles and he waits patiently for her to stop. Finally there is no movement. There is a soughing in the pine as though no one were lying underneath it. His orgasm ensues.

People leave on John's Day. They don't tell anyone they're leaving. Maybe they don't know they're leaving until they leave. When the bell rings they just walk away. The bell is rung in the afternoon. When the sun is two suns above the horizon the children will carry the bell out to the meadow. All threads broken at the bell. To prepare for John's Day, have some packs ready under one of the cedars at the foot of the mountain, for anyone who leaves to take along. Nuts, dried fruits, nutritive moss. If there aren't enough packs, someone will have to set out with nothing. But they'll find things. They won't always have nothing.

When the builder and the lemon peel woman come out of the forest they see the cranberry mash woman working on the fish pond. There is a mound of earth beside the fish pond. The pickled squash woman, rosemary man, honeydew man, pomegranate woman, green olive woman, string bean man, almond blossom man, and sunflower woman are also working on the fish pond. They are lining the fish pond with porous blue-black clay from wooden buckets. The green olive woman is bound to the string bean man. The pickled squash woman is bound to the almond blossom man. The sunflower woman is bound to the banana leaf doll, the banana leaf doll is bound to the rosemary man, the rosemary man is bound to the pomegranate woman, and the pomegranate woman is bound to the celery head man, who is not working on the fish pond. He is sitting on the mound of earth eating figs.

The only work that may be begun on John's Day is that which can be finished on John's Day. Work not finished remains forever unfinished. In fact, work begun any time before John's Day and not finished by John's Day usually remains unfinished. Most people feel it's better that way.

The only stories that may be told on John's Day are those that take place on John's Day.

The builder takes a honey apple. The lemon peel woman pats him once and climbs down to help with the fish pond. The builder wonders whether he should help with the fish pond. There is no room, but he is a builder. "Where will they get the fish?" he says. The celery head man says: "From the ground."

The angelophytist has helpers on John's Day. The angelophytist is the salted plum man. The helpers do not know how to read angelophytes. No one who knows how to read angelophytes is allowed to help. The angelophytist is chewing sage. He is lying with his head between the horseradish barrel and the beanpaste barrel, and he is holding onto the feet of the rhubarb woman and singing, "Beat the cabbage, froth the broth." There are three angelophyte colonies under clear cyclate on the grass. The helpers are also chewing sage. The messages people send on John's Day do not always arrive. The messages they receive are not always intended for them. The messages that are intended for them are not always the right message.

Near the fish pond, nine empty barrels have been pushed together. They are all straight, all hexagonal, and all the same size, and they fit together like honeycomb. On the nine-barrel stage, the beanpaste woman and the kiwi man are handstanding side-by-side, and the whitethorn woman is handstanding on their feet and opening a coconut with her toes.

Farther from the fish pond, on a smaller stage of only three barrels, the nasturtium man is speaking against the purple grape woman.

On the other side of the meadow, on a stage of eleven barrels, the green tangerine man is holding a mosaic depicting a bolt of lightning.

The sweet plum woman says, "They're going to perform a one-act play." She has come up to the builder from behind. She rests her head against his back. "A historical drama," she says, "very realistic. They are scholars. I'm tired. Would you like a raspberry?" She reaches around him and puts a raspberry in his mouth.

"A rendering of ancient times," says the builder.

"A drama after historical principles," says the sweet plum woman.

There are always more barrels of food. There are always more stones in the meadow. Prepare for John's Day by taking all the stones out of the meadow, but they'll find their way back.

"I was walking back from the forest with the lemon peel woman," the builder says, "and she wept." The sweet plum woman says, "I went into the forest with the avocado man, and also the beet green woman and the sour acorn woman, who are reconciled." "She was walking behind me," says the builder, "and when I asked her why she was weeping she said she hadn't been." The sweet plum woman says, "I don't know her well. I don't know why she was weeping. I wouldn't have wept."

Prepare for John's Day by raking the grasses of the meadow, tip to toe.

The sweet plum woman says, "I'm tired now and so are you, but let's spurn each other's love and be bound together, only for a short time." The builder puts his arm around her, careful of her wings. They mount a single barrel together and declare that they spurn each other's love. The avocado man binds their wrists with blue and green thread. They climb down from the barrel. The sun is two suns above the horizon. The children are bringing out the bell. The sauerkraut woman takes a bite of mushroom and passes it to the builder. The sweet plum woman says, "Did you make a speech?" "I did not," he says. He takes a bite of mushroom and passes it to her.

The brine moss man ties an acorn-sized paper basket filled with anemotrophs to a spidersilk helium balloon. He has taught songs to the anemotrophs. He releases the balloon and it drifts up into the sky. A breeze shakes some of the anemotrophs loose; for an instant they hang in the air in a small blue spore-cloud, as though awakening, and then the wind puffs them down the mountain. They and the others will come down, maybe that same day, maybe next week, maybe next month; the nearest angelophyte network will scent them, and then for months after John's Day the community will be getting John's Day songs, some their own and some from elsewhere.

The bell rings. Everyone stands still. Threads snap. The builder and the sweet plum woman stand side by side. They pull gently against each other and their thread snaps. The bell rings again. The lemon peel woman leaves. No one else leaves. The fish pond is not completed. The fish pond will never be completed. The fish pond will have to become something else. The cranberry mash woman stands still. The bell rings a third time. The sauerkraut woman says, "A historical drama with an edge to it, I think. I believe they'll be taking risks."

The sweet plum woman says: "There are *so many ants*." And she's right. Tiny little ones. There are rush-plait canopies to keep off the sun—and designs, black bark plaited against white rush, brown bark against gold bark, salt crystals, blue threads and green; silk canopies, silk and plait canopies, yellow plait with red silk woven through it: not blood but silk, red in color.

4.2 A John's Day Drama
After Historical Principles

Names of the Actors

HAWKINS Commander of the starship *Theseus, Duke of Athens*.
COLETTE daughter to ANGUS OMORTOVIX, beloved of HAWKINS.
BRIGHT chef on the starship *Theseus, Duke of Athens*, in love with COLETTE.
HOLLY science officer on the starship *Theseus, Duke of Athens*, in love with BRIGHT.
ANGUS OMORTOVIX ambassador from the planet Neptune.
ASHE a policeman.
CREWMEN, METALWORKERS, KITCHENBOYS, DEPUTIES.

Scene I: The Starship *Theseus, Duke of Athens*. The Bridge.

Enter HAWKINS, ANGUS OMORTOVIX, with others.

HAWK. I have commissioned a replica of your daughter in stainless steel.

ANG. I defer to your custom.

HAWK. No custom, but something for myself. I will explain. When I was a young boy, I owned a dog. It performed no useful work, but I confined it in a concrete enclosure and compelled it to obey me. I sought intrigues then, and became embroiled in numerous plots for obtaining power. This is a common pastime of boys on Earth, who have no other occupation. In these affairs I entrusted my dog with my most sensitive secrets.

Ang. When a Neptunian boy becomes capable of complex thought, we gift him with a broom. He tells all of his secrets to the broom. He does not use it to sweep the floor (there is no dirt on Neptune), but treats it only as a repository for secrets.

Hawk. And does the broom betray him?

Ang. Boys at boarding school torment the weaker boys by switching one broom for another. The trauma is acute.

Hawk. My dog betrayed me to a girl whom I had hoped to enslave. From a hidden vantage I watched as the dog allowed her to photograph it from every angle. Later it was struck and killed by a drunk driver. The girl relocated to a rural province and became a huntress. I believe that it is because of this incident that I aspired to command a starship: all men thrall to the abyss, but only those of us for whom the abyss is everywhere dare to meet it with open eyes.

Ang. On Neptune, it is you humans who have turned our faces to the abyss.

Hawk. Angus Omortovix, I value our friendship and the friendship between our peoples. I value it as much as a human can value anything. If future generations of men count my life anything better than a quick senseless grumble of photon torpedoes, they will count it thus: that it was I who brought together the people of Neptune and the people of Earth.

Ang. And you hope that our accord will stand fast against all secrets and betrayals. I hope the same, Commander Hawkins: and tomorrow I give you my daughter in love, to be a living symbol of our bond. Although I trust that both you and she will thrive long after I have beheld that abyss beyond which there is no other, I trust also that the friendship between our peoples will survive even the two of you, and many generations to come. My boyhood broom is far from here, Commander Hawkins, in a containment facility deep beneath the quicklime deserts of Neptune.

HAWK. I take your meaning. Do not think that I distrust you; but it is in my nature to distrust all simple pleasant things. That I should cement our friendship by joining myself in love with fair Colette, who renders the dark of space as bright as a spring day, and its cold vacuum as feathery-full as a pillow of silk and down—this strikes me as incredible, even some trick of fate. That is why I have commissioned the replica of which I spoke, which will become the figurehead of my starship: so that the lovely Colette, forever a woman of soft places and rosy hues, may at the same time be as sure as steel. I am pleased to love only Colette and no one else, but I would also trust her, and through her the people of Neptune, as I trust steel.

Enter COLETTE.

ANG. Daughter.

COL. It eases my heart to see you here, Commander Hawkins. I was asleep in my quarters, and I dreamt myself at home on Neptune. I call it home, Commander, not because I was born there, but because I dreamt you there too; and wherever you are, there is my home. But when I woke I did not see you, and my dream seemed more home to me than the small metal room in which my body lived—or rather, in your absence, failed properly to live, but rather aged. I hurried to set eyes on you.

HAWK. Soon we descend into the atmosphere of the planet Venus. In the traditional Venusian ritual we will agree to possess one another. After that I will carry you away in my pleasure-craft: in a verdant canyon where the birds sing always in harmony, we will sport with one another until we forget which flesh belongs to you and which to me. Thereafter we need never part again.

Col. That man!

[Enter BRIGHT, bearing a tray, followed by HOLLY.]

Do you see him too?

HAWK. I see Bright, the chef.

BRIGHT. Eggs of fowls and flesh of fish.

Col. I began to wonder whether I hallucinated him, although it shamed me. Wherever I have gone, even into maintenance closets and ventilation ducts, this chef has been there offering me things to eat.

BRIGHT. I am head chef, the lady our honored guest.

Col. I have had no peace from him. Whenever I arrive in any place I find him there already, as though he knew my movements before I intended them. Meanwhile, this woman trails forlornly behind him.

BRIGHT. I was in the kitchen, carving animal flesh for our supper. I removed the internal organs of birds and set them aside. I recognized the moment when Lady Colette boarded the ship, because at that moment I was struck blind. Somebody screamed: I had carved a kitchen boy instead of a bird's carcass. I put a loaf in the place we put loaves in order to make them into bread, but discovered that I had put offals there instead. The stench and outpouring drove everybody from the kitchen, and lingers still on the lower decks. Each moment I spend without the presence of Lady Colette is a moment during which I am dead; my life is the sum of the moments which I spend in the presence of Lady Colette. It is easy for me to know which room she will come to next, because I can see only the path to that room and no other.

HAWK. He imagines himself in love with you.

BRIGHT. Say rather that it is my love for you, Lady Colette, which imagines me—that a sudden boundless love of you has drawn matter from the careless ether, and articulated limbs and organs into this rag of a man, its instrument, with no other purpose than to come near you.

HOL. Worm! The ship has not slept twice since you said the same words to me.

BRIGHT. Two sleeps ago Lady Colette had not yet boarded the ship, and I did not exist.

HOL. We were roaming the ship's gardens at twilight, and had paused under a trellis where wisteria grew. I believe a swan came into the speech you made then; but aside from the swan it was the same speech you make now. You would make your speech to a sponge if it came in your way. I believe it must be in atonement for a crime so wretched my memory has hidden it from me that I continue to follow you around this ship.

COL. They make a droll pair. But it disturbs me, Commander, that they should intrude on us now, when our own love is so new, and the ceremony of possession so near.

HAWK. They are lesser people than we. There are many on Earth who call love the highest good, and who make it their mission to serve love, yet who know love no better than they know the interior of the moon. Here are two such, crippled in their spirits. Observe the fantastical nature of their thoughts, the rolling of their eyes and the clenching of their jaws, and most of all their misery.

Col. On Neptune the people throng the beaches and all the ammoniacal declivities, where they swoon at the sight of one another and swear garbled oaths to the stars.

Ang. And swallow serpents, knit wings from the whiskers of subterranean creatures, and see things invisible to others.

Col. But all of this avails them not: still they swoon, still languish.

Ang. And would starve but for swallowing the serpents.

Hawk. Such is the defect the weak call love; it is a common flaw of people. But hear me, chef: you must give it up. You and the science officer may woo and betray one another freely, so long as it does not interfere with the operation of my ship; but you must renounce Colette, for she is mine alone.

Bright. I would be more able to renounce my life.

Hawk. Then I will permit you to choose one or the other. On Neptune, love's dupes swallow serpents; let us adapt their custom to our needs. On Venus we will dock under the banyan trees, where it is fair; but the rest of that planet, which is a trackless swamp, teems with monstrous worms striving ceaselessly to poison one another. If you have not given up your folly by that time, I will put you among them.

Col. All he need do is return to his kitchens and continue just as he was; surely it will not be necessary to put him among the worms. I ask you to return to your kitchens, small man, for my sake.

Bright. I am blind except in your presence, Lady. All things other than yourself reek of corruption. The kitchen is as the foulest oubliette.

Col. Then let this woman guide you to the medic, for she appears to care for you.

Enter Ashe.

ASHE. Commander Hawkins. Sabotage on deck 7G. The light has gone out.

HAWK. I will cooperate fully. Colette, Angus Omortovix, let us part from each other treasuring thoughts of tomorrow's celebration.

ANG. When we will bury this grotesque turn of events under friendship and good cheer.

HAWK. Chef, think on the future.

Exeunt leaving BRIGHT and HOLLY.

HOL. He will not put you among the serpents, I think.

BRIGHT. I will send Lady Colette poetry concealed in cake.

HOL. Gone are the days when I thought it possible to overestimate your stupidity. Still, he is no warlord, but Commander Hawkins; and we no tribe of savages, but a unit of civilization, though we be floating in the primal deep. He will not put you among the serpents; and should he put you in the brig, I will commit some trivial offense in order to accompany you there.

BRIGHT. The kitchen boy who took the Commander his supper yesterday found him filing his teeth into sharp points.

HOL. Was it the same kitchen boy who saw a sloth's face in the moon Ganymede, and it warned him never to sleep?

BRIGHT. Since he made up his mind to molest my Lady, the Commander devotes himself to gazing out into open space with furrowed brow; and when the crew disturbs him his mouth foams, and he rails against them. The brig is full and we have canings. Perhaps he has been a just man in the past. But a man's character is as a drop of blood in a river,

BRIAN CONN

which may know itself for a single weightless instant, but swiftly drowns under mortal currents. Commander Hawkins is the slave of time and chance, and of the mysterious passions of matter. His love changes him.

HOL. He is a man weaned of a fusion reactor and stretched thin by the pull of strange gravities; his heart beats not as ours.

BRIGHT. Shall we let him grind us under his heel?

HOL. Would that you had never come onto this ship, but gone rather into the community of Russia, in Earth; for there they scheme without respite and count no day complete without violent revolution, and would greet your clumsy fomentations as the most natural form of discourse. You said in the garden you would never love any but me. Shall we not pretend, until all of this is finished, that we are again in the garden, under the stars, and that you love me and no other? The world was thus once and can be so again; there is nothing to prevent it. And in this way you will be safe from serpents.

BRIGHT. The serpents of Venus are a pale sunless white. Poison sacs, lying beneath the translucent skin, adorn them with spots like the leopard. Each has two heads and each head is provided with barbed fangs, the better to fasten round two separate bits of me and rend my flesh in twain. If the Commander's tyranny will not move you then perhaps you will be moved by this image of my suffering, mine whom you say you love truly, to assist me in a certain matter.

HOL. You mean to compel me to low treason; your heart is transparent to me. Nevertheless I will do whatever you ask. The path of my life kept so long to sound reasonable country that I began to think myself governed by reason; now it twists suddenly, and darkens, and shows me it was never reason after all, but only some mask of chance and whim that happened for a moment to resemble it.

Bright. I will never again love you as a woman. My tongue sticks even to call you woman: there is only one woman, and she is Lady Colette. But if you would have what affection there is in my heart for such as you, ask me rather to love you as I love my knife: as a simple tool that does not fail.

Exeunt.

Scene II: The Starship *Theseus, Duke of Athens.* The Foundry.

Enter three Metalworkers.

1. Met. The statue will not cool.

2. Met. It has rested in the energy mold the better part of a day. Look through the mold: it is still white in color, and no man may approach it without pain.

3. Met. What time has the Commander given for it to be ready?

2. Met. Tomorrow, the night of the ceremony.

3. Met. Bring a coolant, nitrogen or the like. Chill the air neither harshly nor abruptly, for it offends the metal; let the coolant urge Nature subtly toward our case. But is the statue not fashioned strangely?

2. Met. According to the Commander's order. It is hollow within, and swings open like a coffin.

3. Met. A box in which to bury the dead, for we do not like to give them naked to the ground.

1. MET. A coffin in the shape of a woman.

3. MET. During the wars I often saw a woman in the shape of a coffin.

1. MET. When last I was on Earth, I went among the savages of Peru and took strange drugs. It seemed to me then that tiny beings, some of aluminum and others of moss, swarmed over me and attempted to enter my astral body through occult vortices that I knew not how to defend. Since that time all women have appeared as coffins to me, coffins in which the corpses of people rest. The coffins speak and move while the corpses lie still. But I see this statue as it is; and although in truth it is more like a coffin than like a woman, it is the thing most like a woman that I have beheld in many years.

Enter ASHE.

ASHE. Metalworkers.

3. MET. We will cooperate fully.

ASHE. I had report from a crewman, that a stranger was in the foundry.

2. MET. A stranger white in color, in the shape of a woman, who robbed the air around her of all chill?

3. MET. He means that the crewman may have seen this statue, Officer, which is the size and shape of a stranger.

2. MET. It was a jest.

3. MET. The ship grows larger and larger every time they work on her; by now nearly everyone aboard is a stranger to every other. When I came here we fit together like the organs of a single body; but the greater the beast grows, the less of her belly we have to cling to. Soon she will be the size of a world, and each of us will think himself alone.

ASHE. The crewman described the appearance of the stranger. He said the stranger appeared unwell.

Exeunt.

Scene III: The Starship *Theseus, Duke of Athens.*
The Kitchen.

Enter HOLLY, with a thermos bottle, and BRIGHT.

BRIGHT. I have met with as many of these thermos bottles as there are stars in space, for we use them daily to send up soup to the crew. But never before have I heard one growling to itself with the voice of an earthquake.

HOL. There is the current therein that drives our civilization: the last mask of matter's rising motion, that which rends the sky and restores life to the corpses of men: the electrical force, phlogiston's warlock cousin: the bolt of lightning.

BRIGHT. It trembles as though from a turmoil within.

HOL. It is in the form of a gel. In the lowest level of the laboratory, the great socket bears current from the reactor core. The shock that courses from it has scorched black the metal plate and attenuated the thrice-perforated steel until it resembles the wire snout of some bestial mechanical colossus. I have opened the seals and directed the current through the ship's etheric channels into this thermos bottle. You must be quick; for while those seals stand open some current leaks out, and, collecting in remote tubing, piping, and patches of rust, menaces us all.

BRIGHT. And when the Commander drinks of it?

HOL. It will strike him dead—or, again, it may strike him

somehow living: it is a capricious unfathomable stuff; while he in his time has walked the seams of space, and his being is bound up in volatile energies that may mate with the blue ghost to spawn some prodigy.

BRIGHT. If I were divided in my heart, a man who weighs one thing against another, I would grow fearful of this affair I've set in motion. But I have given myself over to love, which is the noblest sacrifice a man may make. Thus I plunge toward my destiny even as a shooting star plunges unwavering toward earth; and if the violence of its passage consumes it, then it was made to be consumed.

HOL. After I had filled this bottle as you asked, I fell into a deep sleep.

BRIGHT. Your face wears a stricken look.

HOL. It was a sleep which descended on me so abruptly that I hadn't time to go to my cabin. I sat in my chair in the laboratory and laid my head on the workbench. Nevertheless it was as deep as the sleep of any deep winter's night. I did not dream, and when I awoke I felt that I had slept for an impossible duration of time, or even that I was awakening from a sleep that began when I first boarded this ship.

BRIGHT. There is a thirst in you for oblivion.

HOL. Since then I have desired nothing but to play by myself with a pack of cards.

BRIGHT. Even when you are coaxed by such as me to work some small act of will in the world, your fearful heart aches at once to resume its inertia: you turn to your cards as an insect scurries from the light. Our civilization teaches its children that we are made for love; but in fact some are made for love, and others for oblivion.

HOL. I climbed the path to the cliff that looks out over

the ship's goat pasture, but all I could think were the cards laid out in cascades and crosses, and on them the tiny hearts; and as they mixed themselves, all in vain, their movements seemed to describe the very seal of oblivion, a blank stamp attesting and affirming that the total transaction of our love has come to nothing.

Bright. All things will come to oblivion. I will too, and Colette, and Commander Hawkins with or without me. But there is some difference, it seems to me, between the oblivion of your fearful heart and the oblivion of the shooting star, which turns twilight into wishes.

Hol. Do you remember the day I joined this crew? It was my first assignment out of camp. The further the cattle truck carried me from the familiar cul-de-sac, the more I felt that I had died unexpectedly, and was now merely filling time in some perfunctory sequel to my real life. When I got here I met a freckled man, I have forgotten his name, but he was named after a cheese; he told me that on this ship I would learn to ride horses, but they would trample me. I should have flung myself on my cot then and sobbed; instead I went roving the corridors, and happened to meet you, and you gave me apples; and I think it is only because of your apples that I remember anything at all of that day, or of days before. When I woke in the morning we were in orbit. I looked out my viewport and saw the vacuum; but I remembered your apples, and then, as though the apples had unlocked a room abandoned and already gathering dust, I remembered all the rest.

Bright. I remember nothing that happened to me before a certain day, not long past; or rather, my mind is filled with images, but I know not whether they are true memories, or dreams, or only the inventions of idle moments. The medics tell me that the sting of a certain wasp disordered my nervous system when we made the expedition to Jupiter; I have no memory of that either, and all that comes into my mind, when I instruct it to remember, is a faded swatch of pale pink velvet, and above it a falcon far away in a blue sky.

Hol. I loved you for those apples, I think; but now the murderous force you have called forth from my hands has re-awakened the vacuum your apples once staved off, and I find myself once again in the state of that first night, gazing, as it seems, into some black whirlpool of space.

Bright. We do not love alike, you and I. Perhaps I seem to have done wrong, but I have been pure of heart. There is a vision in my mind of a cool green place. If I remembered Earth, I would say it was Earth, and some place there in which I first knew love; but because I cannot distinguish, among my mind's images, between memories and dreams, I cannot say whether this one belongs in the past or in the future; but I am reminded of it, seeing a photograph of fallen leaves, or hearing stories of kings. And, although I must have been to many thousands of places in my life, and met many thousands of people, and imagined as many thousands again, and although all the people I have known mingle with the people I have imagined, and both mingle with the people I might become, so that I drink the days through eyes and ears of diverse and unknown provenience, existent and nonexistent, past and future, selves and strangers—despite all this there is one vision that silences all the rest, and that is of the cool green place that is my love's home. I have always kept before me the image of that place, and it is always toward it that I have striven; and if sometimes my vision has placed one woman there, and sometimes another, those are the vicissitudes of my mortal eyes: for my devotion to the tranquil place unattributed in my mind has never failed.

Hol. Perhaps love wears masks, as many as matter's rising motion.

Bright. The black fury gel-bound in this bottle is my love made manifest; the storm therein mirrors that in my heart; and when Commander Hawkins falls, then they may say in truth that he died of love.

Enter a KITCHENBOY.

Kit. An accident in the freezers.

Bright. What accident?

Kit. A wash of blood.

Bright. I will see it. Bring Commander Hawkins his supper, and this his thermos bottle.

Kit. Aye.

Exeunt BRIGHT, KITCHENBOY.

Hol. If it were possible to die of love I would be dead of it. Of all human emotions, it is only grief that kills.

[Enter ASHE and several DEPUTIES.]

Officer.

Ashe. Where is Bright?

Hol. The freezer, I think it was said.

Ashe. You are alone here?

Hol. There is no one here with me.

Ashe. Men report a crimson vapor aboard, roiling like the storm of Jupiter.

Exeunt.

Scene IV: The Starship *Theseus, Duke of Athens*.
The Bridge.

Enter HAWKINS and two CREWMEN.

HAWK. It must be done after the ceremony.

CREW. Aye.

HAWK. Adjacent to the banyan grove of Venus is an antique cannery, now a museum—that is, a kind of structure. They will keep it closed tomorrow in honor of my nuptials, for they celebrate all great events with sloth. Legend tells that a magical fish frequents the waters near the wharf, and that lovers who stroll there alone may earn merit by persuading it to change its color. Colette and I will walk along the wharf in quest of this fish, as is the custom; and, returning, we will pass by the servants' entrance to the cannery. You must hide yourselves there tonight, and await us, and take her then.

CREW. Will the guests wonder, when you return from the wharf without her?

HAWK. They will think her with me still. I have imbued this gold ring with the power to summon a hologram of her, a lifelike illusion: ill-animated, but enough for our promenade to the pleasure-craft.

CREW. Every man should have such a ring, and wash our hands of fleshly women.

HAWK. Indeed, many a man prefers the phantom woman to the flesh, and will desert the honest creature who loves him to pursue an image contrived by fancy; but when a woman vanishes in the dark, as these holograms do, then her lover is sick at heart.

CREW. The guests will keep to the margins of the boulevard, I think, far off; and from a distance this contrivance should please them well enough.

HAWK. Then I in the pleasure-craft to the verdant canyon, and you to watch over the Colette of flesh. Imprison her without atrocity, for she is not yours: she belongs to the ship and to the heavens. Look for me when Angus Omortovix and his retinue have gone, and I will see to the bleeding of her. Then her blood shall slake the white-hot casting, and her body lie eternally within the ship's figurehead; and the beauteous energies which she shall bring among us shall charm us all into a state of surpassing love.

CREW. Perhaps that way is better than each man possessing an intangible woman trapped in a ring.

CREW. But by my reckoning we must soon have one or the other, for I find the ship insufficiently filled with love.

Enter KITCHENBOY with tray and thermos bottle.

HAWK. Descend now in a pod into the sea and make your way to the wharf. Take a tin of preserved flesh to sustain you.

Exeunt CREWMEN.

KIT. Your tray and soup.

HAWK. What news of the man Bright?

KIT. In the kitchen he works unprecedented marvels.

HAWK. It is often so, when a man has passed through some turning of the spirit: having ailed, he returns to the place of his duty and is reborn, and something of new life blossoms in his heart. Perhaps the soup will be spiced with penitence; but, again, it may have a bitter flavor.

[Enter ASHE, with a DEPUTY.]

Here are the police. On Earth a man devotes the eve of his wedding to erotic revelry, or else to reflection; but above the coddling blanket of atmosphere, we confront eve and day alike naked of romantic airs.

ASHE. The deputy and I went into the upper hold.

DEP. Following reports of mists and strangers.

ASHE. Up the mountains we climbed, and up the narrow staircase, where the electricity is much aged and the light seeps dull brown from the hanging fixtures, and dies illuminating nothing. We stumbled on the steps.

DEP. With a deafening clatter we stumbled.

ASHE. It was shoddy police work.

DEP. We listened in case our racket provoked some noise from above.

ASHE. A comet passed outside the window, close so that we saw the pocks and scars on its surface, but dim in the shadow of the ship. I grasped the iron winch to raise the trapdoor, but its cold blistered my hand. I drew on my gloves; the deputy readied an energy weapon. I cranked the winch slowly while he trained his pistol on the widening gap. The hold above ran over with light, for it basked in the white-blue aura of Venus.

DEP. Inside, we discovered undocumented cargo.

ASHE. Coffins filled with earth!

DEP. I took a sample of the soil to the laboratory; all tests show it devoid of organic matter, the dust of a bleak irradiated moon where life has never awakened.

ASHE. I propose to return with backup.

HAWK. When did these objects come aboard? During the mission to Jupiter we packed the upper hold with furs and silks; and when we adventured in the outer solar system I saw myself that it was empty, for vermin are a great danger in deep space.

ASHE. And since then we have visited only Neptune, where we took no cargo but the lady and her father.

KIT. Captain, Officers. You are not the first to see these coffins. I was a child on this ship; my mother manages the supply of copper wire, and my father is a brewer. They were libertines, and, although the teachers fitted my sister and me with collars when first we were able to walk, my mother discovered a way of removing our collars, and allowed us to roam our quarter of the ship freely at night when the teachers had gone. I used to boast to my sister that I feared nothing. At that time the area above the alley of the fortune-tellers, which is now the upper hold, was a chapel; it flooded when I was very young, and was abandoned, and said to be haunted. Whenever I boasted to my sister, she dared me to go into the old chapel; and often I did, although in truth I was afraid. The ruined pews cast uncanny shadows in the gloom, and a pungent mold stirred in the tapestries with the breeze of my passing. Sometimes I saw coffins, and at other times the coffins were absent.

HAWK. If they are there when I come, I will shoot them with my revolver.

Enter three METALWORKERS.

3. MET. Commander, the statue of the lady has vanished from the foundry.

2. MET. Perhaps you ordered it so?

HAWK. I did not.

3. MET. The electrical current surged without warning

among the mechanical hammers, which sprang from their moorings and smote the braziers and basins. When we had contained the hammers, we returned to the workroom: the energy mold had burst apart, and wires writhed hissing and snapping like blue-venomed snakes on the floor.

2. MET. But charred footprints led from the statue's pedestal out the foundry and toward the plains.

1. MET. And I thought I saw its figure, as we passed, far off in the sheep pastures.

Enter several DEPUTIES.

1. DEP. Raw electrical current flows loose on the ship. In the plumbing beneath the radio tower, a twitching heap of bones where once a mechanic walked.

2. DEP. In the cabins at the foot of the mountain they report a dilapidated black chariot drawn by mammoth steeds as black as hell.

HAWK. The ship is filled with wonders. The wonder I had hoped to fill it with was love; instead a white-hot golem walks abroad, tending the sheep or else devouring them; emblems of death manifest unbidden in the upper holds; and all the crew quails before mists and vapors, unbound energies, and half-glimpsed bloodstains. And I feel tired suddenly, as though I were the oldest man on the ship, or in all the empires of men—or if there is one older, then at least I am sicklier than he in my spirit; for these monsters that now flock round recall to me the improbable wonders I dreamt as a boy: these phenomena beyond human knowledge, these grotesqueries from the shadows of understanding; and now that I yearn for subtler foes, and to try my strength against the love of woman, I draw instead the same menagerie of worn out phantoms; as though I had made some choice in my youth, unknowing—as though fate had glanced once in the direction of my heart, and, finding there some naive fancy, furnished my life in its image and looked away forever. You, kitchenboy, fetch me my helmet.

[Exit Kitchenboy.]

All day there has been an uncertain breath in the air, as though the ship herself, though a million strong, were nothing more than a momentary coincidence of currents, and at any moment might fray and unravel into nothing, and we all suffocate in the void.

Drinks soup. Falls.

Ashe. The ship is sound enough; it is the affairs of men that fray.

Alarums.

Exeunt.

Scene V: The Starship *Theseus, Duke of Athens.*
The Cabin of Angus Omortovix.

Enter Angus Omortovix, Colette.

Ang. When you were young I brought you to Nereid, the third moon of our planet, to visit your mother, Colette the elder, at the frontier there. Do you remember?

Col. I remember arriving at night on a cracked plain of white stone. In the distance there were hills like great dribblings of mud, sagging like the skin of the elderly. Mother had cut her hair, and I did not believe she was Mother at all; but you spoke to her as though she were Mother, and then I thought you were deceiving me, and had brought me there to sell me as a slave into the opal mines.

Aɴɢ. It was a frightening journey and a frightening place; I was frightened too. But she was your mother after all, and that place, which seemed distant beyond comprehension, was nearer our home than is this planet of Venus, where tomorrow you will be made new.

Coʟ. If I am to be made new, let me be made without memory of that journey to Nereid.

Aɴɢ. On Nereid we were afraid, because of the rough men on the ship, and the great black chasms deep as space itself, and the opals like eyes therein winking demon-red and ghost-blue in the shimmer of our reactor trail as we passed above. But we were among our family there; and in truth we were safe. Now we cruise far from home in the power of a warlike race, yet my caution dozes, careless of the distance and careless of our vulnerability. Our hearts know not when to fear and when to open; we teach them caution against their natures. But I did not bring you here to caution you. Go to the red velvet curtain there, and behind it the alcove in the wall.

Coʟ. The window looks out on the Commander's own courtyard. It is snowing.

Aɴɢ. There is a meadwood chest in the alcove. The meadwood comes from the forest near our home.

Coʟ. I recognize the wood and the chest as well; for I remember you making this chest, each night for an eternity of nights by the last light of the luminous coil: I remember the dry pumice with which you sanded it, the sharp-scented sinew with which you bound its joints; and you polishing it until it shone like butter, and fitting it with fittings of antler; and the stag blazon mosaicked atop; and I sitting nearby stringing together the shells of oysters to decorate the garden.

Ang. You have grown into a woman so different from the child you were that I hardly can reconcile in my mind the woman with the child; yet the child's memories are also the woman's. Open the chest—it is not locked—and there under the dry straw and the preservative herbs, find a pouch in the form of a disc of white fur, six hands in diameter.

Col. It is soft as down, yet abrades subtly my skin that strokes it.

Ang. As will the snow, child, brush gently a maiden's eyelash, yet also burn.

Col. A handle of horn lies within.

Ang. It is your mother's sword—draw it, it is yours now—your mother's and hers before her, the silver sickle-moon sword traditional among the great houses of Neptune: your grandmothers' back unto the Duchess of Old Omortovortes, who scaled the mountain Ul-noumen and with this sword overcame the dictator Noth in his fastness.

Col. When I hold it I feel her hand clasped in mine.

Ang. It was with this sword that your nine-times-great grandmother slew the frosty furred lizard, last of its kind, which dwelt in a house of edible vines yet by choice ate our kin, even as we eat other animals. She sewed its fur into this case, which yet warms and oils itself with the life of the lizard. And it was with this sword that your thrice-great grandmother sliced open the tapestry in the Palace of Aromatic Compounds, unmasking the spies who conspired in its shadow, and so preserved the Republic; and the twin slender bones of the case's hasp are the tips of the forefingers, right and left, of the chief of those conspirators, which he forfeited in punishment for his crime, so that he should no longer be able to point.

Col. It cools my body to hold it; and, as though limpid coolth flowing through the half-loop of the blade dispels a haze within my eyes, I seem to see farther than before, out into the snowy courtyard—and to see the back of you, Father, and all sides of the objects around me, as easily as once I saw their fronts.

Ang. The sword is named Colette, and the women of our line take their names from it.

Col. Suddenly I am uneasy.

Ang. It made Colette your mother uneasy too.

Col. As though my name were but lent me by this object; as though that which I had long taken for my own were not my own, and I were less substantial than I had thought.

Ang. Tomorrow you will be wed, and leave the cloister of childhood, wherein you were free to bear a name of your own: tomorrow you cast yourself into the web of the clutching world, where all you would make yours will be so only contingently. You will negotiate for all things then, for your body and your thoughts, for all your comforts and perhaps for some counterfeit of freedom; but negotiate your first peace between yourself and the weapon whose name you share, your first and last defense against all things, and let this bond be stronger than all others. I give you this thing today, that the bond between you and it shall surpass by one day that between yourself and your husband.

Col. I shall find peace with it. But allow me to wish for one moment that I had found something else in your chest, or nothing at all, and that I might fall defenseless into the world's web, and feed the mouths of earth, and so be spared this struggle—and yet the husk of myself, no longer home to any will of woman, recall fondly this chest as I knew it in our home, and you my father handling it with homely touch by the last light of the luminous coil; and recall too this night when I opened it, and found it empty, and so vanished.

Ang. I went to the foundry today, to see the statue they have cast in your likeness. It glows white to make a shadow of the sun, and the air around it shimmers with uncanny vapors. Its light impressed itself on my eyes, so that even now I see it before me wherever I go; and it seems to me that the image of this object, this smoking terror filled with violent energies, comes nearer and nearer to me, even as you my daughter move away.

Col. Do you know that there is a red liquid here, seeping under your door like a wicked thought into a righteous mind? In the corridor too, in dark crooked rivers.

Exeunt.

Scene VI: Underground.

Enter Holly, manacled, and Ashe.

Ashe. Respect the power of the law.

Hol. The instructions we write lest people no longer know whether they do wrong.

Ashe. Those who act not according to the law, by misdirecting the electrical currents of the ship and by murdering, we imprison here in the meanest of rooms, in which all furnishings are steeped in human waste; and we give them only that food they will not eat, because we hate them.

HOL. Then Commander Hawkins is dead?

ASHE. He is not, though nearly so. It was his practice to anoint his body each morning with an oil of vitamin, and this preserved him from the worst.

HOL. It is strange to say, but I welcome the horror of this cell, and any other horror you offer me. For there has been a trading of horrors lately in my heart: this morning I loved Bright, as low a creature as ever woman loved; then after I had committed this crime I did not love him anymore, but the crime tormented me neither more nor less than had my love; and now as I step into the cell I seem no longer to bear the crime's weight, but only the burden of the time ahead, during which I will be confined here; and I begin to think that, so long as one horror moves always into another, there is little harm in them.

ASHE. Horror will sustain itself to the end of things; it is the duty of the police to chronicle its progress. Bright has stolen a capsule and launched himself into space. He can land nowhere else but Venus; we have asked that the authorities there send him back to us, but they will surely stone him first.

Exit.

HOL. After all it is not so awful a place—here is the pallet of straw, and there the basin of filth—different in kind but not in essence from any of the homes we build on Earth; and already my nose accustoms itself to the odor. But there is this difference: that all the cells are alike here, neither painted nor adorned, and the corridors are like the cells. And in addition there is no clock. But there is a slow regular drip of blood from above; I know not whose, or why, or what events now unfold in the territories of the ship, for already all those intrigues wash into one another in my mind, like old tales made for forgotten peoples; but I might count the drops of blood that fall, and when people ask the duration of the time I spent in the cell, I will recite the number of drops.

Hol. I recall my activity of old, that of wandering the streets and looking at the houses. The dark houses were the least of the houses then; greater than those, the houses with light but no people; and greatest of all, the houses with both light and people, either silhouettes of people or visible illuminated people in all their dimensions, manipulating objects and talking to each other. To look through a window on the other side of which people were talking to each other, that was the greatest accomplishment. And if they were eating at the same time, or folding linen together, those also were worthwhile things; but that there should be more than one and they talking to each other, that sufficed by itself to be the greatest accomplishment.

Hol. The way to dream myself into the house then was not to dream myself one of the people, but to dream myself separate from them yet closer: dream myself for example in the room with them, hidden, perhaps under the table, or in a wardrobe, listening to their conversation and watching them in their private moments; or perhaps, better yet, inhabiting the walls of the house, not within as an insect, but surficially as a flat intangible presence able to flow invisibly from room to room and from person to person, watching as I liked. But if they should happen to glance out and see me looking in

BRIAN CONN

their window from the street, the house became of no use whatever.

Hol. When I return to earth I will take a large house, I think, but confine myself to the threshold. I will invite everyone I know, and they will be obliged to climb over me to enter; and I will forbid them from referring to my presence on the threshold, but call on them to move about in the house as they ordinarily would, and sometimes to leave the house and return again, climbing over me both coming and going. And watching them thus I will be comfortable for some time: making sure, in that way, of my presence on the structure's threshold, neither coming nor going like the rest of them, but having peace.

4.3 The Lemon Peel Woman

Empty barrels get taken into caverns and sheds. Full barrels get taken into the forest to anchor the corners of blankets. There are fine cotton blankets on John's Day, blue and green. The mushroom is finished. Sage in the day, mushroom after the bell. There have been speeches and artworks and now there is lying in the shade. There is eating of salt carrot. It is time to move the canopies into the forest. That moving of the canopies into the forest was well done. If you lie looking at the sky through the leaves of trees there is the aroma of clean sun-warmed blanket. The butterflies are white. All voices are murmurs. The wind did not know you were there and is curious about your body. It is time to rake the meadow. That raking of the meadow was well done. The meadow is empty. It will be dusk soon. There is phosphor under the trees. There is a breeze from one direction or else the other. At first there are stars and then the clouds cover the stars and the moon is a pearly smudge in a certain quarter of the sky. The nighttime silks are pitched overhead: the vault of night is the work of people. Under rearing horses on a blue silk canopy they pass round a mushroom made of marzipan. Under a green salt-spangled porpoise on a yellow plait canopy they are wrapping a woman in a silk cocoon to her murmured delight. Three of them carry her away and the rest paint each other's bodies with phosphor. Pickled cabbage is luminescent in the phosphor light. Rain drums on the silks. In the middle air between canopies and blankets hang paper phosphor lanterns. The paths are dark nevertheless: follow the trail of blue-green ribbon in the treetops and the pale gray ellipses that are barrels of salt. The path splits and splits and splits. Dark dangling vegetation fondles your ears. Faces in the trees, faces in the moss. Salt mango. Phosphored lemniscates on salt barrels. Phosphored elm branches join to make a blue bower under which two women share a coconut. Phosphored bodies approach you on the path and move against you in the dark of the forest. Now your body is phosphored too. They are carrying away the silk-wrapped woman, who wiggles. Salt walnuts. Everybody is thirsty on John's Day. The rain starts again. You find yourself under a canopy depicting a celestial pitcher from which the sea wind blows. Here they have phosphored only their genitals. They move sluggishly. The frogs sing:

> *This rain, it hath but middling vigor.*
> *The king of the moon,*
> *The king of the moon.*
> *My beard is come unkempt.*

The crickets sing:

> *She journeyed to a fountain*
> *Where her lover bade her go;*
> *The queen was long recounting*
> *The last time there was snow.*

Drums and pipes. Sounds of breath. The canopy laughs in the rain. Smell of phosphor, wet earth smell. Pots of oil and pots of water. Four hands oil and knead your back and shoulders and the hollows of your elbows. Blue-green midnight paths. An oiled scapula finds your own hand. Phosphor spiral round a tree trunk. Six maple leaves phosphored for a constellation. Whirligigs among the leaves. Ribbons, banners, silver foil, white salt plain, the bottom of a ship, the top of a ship, three masts, waves slapping the sides, octopus, moon in mosaic of yellow mineral. Paper sculptures. Boxes and spheres. Smell of sea spray. Neighbors approaching on the path. They have phosphored their eyelids. Closed eyes glow. Open eyes vanish. Everybody closes their eyes at once. Chewing of licorice. Honey pecans. A breeze blows warm rain in under the canopy. Everyone is wet. It's warm and cool. Games with string. Chewing of peppermint. The rain stops and starts and stops again. Games with lights. Games with apples. Head on your neighbor's breast. The ants are asleep: trails of honey unmolested on the forest floor.

4.4 The Golden Mountain

"It was intolerable," said the man like a bear; "it is intolerable. Of course I'm glad I've found you. But it's made me sick and I don't think I'll ever be the same again."

"This is the way," said Molly. "I'm sure of it now."

Behind them lay arid wild ranges inhospitable to people. At dawn they had crested a steep pass, where their voices had echoed before and behind them. Now they were descending a high mountain road, which, Molly said, would come out behind the arachniary. The air was cool but insubstantial; the sun reaching through it pricked sweat from their skin.

"Was there a road behind the arachniary?" asked the man like a bear.

It was little more than a shallow ledge in the mountain-side, and if they had stood straight on it, one foot beside the other, their small toes would have dangled over the abyss. They crept along, fearing the wind. Falcons rose up, soared level with them, and subsided back into the blue-gray haze. The sun warmed the rock until it blistered their feet, and the man like a bear trailed his hand along the cliff face to reassure himself that he was not treading on burning air.

"I was kept in a small golden box," he said. "As though I were a jewel, which people once feared, and kept in golden boxes lest the sun strike them."

"As for myself," said Molly, "I built a wooden canoe and explored a series of small islands. But now we near once again the community of people; think no longer of your passage through the unearthly regions, but rather of the people below whom you love—the man who paints silks, the woman who nurtures camelids, the cooper, and the rest of them— for those other things that befell you befell you alone, and if you speak too insistently of them the community will reproach you."

They had met no one all day. But the trail widened as the afternoon wore on, and they began to pass tiny triangular pens, nooks in the rock closed off with precarious fences of sun-parched twigs and occupied by two or three goats. The goats watched them carefully; the declining sun, which loved the yellow of goats' eyes, splashed it everywhere, as though to place the mountain and the trail, and Molly and the man like a bear, and all the world, into the eyes of goats.

"Then what are these goats?" said the man like a bear. He stopped suddenly. "Were there goats, then, on the trail behind the arachniary?"

"The flocks of those who subsist on thorn," said Molly.

The man like a bear raked his hands through his beard, quickly, one and then the other. A cloud of yellow dust rose around his face. "I suppose you will tell me they drink the milk of goats, these people, though they be grown, for they have forgotten that it is childish to drink the milk of goats— and you will tell me that they boil their thorn before eating it. No," he said, "there were no such people. This is not our mountain."

He turned around and started back up the trail, kicking a stone loose as he did so; it clattered over the edge and they heard no more of it. Molly pursued him as quickly as she dared. "They keep the goats for dung," she said, "to nourish their mushroom colonies. I came here often for pleasure. I recognize the goats." She caught him up. "I tell you these goats are well known to me. It is our mountain and no other, and in its hidden caves and crevices dwell the thorn-eaters, whom you too would recognize if you saw them, for they sometimes came into the community for medicines and for the sight of people."

The man like a bear stopped and looked out into the sky.

"It is near," Molly said, "nearer than it has been to us for a long time. I will go and bring people back to help you, if you like. Even so I think we will arrive before night."

"I am only afraid," he said. "Earlier, before I found you, I supposed for a time that I had come back into the ancient world, where they left no place behind without first reducing it to cinder and rubble. Our civilization did not exist then, and they never had the opportunity to leave our community behind; but nevertheless I feared that they had contrived somehow to reduce it too to cinder and rubble."

Molly laid her palm on his chest to steady his trembling, and then they resumed the trail downward together.

"I hope it is not making too much of myself," she said, "that I recognize the goats and guide you down the mountain."

At that, without a word, the man like a bear sank to the ground. Molly looked at him for some time, then continued alone.

The man like a bear sat first with his back to the mountainside, but he could not bear the sight of the featureless blue in front of him; then he sat facing down the trail, but felt, at the limit of his right buttock, the place where the rock fell away; then he lay facing the mountain, but found it worse than ever with the drop invisibly behind him. Finally he lay on his shoulder, wedged between trail and mountain, with his head turned to look up toward the peak and all the vanishing loops of trail they had already descended. His shivering soon subsided, and he lay peacefully. There was no sleep in him, but only the desire to lie very still and gaze on simple things such as the sky.

Molly returned as the sun touched a fogbank that lay

along the horizon. She had a small cyclate vial, colored amber, and she carried tucked under her arm a great fleecy disk the size of a large barrel-top.

"Objects I buried here long ago. They are still here, just as I left them; and so this is our mountain and no other," she said, "and objects are here, and likely people too—just as we left them."

He raised his head and looked at her.

"I am well," he said, "only very tired."

"Shall we continue? I think we will soon be hungry."

"Very well." He did not move. "I would prefer it if you did not refer to the details of our community, or indeed our civilization, in any way. We have been long absent, and when I call to mind the image of our home it seems strange to me; and the closer I call it the stranger it seems. And so I would prefer it if you would guide me there, if it will please you, but tell me nothing about where it is you are guiding me, and when we arrive there I will see it. But it may be that at times I will close my eyes."

He got to his feet and stood swaying. "Perhaps it is wiser that I walk ahead of you," he said; "otherwise, should I stumble and pitch forward, I may carry you with me over the cliff."

"Except it is not possible to pass each other," said Molly, "and I am already ahead of you." She turned resolutely down, and after a few steps looked behind her and saw him following with a jerking motion, as though not entirely in command of his limbs.

"Since I lived in the golden box, I have felt as though all the interior of my body has been replaced by tiny workings of gold. Ordinarily they move smoothly together, though not as flesh moves; and sometimes they move less smoothly together. And though I am eager to be home, I doubt how the interior of my body will move in that context."

"We might bathe in the creek tomorrow morning," said Molly, "with fishes swimming round our knees and river turtles looking on from the mudwallow. And the man who massages bodies will be there," she added, "to see to your interior."

The sun soon vanished behind the fogbank, but the sky's light held. The trail widened and the air warmed despite the hour. They rounded a bend and saw, for the first time since they had gone away, the mountains in which people dwelt: a long low range, clothed in green and adorned with a dark intimate meander that was the creek. Molly pointed. "There, you see: there are the canopies of the spider handlers nearest to us, and there beyond them the proscenium meadow, and there the cauliflower rows."

"The canopies are dark," said the man like a bear, "without glow of phosphor, though the air is dimming. There are no people on the trails. And they have dug a pit in the proscenium meadow." And indeed there was a pit visible in the proscenium meadow. He followed her slowly, glancing from the trail at his feet to the trails of the community, which, however, continued empty.

"Molly!" he called; and, when she waited for him, had nothing to say, but held her hand down the last stretch of trail.

They came out, as Molly had predicted, behind the arachniary. The trail threw its last loop around a bulwark of gray rock, and when the man like a bear looked back he could no longer see the high mountains and the knife-edge on which they had come. From here it became a road, dusty and not wide, but a true road that people walked every day. It led from the great cavern of the arachniary down among cedars. Only the handlers of spiders dwelt here, and certain chemists; it was a remote place at the best of times, but silent now with a silence deeper, it seemed, than the silence of the trail; and although the breeze blew, and the trees waved, and the evening insects mobbed his face just as they had in the memory that seemed no longer his own, there was a mocking in it all, and a presentiment of some horror very near, and perhaps a stench.

He swept aside the black silk curtain of the largest canopy: a blue hemp rug lay within, three hammocks tied with rosemary-scented silks, a pouch of contraceptive moss hanging from the roof pole, and a ball of beeswax half-carved in the shape of a ship's prow. But no people; and no people, they soon found, under any of the canopies, neither the canopies of the chemists nor the canopies of the nurturers of spiders. The man like a bear called down the road, where the canopies of those who nurtured cauliflower and cabbage were visible; but no reply came. In the devouring emptiness there was not even an echo.

Molly brushed dust from the fleecy disk she carried.

"There has been a contagion," he said.

"Perhaps we are in a place not quite the same," said Molly. "Perhaps I was mistaken. I did recognize the goats; but this sickle, which formerly was of silver, is now of some blue-gray metal, with a handle of ebony. And the pit in the proscenium meadow—"

As she spoke, the sun, which had set behind the fog on the horizon, entered a narrow band of clear sky between the bottom of the fog and the edge of the earth. It was as though a fiery eye had sprung open for a final glare at a world empty of people. Everything turned to gold. At the same moment a wind sprang up and caught the yellow dust that lay thick along the arachniary trail; the dust swirled in the sun, and they were enveloped in a sulfurous gloom.

"The mouth of earth," said the man like a bear, coughing. "The proscenium meadow is a grave." He could not see Molly for the dust, and it seemed to him that he was addressing the gloom itself.

"Can it be that the same goats are here," Molly's voice said, "but not the same people?"

"All have perished," said the man like a bear. "How can we escape this dust?"

"We might look farther," said Molly, looming suddenly and then vanishing again. "After all they are people, and it is our duty to learn their end."

The man like a bear did not answer. His nose and mouth were filled with dust. He squatted so that his beard brushed the ground, closed his eyes, and vomited. He had eaten nothing all day except dust, and he felt certain that he now vomited dust—if not trail dust then gold dust, as the clenching of his stomach ground to dust the golden mechanisms within him. Molly was speaking. She took his hand and tugged it as though to break him.

As she pulled him to his feet the wind died and the air began to clear. The sun had set and the shadows taken hold.

"We might look farther," Molly repeated; and she opened her mouth as though to say something more, but instead shivered and pointed down at the trail. The dust there bore a fresh set of footprints. They led past the place where the two of them stood, back up toward the arachniary; they had not been there before.

Molly and the man like a bear observed the footprints together in silence. They were large, much larger than Molly's feet, and her feet were larger than his; and they were deep, although a great deal of dust must have settled over them only moments ago; the feet had been shod, peculiarly long and peculiarly broad in the toe.

The man like a bear suffered a coughing fit. When he had finished, he said: "Someone passed near us in the dust."

"And must have heard us," said Molly, "but passed by nonetheless."

"They are deep as though he bore a great weight." He reached down and took a strip of lemon peel from where it lay beside the prints. "There has been a contagion which renders people—" he stopped. He had been about to say "deaf," or else "mute," or else something to do with lemons. Thoughtfully, he began walking the path of the footprints toward the arachniary.

"Wait," Molly said. "It is some spirit of darkness, which commands the dust and the red sun. There in its solitary stronghold—"

She broke off, and the man like a bear looked up the trail and down the trail. All the world was the solitary stronghold of the spirit of darkness.

Together they followed the tracks up past the canopies of the chemists and the nurturers of spiders, and down the dusty stone steps into the cavern of the arachniary.

Inside, it smelled of every kind of metal. Several thick strands of the web of the Marietta spider, which transmits light a little, caught up the twilight at the threshold and carried it in a dim and fading dendritic arc to the far end of the cavern: a dim reproduction of a dim light, as though the scarce luminescence of the sky's dimmest star, alighting near the entrance, had been smeared through the air by an ethereal thumb. The only things visible were those things that gleamed: the compound eyes of the larger spiders winking like stars; an obscurely shimmering nebula of deep red, a heap of some mineral; and, brightest of all, a dozen gloomy galaxies of silver-white droplets of liquid metal, suspended in the webs of the Kloss-Ring spiders and wicked thence down to waiting beakers in a dozen dangling capillaries like a dozen chutes of moondrops.

A wailing arose in the back of the cavern and ended as soon as they became aware of it. With a soft homely rustle Molly drew her sickle.

4.5 Fog & Mist

The young builder is working at a table. In a compartment under the velveted bench he found a roll of thick white paper, an inkstone, a handful of brushes, and four fat idols of yellow metal to weight the corners of the paper. There is a swamp outside, or else a jungle. Three walls are rice-paper screens; the fourth is open, not a wall at all but a redwood-framed rectangular absence; thick fog curls in over the deck. His work takes up the surface of the single table, and his body takes up the single chair. It is raining again: the air sits heavy on his skin, the paper warps under his brush. The rain and fog, being of a slick suffocating consistency, favor sludges and black liquids. The ink takes on a fever sheen. There is a white cat here, missing one leg.

The cat says: "Lucky thing too."

The cat is not the single most disturbing element of his situation, but it is among the most disturbing. He was on the road, he thinks he remembers, walking from one place to the next; and one night, finding himself pursued by a wolf, fell down a steep grade and fetched up against the closed door of a structure, which he entered. Was it that way? It may have been a year ago now, but there are no years here. It was that way, he thinks, or some way like it; but, searching all the short simple length of the three walls, he can no longer locate the door through which he imagines he entered.

The room is raised high on wooden pylons, black with rot. Far below, visible through gaps between the planks of the floor, yellow scum bobs on the surface of water. There is no door at all in fact, nor stairs down from the deck, nor any gap in the railing. Through the fog he sees neither land nor vegetation. Swamp or jungle? he wonders idly. He supposes they smell much alike. A hammock of greasy gray rope hangs outside, under the eave. When he awakens there is a shallow ceramic dish on the chair—his work still occupies the table—and in the dish what he takes to be food: a vegetable like broccoli, but softer, darker, and sweeter; a mass of pasty white grain; and something like animal flesh, which he scrapes into the water. The sound of the splash vanishes in the rain. There are a metal fork, a metal knife, and a ceramic mug filled with fruit juice. The food is hot, and he leaves it on the bench until it is the temperature of ordinary things. The fruit juice is not hot.

He has seen neither mice nor insects; the cat, he supposes, is a pet cat.

It says: "People with pets live three point six years longer than people without pets."

This place is old, perhaps some mechanical quarantine of the late capitalists against the contagions peculiar to them. In addition to the pet cat, an atavism in its own way, there are books: bound books of paper filled with crisp tiny letters: authentic ancient books printed with metal type. They fill a low ebony case ornamented with simple scrollwork. The smooth metal-cut edges of the pages are painted gold. Everything is well dusted. He does not read letters. In one of the books is an illustration, one full page, thicker and glossier than the rest, of a weatherbeaten green door high in a chalky gray mountain pass. The light in the room is an orange-brown glow of unfamiliar luminescent organisms, emanating from channels where the walls meet the ceiling. He takes the illustrated book out onto the deck to look it over by the white light of the fog.

"Do you read letters?" he asks the cat.

"Cats can't read," says the cat.

"Cats can't talk," he says.

"That was a very clever thing to say," says the cat. "I appreciate that remark."

Swim for it, he thinks. But it is a long way down.

He unties all the knots of the hammock, splices the ropes together end to end, loops one end like a noose around the neck of one of the fat metal idols; rope in hand, he throws the idol over the edge of the deck. This splash is audible even over the rain. He plays out all the rope and the idol still tugs: the water is deep, deep enough, he hopes, for a dive from this height. He lies for several hours, head dangling over the edge of the deck, watching for signs of snakes. There are none. He dives. The water is warm and clotted, like a fluid of the body; he chokes on the miasma lying invisibly above its surface, and founders. Marshaling his strength, he strikes out away from the pylons. His lungs burn. He washes up on a black clump of mire overhung with every shade of greenery. It is a jungle after all. High up in the canopy, rope bridges rock to and fro as though hastily deserted. A monkey watches him from behind an orange-flowered vine, and another from behind a banana leaf. A third screams. A centipede disappears with a twitch under a scale of bark. Numerous hidden monkeys join the screaming. It may be a road shimmering ahead, but he is weak from heat.

The cat says: "That was a powerful experience. How are you feeling now?"

"I feel fine," he says.

"And I feel like a cat," says the cat. "Let's look a little deeper."

The cat is not entirely insubstantial—he has held it in his hands—but it is capable of transforming itself into a mist.

He gets up from his work and goes to sit on the deck. There is no chair out here and nothing to look at but the fog and the hammock. Half the deck is wet with rain and the other half is dry under the eaves. The rain has stopped for the moment, but drops still plink from the corners of the roof.

He tears the illustration of the green door out of the book and lays it on the table beside his work.

At first he thought this place an illusion. He trod carefully, not wanting to be one of those who walk, mesmerized, off a precipice; he touched nothing, lest he grasp a viper thinking it a deck-rail. Later he supposed he would perish of solitude. It was then that he began his work: a talisman or mandala, incorporating whatever ideographs his imagination yields—

though, as he paints them, they impress him less as objects of pure invention and more as indecipherable records of memories he can no longer bring to mind: dead memories, memories of dead events; or perhaps memories of forgotten imagination-inventions never realized, extruded finally into dead glyphs and dropped onto the paper as a tree drops its leaves when they are filled with yellow.

A clot in the road, he thinks, a place of coagulation. He did wonder when he began walking whether there must be such places.

The cat says: "I've a touch of the claustrophobia."

When he tires of working he sits cross-legged on the deck and pages through the books by the light of the fog. Although he does not read letters, he turns the pages without haste, taking care to omit no page. He finds an order in the ancient numerals printed on their corners and watches them to ensure that nothing slips by. When he tires of turning pages he closes the book and watches the fog. The watching of fog takes up more and more of his time, and his thoughts increasingly resemble fog.

Also in the compartment under the bench is a pot of glue, yellow-orange with an acrid scent. He empties the ebony case of books, knocks out the shelves with his feet, and paints it inside and out with glue. It is well constructed and of sufficient size to hold a person. When the glue has dried he applies a second coat. When the second coat has dried he leaves it overnight in the rain; in the morning the glue is still hard, the wood underneath still dry: waterproof. He splices the hammock cords into a rope, ties one end to a beam of the deck and the other to the glue-finished bookcase, and drops the bookcase into the water. It floats on its back. He knows very little about rafting. Taking the shallow food dish for use as an oar, he slides down the rope and seats himself in the bookcase. The craft is not as steady as he would like. He unties the rope and launches himself. He overturns immediately. He is in an undersea kingdom—or rather, an underswamp kingdom. A princess approaches on a giant seahorse. Swamphorse? Tiny iridescent bubbles pour upward from its head. She snares him in a net and tows him to a stone tower, inverted underwater: its base rests on the water's surface and it extends down, interminably down into the black depths. She opens a door at its base, or rather peak, and, as though her net were a sling and he the stone, whirls him nauseatingly around and hurls him inside. He hears the door lock behind him. The stairs wind down to the tower's peak, or rather nadir.

He puts aside the last of the books. He has been through every page of every book and there are no other pictures. He incorporates into his talisman an ideograph he invents to represent the green door in the high pass; it becomes the only ideograph in all his mandala whose meaning he knows.

Night never comes. He sleeps when he feels tired and awakens to the fog. Sometimes he pretends to sleep and listens for the sound of the people who bring the dish of food. It must, he thinks, be brought by someone—unless the cat brings it, perhaps in the form of a mist.

"How would a cat carry food?" says the cat.

"A harness of some kind," he says. The cat sniffs and looks away.

Lying awake in the hammock, he hears the tap of a ceramic dish on a redwood floor, faintly, as though far away through the fog. He opens his eyes and sits up. There is no dish anymore. He goes into the room and watches the fog from the bench.

The cat says: "A harness for mist?"

The builder says: "In our civilization we harness all creatures, mist or not."

His ears again pick out the tap of a ceramic dish, distant yet at the same time quite near, as though space were folded into a tiny square and all far-off events' recurrences or precurrences of the events in his own orange-brown-lit room.

Coagulation and dissolution both, he thinks: both, of kinds. More, he supposes, of a soup, like something his mother used to say, or else something he intends to tell his daughter.

"Birds?" asks the cat. "Do you harness birds?"

The deck railing is nothing but a row of wooden posts with beams nailed across their tops. The nails are metal. He pries them up with the metal eating-knife. He tears strips of velvet from the velveted bench and wraps layers round his hands as gloves; he kicks out and pulls up the posts like rotten teeth. He saves the nails. One of the idols suffices for a hammer. He builds a ladder out of posts and beams. He transfers his talisman from the table to the velvet-denuded bench, along with the illustration of the green door in the high pass; standing on the table, he punches a hole in the ceiling with the idol. Rain pools on the floor. He punches a hole in the floor under the hole in the ceiling and the rain passes through the room unimpeded. He works one end of his ladder up through the ceiling hole and sets the other end just outside the floor hole, bracing it against the bench below and a roof beam above; when he mounts the ladder it shifts, settles, but finally holds; he climbs onto the roof. Footing is uncertain here: the red tile is slick with rain. The fog is as thick as ever. From the deck, the white cat looks on with twitching tail. The builder climbs down, pries up the nails of all the decking, builds another ladder with the planks, and nails its bottom to the roof beam so that it rises into the air like an antenna. He climbs to the top but finds the fog undiminished. He buttresses and extends his antenna-ladder with the help of the bench, the table legs, the chair, most of the floor, and every roof beam except that to which his ladder is fixed; the talisman and the illustration of the green door fall through gaps in the floor and tumble into the water; what there is of the room is awash with rain; the fog at the top of the ladder is as thick as ever. The white cat paces the last of the floor-beams. The builder splices the hammock cords together and hangs the rope from the sole remaining roof beam, creating a second route to roof level and allowing him to draw up his original ladder from the floor and further extend the rooftop ladder. Is the fog lighter? He nails the tabletop to the top of the ladder, piles the books on it, and stands on the books. The fog is lighter, distinctly lighter; but still impenetrable. The ladder teeters and he descends back to a safer altitude. He has converted the whole room into a ladder and the fog is still impenetrable. Not far above, he tells himself, there is clear air and a view to the ends of everything. The white cat mews below. It leaps from floor-beam to floor-beam, pawing and finally clutching the rope. He pulls it up, it penduluming at rope's end, and carries it in his arms to the top of the ladder. Standing on the books on the tabletop on the ladder on the roof on the room on the rotting pylons, he holds the cat high above his head. The cat balances on its hind legs. "Ahoy!" it cries; then, with a terrible scream, it is torn from his grasp.

The knife slips as he pries at the first nail. It is not sharp, but the serrated edge opens a shallow gash across the back of his thumb and a single drop of blood flies across the deck and lands on the cat: one red drop on a field of white. For a moment, builder and cat alike are transfixed; then the cat's pink tongue darts out and laps up the blood. Its coat is white as snow. Its eyes are green. The builder feels embarrassed, as though he had caught it in a shameful act.

4.6 Stories for Children

"We might bring it to the laboratory of the deliverer of infants," said Seamus. "Perhaps it is the blood of people and perhaps not; but whatever blood it is, there is inscribed in it the great language of all bloods. So small as to be invisible even to the eyes of children, it is written there nevertheless, in helices coiled together two by two, in numbers beyond counting even in the smallest drop of blood. In the laboratory this language is easily read. Moreover, the deliverer of infants, who enjoys such things, writes in ink something of the blood's speech of each infant he delivers before sending the infant away into another community; and he does the same for every child who comes here after being delivered elsewhere; and he keeps all these records in a cotton sack in the cabinet of prostheses. He will tell us, I think, through what creatures this blood once flowed; and if they be people whom he delivered as infants, or people who came here as children, then by matching the speech of this blood with the blood-speech he has recorded in ink, he will tell us also which people."

"It cannot be the blood of only one person," said Andrea.

"I should think it impossible."

"Surely one person holds no more blood than will fit in a barrel," said Thomas. "How many barrels of blood are here?"

They surveyed the blood.

"In the fishpond," said Andrea, "there are very many barrels of blood. On the meadow and in the stand of lindens there is additional blood, but we cannot know its quantity: for how much has the earth drunk?"

Atop a faint rise in the meadow, between the arcade and the mouth of the trail, the yellow grass bore a teardrop-shaped stain of blood, of a size that an ox could comfortably have curled up in; from this stain, short trails of blood radiated outward like the arms of an octopus; and one longer trail, or perhaps two close by each other, zigzagged all the way across the meadow and terminated without further sign at the base of the second-largest cedar. In addition there were free patches of blood, here and there, with trails neither to nor from, and one long streak in the shape of a hook; the nearest lindens were black with blood up to their lowest branches; and the fluff of certain dandelions, though quite intact and far from the major blood patches, was nevertheless tipped with blood.

The unfinished fishpond was perhaps a hand deep in blood, the level of which appeared to have fallen somewhat since it had been deposited: black dry blood rimmed the pool of red liquid blood to the further depth of one fingertip, and this margin seethed with flies, twelve thousand or so. The mound of earth beside the fishpond appeared free from blood, although it was dark in color, and loose, and much blood might easily have vanished into it. Although it was early in the morning, the sun was already hot, and the scent of the air was less than fresh. The flies swarmed the children, biting them.

"I am glad for these flies," said Thomas, "otherwise someone would doubtless wish to bathe in the blood."

Deirdre nodded pensively; Andrea scooped up a sample of fishpond blood in a pear leaf.

"It is not an opportunity we often have, bathing in blood," said Thomas. "Once in a lifetime, perhaps."

"Is the deliverer of infants awake?" asked Seamus.

"I think none of them is awake," said Andrea. "Thomas and I came here to look at them while they slept in the forest, and to take away what food remains. Instead we found this blood. We have not yet looked on any of them, nor discovered any food; but I have heard none stirring. I will leave this pear leaf in the laboratory of the deliverer of infants, for if he is not yet awake then he will awaken soon enough."

The man who made needles staggered from the forest. He was covered in blood. He saw the children, screamed once, and collapsed at the edge of the meadow.

Andrea left with the pear leaf full of fishpond blood, and Seamus went to fetch Ulrika from the crèche; she was friendly with the deliverer of infants, as well as all the others, and would, he thought, be able to calm them when they woke. Thomas examined the man who made needles, and found him without wounds: the blood that covered him, front and back and head to toe, was not his own.

His scream had awakened others. Thomas circulated among them. Some were touched by blood, others not. They peeled away limbs blood-stuck to blankets, to other limbs, and to other people; they began to roam the forest with gaping frowns; they did not yet understand whether they were awake or not, or where they had awakened. None were harmed.

Soon Seamus and Ulrika came. The deliverer of infants was untouched by blood, and they sent him to the laboratory; everybody else, blooded or not, they sent to bathe in the creek. The man who wove hammocks began to gibber, but Ulrika held his hand and led him to the creek herself; he dove in, and the gibbering did not spread. Everybody was fatigued from the activities of the night. They came properly awake only once they were in the creek; and all the rest of the summer, whenever they happened to think of the morning after John's Day, they thought of the fine blue sky, the breeze that tumbled down from the mountain, and the people, all except the deliverer of infants, together in the creek—some of them with a crimson tint under their nails or behind their ears, but clean on the whole, cool and frolicsome, splashing each other while turtles looked on from mudwallows.

The young builder, also untouched by blood, left the creek and found the children gathered around the fishpond and the mound of earth beside it. They had brought goats from the crèche, and the goats were busily devouring the blood on the meadow and the blood in the forest. But the blood in the fishpond was a very great quantity of blood.

"We might siphon it," said Thomas. "The path descends from the edge of the meadow and the ground soon dips below the level of the fishpond; we might siphon it into barrels there."

"And when we have it in barrels," said Ulrika, "what will we do with it?"

"It might be made into a fertilizer," Deirdre mused.

"Or an artwork," Thomas suggested.

Andrea went after a goat that was straying up the mountain.

"Perhaps we ought to bury it here," said the young builder. The fishpond, he noted, would never be finished. It had not been finished on John's Day: no curing colony had been introduced into the clay with which it was lined, and it would soon return to earth. It would have to be filled in anyway. "Let us fill it in now, and the blood with it."

"As though we were burying a person," said Deirdre.

"A person," said Thomas, "who is made entirely of blood."

"Shall we make sandals?"

That confounded them—if it were like a person then it required sandals, and if not then not—until Seamus observed: "It has no feet."

Thomas fetched spades and they set to work. The first spadefuls of earth splashed blood up into their faces, and raised clouds of the black flies, many of which settled on their skin where the blood had spattered. But the work went quickly; soon the substance at the bottom of the fishpond turned from blood into mud, and splashed less; and then sweat rinsed their bodies clean. The black flies did not like to leave the blood, and had almost to be scraped off with the edge of a shovel lest they be buried and killed.

As they were throwing down the last spadefuls of earth, both Andrea and the deliverer of infants returned, from opposite ends of the meadow.

The deliverer of infants reported that the blood came from many different sources: some were people unknown to him; some were creatures not human, and also unknown to him; and many were individuals who had left the community and never returned—one, he said, was the lemon-capped woman who had left only yesterday.

At that, the young builder went away down the trail that led to the road, and they did not see him again that year.

Andrea reported further bloody marks, both on the ground and on the lower leaves and branches of the trees; they led, after twists and turns, to the arachniary, which was itself undisturbed. She conjectured that the spiders, having scented the blood in the dark of night, had come to the meadow to play in it, and subsequently tracked it through the forest.

"Though perhaps not," said Deirdre. "The appearance of so much blood is after all a prodigy of sorts, and so perhaps the trail of blood is a corollary prodigy; for we may easily mistake where any chain of prodigies begins and ends; and so it may be that the best explanation is some other explanation, something of which we have no knowledge. I mean that the affair defies conjecture."

"Let us nevertheless recall this day and all its details in the history of the crèche, and know hereafter that such a thing may occur," said Seamus.

"But let it be told in the crèche's history," said Lemuel, "as a thing of which we have no knowledge."

Deirdre and Andrea went to the creek, Thomas took the spades back to the toolhut, and the others led the goats back to the crèche.

The deliverer of infants was alone. He climbed the low packed mound of earth where the fishpond had been and sat down. He did not enjoy reading the language of blood—or rather, he did not enjoy feeding blood into the nucleolexic gel, lavender in color and smelling like an infected wound, that read that language for him. It was invisible, what the gel did to the blood, but it disturbed him to know that, in order to read the blood's helices, it tore the pairs of them asunder: what had been a carefully coiled helix wrapped in the snug embrace of its opposite number, it left a tattered strand of waste; what had been the name of a person it left an unintelligible stutter. As he sat on the mound of earth, hearing faintly the joyful cries of those still bathing in the creek, and musing on tiny violences, he stirred suddenly and shook himself: for in his grief over the blood's small helices, he had forgotten already the reservoir of unsundered blood beneath him, and the people who had left the community, whose blood it was—forgotten them like he would forget the wind when it ceased—and so forgotten the other violence of the morning or night, invisible in a different way from the invisibility of the blood's language: for it would be told in the crèche not as a story of violence, as would the sundering of the blood's helices, but as a thing of which they had no knowledge.

CHAPTER 5

THE SNOW PAGEANT

5.1 Stories for Children

The children took their history lesson in the field behind the crèche. In the late summer they drank afternoon milk and sat under the dead tree. Then the older children instructed the younger children. What kind of tree was it and how did it die? It was the mightiest oak in the forest and it died of blight.

Ute was the oldest of them, old enough to remember a time of limitless potentialities, when new people arrived in the community every day. It was not yet known then where the wells would be sunk or where the roads worn, and there was no thought of art. She was not old enough to remember a time before the crèche was built. For her the afternoons under the blighted oak possessed the quality of a ritual outing which she had performed her whole life. She seldom left the crèche anymore, and the very young children did not remember a time when she had gone forth from its grounds; but in the late summer she walked to the oak in the little field and allowed the sun to strike her.

This was the way she addressed them: she sat, casually at first, with the dead tree on her right, and looked past it toward the mountains. While she reviewed the facts of history and guided the children in their discussion, she never allowed her gaze to waver from the mountains. Nonetheless she was perfectly attentive to everybody. As history poured out of her, her spine straightened, and even lengthened, and she sat taller at every moment; and finally she assumed the lotus position in order to sit as tall as a child can sit. She sat so tall (the young children told each other afterwards) that, had she sat any nearer the oak, it would not have failed to pluck her up in its blighted branches and consume her.

Her reason for not looking at the others was simple: she feared that they would not be the children she thought. For she had instructed so many children over so many summers, and always about marvels of which neither she nor anyone had any knowledge, that it was no longer possible for her to remember which summer she was in, the present summer or some other summer. She feared a trick of the season. As she carried on addressing the mountain she pushed the other children from her mind, and soon perceived nothing but a bleak expanse. Her voice rose and her body drew taut as a harpstring.

At that moment one of the other children would touch her, on the hand or on the knee. None of them could resist the impulse to touch her in that state. She turned on the one who had touched her with a terrible expression. Then all tension drained from her body and she fell laughing onto one or the other of her neighbors. Someone nipped at her ear and the situation soon developed into sex play. It was never necessary for her to say that she loved them all.

BRIAN CONN

*

How did the deliverer of salt arrive in the community? The children did not escort her; she found her own way and arrived cloaked in the scent of dung. The oxen charged up the forest path with lowered heads, like bulls; the wagon careened behind. The hatter fled the oxen and fell on the road, and the deliverer of salt rode over him. He was crushed. The deliverer of salt clung to the reins with hands like boulders.

Two women brought the hatter to the canopy of the medic; the medic shook her head.

The oxen suffered from an intestinal disturbance, all four of them. They were ill. That accounts for the dung, which dribbled unceasingly down their hindquarters and flung itself in gelid clots to right and left, and also for the fury of their charge: they were goaded thereto by their complaint.

When they neared the bridge, the deliverer of salt stood on the platform. She assumed a stable posture with her thighs spread wide. She towered over the oxen even as they turned aside from the road and plunged into the creek-bed. Had it been a different season she would have raised a gray spray of creek-water; and perhaps she would have fallen, and found nobody to draw her from the creek, for she was alone. But it was the six days of summer's dissolving heat, and the creek was dry. The people were as burnt as the grass. The mountainside had burnt too, and the stone had the appearance of cinder. The deliverer of salt rode the wagon up the opposite bank. When she opened her mouth a blackness lay beyond her tongue as though her jaws were the jaws of a cave. She cried the word to the oxen, and they staggered as though roped and came to a halt on their knees before the larder. They kept still with rolling eyes as she dismounted.

*

The light was dim in the larder. On the arms of the sorter of the larder the veins stood out as the blood sought to rise toward the sun, which thirsted for it. Likewise the veins of cinnabar stood out red and sweating on the walls of the larder.

The sorter of the larder considered that he had had one great piece of luck in his life, and after that none. He had been lucky to be born into a world in which people required foods to be sorted. He loved foods, and as far as he knew he loved nothing else. If he loved barrels and bottles it was only because they facilitated the sorting of foods; cedar shelves and sweet oak casks likewise, clay pots for honey and tree-syrup, burlap sacks and creaking openwork baskets hanging from the ceiling; and if he loved people in passing it was because they took the food away and made room for him to go on with the sorting of more. He was otherwise of insurmountable laziness, and he considered that without the larder there would have been no work for him in the world.

The larder was a natural cavern, with floor lithotroph-smooth and walls of unfinished stone. All the flies had died in the heat. The sorter of the larder was oppressed by the quantity of sweat that poured from him. He had a choice in the matter of the sweat: whether by sorting with arms wide and torso unmoving to allow it to run down his flank, or whether to sway to and fro in his sorting and so coax it to run down the inside of his arm. One or the other. But the sweat was intolerable whatever route it took. For many days he had not seen the sky. He kept his eyes to the ground when he ventured from the larder. It was intolerable in the larder, as though existence were merely a pretext for suffocating all creatures; yet it was more intolerable everywhere else. The sky would be white were he to look in that direction. He directed his gaze instead toward yams. He imagined the situation might improve were he only able to remove his head; and he imagined that, in doing so, he would reveal not the interior of his body, but a sharpened stake of white wood, for thrusting into the sun. He stepped back from the table, which groaned under the weight of the heat. Sweat trickled down his inner thighs, the sweat of his reproductive organs.

He heard himself called to take a delivery of salt.

*

The avocado gatherers had brought avocados that morning: the great sorting table sagged under black reptilian mounds of them. The scent in the larder, which had been the scent of avocado, now became the scent of avocado mixed with the scent of dung. The sorter of the larder did not immediately associate the scent of dung with the call of salt; the rapidity of events confused him; the wagon clattered and the oxen huffed, a hoarse stony voice shouted salt, and he was dizzy. The heat smote him anew though he stood very still. He thought at first that the woman on the threshold was a woman he knew, that she had unearthed a forgotten sack of last year's avocados, rotting, and that it was from these that the stench proceeded. But suddenly he saw that she was a stranger.

He followed her out into the yellow afternoon. A dark accretion of dirt spanned her shoulders, descended the channel of her spine, and drew up short, in a black line, where the top of her buttocks had met the seat of the wagon. The hair on her head supported great crumbling clods of soil, and as she turned to roll the first of the salt barrels from the wagon he saw that she was muzzled in red-brown grime, as though she had been rooting in loam. Her nails, both finger and toe, were impractically long, and he wondered, as the two of them unloaded the barrels, that they did not break; but they were strengthened, perhaps, by the bulwarks of dirt underneath.

They unloaded twelve barrels of salt together, and afterwards shared an avocado, and coupled on the floor of the larder.

When first he embraced her he gave a start: under his hands he felt an unexpected texture. Indeed, he did not know what to think, and would have concluded that he was dreaming, except the sensation was palpable in his fingertips and under his palms, as no sensation is in dreams—unless, he thought, he were unaccountably being nuzzled in his sleep by a boar: for what he felt himself touching on the body of the deliverer of salt were boar's bristles. What he had taken for grime on her shoulders and spine was only partly grime; the other part was boar's bristle.

Meanwhile, her coupling had in it what he thought an unseemly greed. She pressed his back against one leg of the sorting table, atop which the avocados overspilled their sacks, and straddled him. He had coupled against that table before and thought it good for the purpose: low and thick, one long edge flush against the wall, quite immobile. But no sooner had she penetrated him than, with scarcely an exploratory thrust, she began to buck so violently that the table took up her bucking, and the sorter of the larder, whose body formed the fleshy medium between woman and wood, could scarcely keep from crying out in pain. Avocados rained down on them. The table leg ground against his spine. The boar-bristle woman cooed in the back of her throat but did not open her mouth; her nails gouged the wood to the left and right of his head; he became aware of an odor of corruption beneath the dung, and of the table leg splintering behind him.

*

The binder of brooms appeared on the threshold of the larder. She had come to confront the sorter of the larder about the state of the small hemp crop that was their joint responsibility. This woman was not far from deaf, having lived the earlier part of her life underneath a waterfall; and, although she had seen the four oxen and smelled the dung, and wondered idly what dunglike commodity had been delivered (for she thought the odor could not be due to the oxen alone), she had failed to hear the splintering of wood. When first she glimpsed the situation in the larder she made up her mind to withdraw. She would wait on the larder path, among the daffodils; it would not be long. But even as she turned away the sorter of the larder cast her a look of such despair that she paused on the threshold and looked: the boar-bristle woman was evidently possessed by some fury. One of her fingernails had split down its center, and a thin stream of blood ran down her arm. Steam rose from her head.

The binder of brooms leapt into the room and struck the boar-bristle woman behind the ear with a young pumpkin. The blow accomplished nothing; the stem of the pumpkin snapped, and the fruit rolled onto the floor. The sorter of the larder struggled to displace himself in one direction or the other, in order no longer to be trapped between the boar-bristle woman and the table leg, and so retreat; but the boar-bristle woman wrapped him and the table leg both between her thighs and squeezed like a vise.

A sack of unshelled peanuts, not smaller than a large child, leaned against the wall on the other side of the larder. The binder of brooms could scarcely lift it, but she wrapped the cloth of its neck around her hands and began to spin. The sack gained in altitude as she whirled across the larder. It tugged fiercely at her elbows and shoulder. She timed her spin with mincing steps; after nine revolutions, over the course of which she attained considerable momentum, so that the sack seemed likely to tear the arms from her body, she clobbered the boar-bristle woman high on the head. The sack burst. The forehead of the boar-bristle woman cracked against the table and bounced, and a second crack followed as she struck the floor. Peanuts showered the three of them.

The sorter of the larder extricated himself. He and the binder of brooms stood looking at the boar-bristle woman where she lay unconscious. In repose there was a softness to her features. She was still alive. Blood streamed from the wound in her forehead; together with the filth that covered her face and clotted her hair, it gave her the appearance of the last survivor of some great calamity.

*

—Is she contagious? said the binder of brooms.

—She was maddened by the season, said the sorter of the larder. A blue pill will bring her to her senses.

He left the larder and directed his steps past the four oxen toward the bathhouse, leaving the binder of brooms alone with the boar-bristle woman.

*

BRIAN CONN

The binder of brooms had not been the only one to arrive at the larder just then. It was the six spare days; the snow pageant approached: the children had sent one of their number to steal chocolate in preparation for the feast.

Hector had arrived unseen. The children had recently completed a secret tunnel between the crèche and the larder, for their convenience in stealing those foodstuffs they did not grow themselves in their croft. The tunnel came out under one of the fermentation compartments in the floor: in the dead of night they had fitted the fermentation bucket with a system of wooden gears which allowed them to lower it into the tunnel and at the same time cause a retractable cyclate cover to extend over its mouth. It was on the cyclate-covered bucket that Hector now crouched, steadying himself on the winch. It was late in the day and he had expected the larder to be deserted; he had not reckoned with the delivery of salt, which had kept the keeper of the larder past the usual time. Instead of the empty larder, he had observed violent passions; avocados and peanuts. When the spectacle was over, and the sorter of the larder had gone, and the binder of brooms was watching nervously over the boar-bristle woman, he let the flap close over his head, turned the wheel to raise the fermentation bucket, and wriggled through the tunnel back to the crèche.

The children had been cleaning all day and the previous day besides. Every surface had been swept, scrubbed, and waxed, and all the air sweetened. When Hector returned, everybody was awake. They were eating at the great table. He might have preferred it otherwise, but, since it was not otherwise, he strode boldly to the peg by the front door and took down the welcoming hat.

—Has anybody come? said Ute.

—Sister, said Hector, the deliverer of salt has come.

And, when Ute seemed about to object, he went on:

—I know well that we do not ordinarily greet the drivers of wagons, or we greet them with less than our greatest hospitality; for they depart as quickly as they arrive. But it seems to me that this woman is something other than what she appears.

He described to Ute, and to a growing circle of children around them, what he had seen in the larder.

—You think her a spirit of darkness, said Ute.

—I do. And because she has no community in which to dwell, and because all around us the mountain itself sighs with loneliness, I desired to welcome her. For are we not people, and do we not welcome one another, even those who lurk in solitude? And it seemed to me that, should we fail to welcome her, she too must depart and continue in her solitude; but if we welcome her, she may enter among us, and stay.

—But in that case, said Ute, perhaps it is I who should welcome her.

Then she too took a corner of the welcoming hat, and they began to discuss who would welcome the spirit of darkness.

*

The binder of brooms gathered the bruised avocados in a basket, the unbruised in a hamper; the peanuts she swept into a new sack. She replaced the pumpkin. It ought to have been she who left to fetch a blue pill, she told herself—or something more pertinent than a blue pill, which seemed to her a poor remedy for open wounds—and the sorter of the larder who stayed behind to care for the larder.

A fear touched her. The sorter of the larder had not, after all, answered her question whether the woman was contagious. Ought she to quarantine herself? She squatted beside the boar-bristle woman—or rather, the deliverer of salt, for the binder of brooms had not yet touched her, and still

5.2 Mercury

mistook the bristles for dirt—and reviewed in her thoughts the signs of contagion. But the sorter of the larder, who was the most likely to be infected, was even now walking the road to the bathhouse.

She bound the woman's wounds and pushed her under the remains of the sorting table, where, she told herself, she would be safer. Then, uneasy that she might awaken, she went out onto the larder patio.

The four oxen knelt there, still in harness, unmoving but for the dung that trickled from their anuses. The dung of the front pair pooled beneath the noses of the hind pair; also beneath the noses of the hind pair, brown against the pale dung, a human toe was visible.

The binder of brooms could not bring herself to step nearer, not at once. She craned her neck from where she stood. They were large oxen, lying close together, and between them was a kind of oxen-valley, and in the valley was nestled a man, much burned by the sun. He wore long black hair and a long black beard. Because he was narrow, and hidden, and because his gaze fell so sharply and unexpectedly onto hers, she thought him, in the instant, thornlike: a man like a thorn. Having seen her seeing him, he climbed over an ox and stood before her tossing his head. When she addressed him, he announced with great solemnity that he would like help cutting his hair and beard.

The binder of brooms found no reply. His hair and beard had grown, he went on, over the course of the year. Because he had loathed children even as a child, he had left the crèche early and so never completed the course of depilatory drugs; now hair grew on the bottom of his face as well as the top of his head, and even a little around his genitals, which the binder of brooms, looking closely, now saw; she had mistaken it for the shadows of evening. He had no blade where he lived, he said, only thorn, and at this time of year the hair on his head and face became unbearable to him. But he knew that here in the community there were blades; and there was even, if she had not left and if she would consent to see him at such an hour and on such a day (here his voice quavered), a barber.

He had come from the mountain, the binder of brooms realized—high on the mountain. He pawed the ground and then stood still, but even in stillness his body seemed to tremble with a restless motion. The binder of brooms did not believe that he had no blade; there were stones, sharp stones up the mountain trail—flints. But if she herself felt the loneliness of the spare days, she who was surrounded by the community of people, how much worse must it be for those who were friends only to the wind?

—That we be as a river with innumerable currents, she said.

He seemed pleased at that, and replied:

—That the currents of our civilization be not of steel, which decays, nor yet of words, which deceive, but of flesh, which is born anew.

—And blood, the binder of brooms said. Flesh and blood.

*

The sorter of the larder had gone halfway to the bathhouse when he came to a man scrubbing the stones that lined the trail.

—Scrubbing away the blood, the man said: a wagon passed this way recklessly, and a man was crushed. He was the man who wove hats. He was also, he added when the sorter of the larder appeared uncertain, the man who preserved berries.

—The man who scrubbed stones, said the sorter of the larder.

—The same man, said the man who scrubbed stones; and now that he is crushed it is I who scrub stones.

The community would meet that evening, the scrubber of stones said, to discuss whether to ask the driver of the wagon never to return.

The sorter of the larder understood at once that the woman who had crushed the hatter was none other than the boar-bristle woman. Now that he was away from the larder, and no longer smelling her dung-scent, nor feeling her bristles under his hand, he found in his mind an image of her different from that which had been there before: he saw her not in the doorway as he had first seen her, but lying on the floor of the larder as he had left her; and he felt a duty toward her, as toward all the contents of the larder, and regretted to have left her there in such disarray. Abandoning without qualm the notion of a blue pill, he turned and started back toward the larder.

—The extra time, the man like a bear had told him, when there had been a man like a bear: the six spare days. Or they may be more days, or fewer; the quantity of days is not the product of a calculation, but a fact of life: when we feel that we are no longer people, and can do nothing but wait until we become people once again, then we are in the spare days. And we never know, when we think during those days of all those who have left us in one way or another, whether some of them might return before the winter, or new people arrive; and if any arrive, we never know of what kind they will be, beloved or loathsome. Or indeed it may be that yet more will depart, and we will find ourselves quite alone.

*

The blue pills were a recent innovation, dispensed by the small doctor who loitered in the bathhouse and sometimes seemed to reside there. It was not true, as some said, that they had no effect whatever; at the very least they worked as a physical purgative. They also left many with a sense of peace—or, as others described it, of emptiness. In fact it hardly mattered what their effect was, or what was in them, or whether they did anything at all: it was the time of year when any kind of pill was attractive, particularly one midnight blue in color, in order to break up the feeling of being made, inside and out, of lead.

People sat out the long afternoons on the woodbine-draped stoop of the bathhouse, on the roof of the observatory, on the parched redwood platform at the end of the ridge, on the lichened boulders under the orchards; they looked out over the valley, smudged and greasy under the heat; and as evening fell they looked out into space and became unconscious of the frail sickening year and the aging of their internal organs. Looking upward they felt a kind of falling. They took blue pills and lay sleepless in their hammocks.

*

The children were connoisseurs of rhetoric and would ordinarily have listened carefully to Hector and Ute; but they had spent every minute since dawn cleaning the crèche, and they were weary as well as filthy.

—We ought not to lie down, said Deirdre, for we are dirty and the sleeping mats are clean.

—But perhaps we might lie down on the bare floor, said Seamus. It is clean there too, but the floor will not take on so much of the dirt of our bodies; not as much as would the sleeping mats.

—There ought not to be any dirt at all in preparation for the snow pageant, not on the floor or anywhere.

—There is the dirt of food in the places where we prepare food.

—But there oughtn't to be any dirt of the body.

—Then we must bathe, said Ulrika, using the barrel-water which we stowed in the bathhouse against this day.

They began to gather their towels.

—Shall we bathe the beneficial animal? said Andrea.

It was the first time the question had been raised. They had cleaned everything else and presently they would clean themselves; but there was another animal than they in the crèche, and they had not cleaned it.

—Perhaps it cleans itself, said Seamus.

—It is part of the crèche like the rest of us, said Ulrika, and we ought to bathe it in water.

It took ladders and hooks for five of them to scale the dome and wrap the animal in a rug. By the time they set out for the bathhouse, the moon hung huge and yellow on the horizon, and all that remained of the day's light was a lavender quality in the darkness. They carried the beneficial animal in the rug, where it lay still.

Hector and Ute remained in the crèche, each holding a corner of the hat: their discussion had made no progress.

*

The barber was also the surgeon and the weaver of linen. The binder of brooms and the thorn man did not find her under her canopy, but they heard an ululation nearby, which the thorn man declared was certainly her voice. The voice of the barber, the thorn man said with pride, carried farther than any other voice he knew. They followed it through the forest and found her alone at the bottom of a broad shallow scree, calling up at a pair of sheep huddled together in a nook on the mountainside.

The tender of sheep had been overcome with despair, the barber explained to the binder of brooms—it was the season—and these two had wandered while he lay face down in a crevice. She had found him, and having comforted him had also found the sheep, but she could not coax them from the nook. The tender of sheep had gone to fetch a woman who was capable of mesmerizing sheep from afar.

It was only after she had finished this explanation that she caught sight of the thorn man, who stood behind the binder of brooms and seemed to do his best to melt into the scree. She fell silent; a bashful expression came over her face, and the three of them stood there in silence.

All year, as the thorn man sat on his stony outcropping and gazed out at the sky, up at the pass, down at the eagles—all year, all he thought about was this woman. And every day of the year, except for the six days before the snow pageant, he told himself that he would not go to see her this year, that he would do without her, because of the agony it brought him to come into the community and endure the gazes of so many people, and because of the special agony it brought him to see her. But finally, on that day when the last grueling heat of the season seemed, paradoxically, no longer to be the last of anything, but the beginning of an eternity of grueling heat, and it became certain that there would be no further existence, he would admit to himself that the only thing that mattered, now that the end of the world was at hand, was to go and be seen by the barber.

Because his visits fell during the spare days of the year, the barber forgot them as soon as autumn came; but once she saw him again, as now when he stepped out from behind the binder of brooms, she remembered them again.

—My old friend, she said at last.

—I have come late in the day, the thorn man said. I was delayed (here he paused to consider the reasons for his delay, and finished—) by numerous emergencies.

—But I see you came at last.

—I came at last.

—At any rate you are here.

(This was the burden of their conversation; but it was not conducted in precisely this way, but rather filled with strange pauses and lengthy stammerings, which, stretching on, suddenly dissolved into the two of them speaking at once and then each urging the other to speak first; all while the binder of brooms shuffled her feet.)

—Had you a cool winter? the barber said.

—Not very; for the mountain breathes steam into the cave.

—Here it was most cool.

They gazed at one another.

—Perhaps with me it was a little bit cool.

—Everything was covered with snow, she said, the road and the trees and all the meadows; the river froze, and we all slept together under thick blankets, and people neither came nor left.

—Also with me nobody came, the thorn man said, or left.

At length he asked her whether it was too late in the day for her to cut his hair. The barber assured him that she would cut his hair whenever he desired.

—Though it has been a full year since last I came to you to cut my hair?

—Even so, she said. Indeed, now that he had come, there was nothing in the world that could prevent her from cutting his hair; however, she added, it would likely take all night, because there was such a growth of hair. But she had discovered a place in the community, high above every other place though not appearing to be so: a secluded place that would fill him with gentle thoughts, and her too, where they could be alone together and look out over the valley: a place ideal, in other words, for the cutting of hair.

—It would be most kind, he said.

They left the binder of brooms to look after the sheep.

*

When the sorter of the larder arrived again at the larder, the binder of brooms had already gone; and so, it appeared, had the boar-bristle woman. Perhaps, he thought, the whole incident from beginning to end had been a delusion brought on by the heat. Outside the larder, the night closed in.

As the sorter of the larder was gazing into the gloom and meditating on delusion, the boar-bristle woman crawled out from under the sorting table, where the binder of brooms had concealed her. He saw her when her hindquarters were yet beneath the table, and she looked up and met his eye; and this time, the second time in his life that she had come into his cognizance, he mistook her not for a friend but for a stranger. Her head was wrapped in a bandage and she wore an expression of fury. But he soon smelled the dung and understood that it was she. He scooped from the floor the same pumpkin with which the binder of brooms had struck her earlier, and struck her again. His blow was surer than that of the binder of brooms, for he gripped the pumpkin by its body rather than by the stem; and moreover the boar-bristle woman was now weaker. She fell senseless, half under the sorting table and half out. The pumpkin shattered, and a clod of pulp slopped over her neck and mandible.

The sorter of the larder lifted her briefly, arms-under-armpits, but let her drop on account of the stench. When he had bound a sachet of lavender under his nose he lifted her again, dragged her out into the twilight, and heaved her onto the bed of her own wagon. The rear pair of oxen had died; he unyoked them, and, mounting the platform, said the word to the front pair. He turned them toward the bathhouse, thinking as he went of the difficulties of bringing buckets of water from the well now that the creek was dry.

*

The children processed over the bridge bearing black towels and the rolled kitchen rug. At times they had been struck by the sun and now they were struck by the moon. The creek-bed below was filled not with water but with silver. They swatted at insects, and spots of blood appeared on their hands. How did the children process toward the bathhouse? They remember and always will; in their histories they recall it to each other.

*

It was a narrow staircase winding forever to the right. Above them the walls pinched together into a low vault, so that as they climbed higher they were forced to duck. The barber carried a phosphor lantern, which threw a bright light onto the ever-curving wall above them but left no light behind. A faint wailing, truncated, reached them from deep in the walls.

—Mice, said the thorn man.

A rasping followed on the wailing, as of stone on stone. The walls were wooden panels, yet seemed to have a patina of verdigris; in the blue light they appeared diseased.

—Year after year your body grows stronger, he said, watching it. He reached for her but she stepped up and away.

—And yours leaner.

They were objects of skin and sinew, lean

5.3 The Operable Window

and sharp both, like twin blades.

A single bat tumbled from the narrowing staircase above; and, in the wake of its squeaks, a rain of soot and an unfamiliar smell.

—We call this staircase the chimney, she said.

At top, a circular chamber carpeted in crimson, a dry fountain in the center and a bench looking out onto the sky. Sea creatures in silver miniature ringed the ceiling. Starlight struck the scissors.

*

Into each of the thirty-six chambers of the bathhouse the children rolled barrels of water: slick and sticky water, warm as the fluids of the body, but water nonetheless, long-concealed in a crawlspace sized for children: the bathwater of the six spare days.

Two by two and three by three they knelt on smooth tile of brown, pink, and green and massaged each other's scalps, while the beneficial animal paced the ceiling of the long hallway. They chewed strong herbs until they no longer saw the phosphor-light but their irises brimmed over with the moonlight that poured through the high windows. In the hallway and the chambers as they exchanged caresses their limbs hung heavy and sticky; but when they descended into the water it bore them gently up.

Claudia stepped out into the hall to call to the beneficial animal. A draft from the outer antechamber raised sparkles on her body. She followed the draft, past the scents of peppermint soap and the sounds of splashing, into the outer antechamber where the gloom was impenetrable, and finally to the outer door of the bathhouse, which stood open.

On the threshold a fat man bore a fat woman across his back. She was bleeding on the steps and they both smelled of a thousand things.

Here, with her dark-eyes in the night's light, Claudia could see the world outside: the trail lined with creek-stone, the empty arching footbridge, two oxen collapsed beyond it, and a wagon; and around it all, like a frame, the two door-posts of cedar and the lintel of vinebraid stiffened with cedar sap; and around that nothing.

—You are welcome to bring her in.

She closed the door behind them. When, after lengthy puffing and thumps, they reached the phosphor-lit hall and the murmurs of children now drying themselves with their shaggy black towels, the sorter of the larder asked them whether they had any of their water to spare, and any of their peppermint soap, and also whether they might advise him how best to bathe an unconscious woman; then they thought again of the beneficial animal, which, like the woman, had not yet bathed. It no longer paced the ceiling, nor any other part of the hallway.

Claudia inquired of the other children whether there was not a stairway ascending from the outer antechamber, broad and straight and lit from above: four steps to a door. All denied it.

*

The tip of the scissors pricks the thorn man at the base of the ear and draws a cold bead across the occipital ridge to the nape of his neck: snip. A lock of hair falls on the rug. The barber snares another lock with her fingertips, without touching his skin; tugs it straight: snip. The hair piles up. There is no moon. The room is illuminated by starlight and out over the valley there is nothing to see but the stars, one of which falls; he closes his eyes and follows her path round him by the snip of the scissors around his neck and up over his cranium. Warmth falls on his shoulder, and his head feels lighter.

—The hair I took from you when last you were here, she says, I wove it into a cord. Yours is the finest hair I know. I knotted it round my wrist and stroked it nighttimes to pacify me before I slept. In the end it came apart.

She is pausing in front of him; he feels her breath on his eyelids. The back of the scissors gathers up the hair above his brow and delivers it to her waiting fingers, which tug once: snip.

The scissors curve in a slow snick over his pinna. She leans close to navigate the arc and her breath tickles his ear canal. He is sitting rigid on the bench; she tugs at the hair on the crown of his head, he leans forward, and in the midst of it the invisible downy fuzz on his shoulder brushes against some bit of her flesh, something around the middle of her.

—I sat many days in the sun, he says. I feared I would boil away into a gas.

She is working on his beard now, around his mouth.

*

—Perhaps it went forth into the world, said Seamus.

—When the door was open.

—But it rises by nature, and rests on the ceiling. In the world it would fall away into the sky.

—Could it not cling to the trees?

The beneficial animal was neither in the hallway nor the vestibule nor the atrium; nor in the antechambers, outer or upper; nor in the second or third atria, nor the additional vestibules, lockers, staircases, parlors, foyers, cellars, closets, chambers, or secret rooms. In a claustrophobic studio at the top of a spiral ramp they had found a cask smeared with the oily black powder that was its waste.

—I tell you there was a set of stairs, said Claudia, illuminated from above.

Margaret smeared a pinch of the powder between her fingers and painted her cheekbones with hunting stripes.

—We might open the cask, said Thomas: perhaps there is something within that it desires.

Deirdre knelt to sniff at the lid of the cask.

—Unopened rooms.

It was not sealed. Thomas and Deirdre together lifted the lid off and set it aside. None of them could identify the blue mass within. It had the consistency of honey and the color (in the moonbeam streaming through the sexpartite spiral skylight) of midnight.

—Licorice, said Andrea, dabbing a bit on her tongue.

—Those blue pills, said Ulrika.

—Some composition of mercury, said Deirdre.

—That doctor, said Lemuel.

Andrea spit out the blue mass.

—Wisdom comes from those who speak it, said Deirdre. Although Ute is the eldest, and after her Hector, their discussion keeps them for the moment in the crèche; it is for us to respond to the state of affairs. We bore the animal here and we must bear it away, though it take wit and strength beyond the ordinary.

—Then let us search again, said Thomas, and more deeply now.

—But wait, said Lemuel: wait quietly to cool the blood before we search deeply. And when we go forth let none pass up or down through trapdoors into the adjacent bathhouses, where people are lost; for although we lose ourselves there not as easily as some, it is nevertheless night, and we are many; and the snow pageant approaches. The beneficial animal opens no doors, and we need open no doors to discover it.

—I shall remain here, said Ulrika, with the blue mass, to welcome the animal should it return. And I implore you all that you will return here to me after a period of time.

*

Only after he had filled the bath with the children's water did the sorter of the larder understand that to submerge the boar-bristle woman as he would submerge a pumpkin would be to drown her. He retraced his steps to the hidden closet where the children had shown him their supply of peppermint soap, and returned this time with sponges.

In the bath-chamber he struggled to raise the woman onto a marble slab. He worked by phosphor-light, and alone, the night being moonless and starless and black. When once he had heaved her shoulders atop the slab, he paused to rest, and then she slipped from him and fell, and her head bloodied the wall. In the end he broke the door from its rope-hinge and lay it down as a ramp and dragged her up by a towel around her feet. Then he took away the door and left it in the hall.

Even under the onslaught of the peppermint soap her

stench was slow to break. In the last bath-chamber off the empty hallway the water sloshed in tempo with his breathing, the sponge rose and fell, and the tile grew slick with soapy water. Never had he scrubbed any turnip so.

Having made a third trip to the hidden closet, he massaged her with oils.

As he kneaded her, his thoughts turned away from the larder, away from the bathhouse and the chamber drowning now in tainted bathwater, and toward a razor. Her bristles threatened to scour away the skin of his palms. He would ask the children for a razor; they knew many hidden things. But he did not hear them any longer, and had not been hearing them.

Was it her bristles that cut him, or a subtle barb under her skin? He maintained afterward that it had been the razor in his thoughts; in the children's history it is told as a thing of which they have no knowledge; but when it was over, said the children who carried him out, his hands were a welter of tiny lacerations, and swollen to a monstrous size.

When she began to stir she found herself anointed head to foot with aromatic oils and traces of his blood.

*

—Claudia spoke of stairs leading up, said Thomas, but these stairs lead down.

—Moreover they are unlit, said Andrea.

They reached for each other at the same time and descended hand-in-hand into the room below.

It was square and empty. The full moon staring in through the single window lit it chalky white. The window had four panes, and the mullions cast rectilinear moonshadow over the white field. The greater part of the floor was strewn with pine needles. In the diamond of moonlight nearest the window a small pine tree stood straight up, and in the next rested a large stone of the type found in the forest. As Thomas and Andrea watched, a bowlegged woman with a misshapen face raised the sash of the window from without, using her elbows; as the sash moved, so did its shadow move on the pine needles. The woman climbed in with difficulty, for it was some distance up and she went on elbows and knees without using her hands: she carried fistfuls of pine needles. She slid down from the windowsill and let them fall on the floor among the rest.

The children had remained in the darkness of the bottom step. The woman had not seen them. She sat down beside the tree, scooped up a plug of needles, and began twisting them idly together. She gazed out the window, moondreaming.

Thomas squeezed Andrea's hand and she squeezed his.

—An operable window, he whispered.

—I have seen them before, she whispered back, in drawings.

—I never. But this certainly is one, and glazed too: see the moon's image floating ghostly in the upper pane. But even the builder when he was here cannot have had such knowledge of structures as to make and install an operable window, nor have suffered such abjection as to have desired to; for only in the world of late capitalism did their prison crowd them so closely that they must open and close a glazed aperture in the wall for their only joy.

A cold wind blew in through the window. They felt the chill and wondered whence it came, now during the year's hot spare days. Both of them saw suddenly in the carpet of moonlit pine needles a field of winter snow, overcast with uncanny bars of shadow.

—She endeavors to bring the forest under a roof, said Thomas. Let us greet her as people greet each other, and ask after her health.

The needles stung their feet as they stepped out into the nearest patch of light. The woman turned at their rustling. She was wearing an owl mask; it was for that reason she had appeared disfigured. The beak cast a cruel shadow over her face, and two tufts of feathers shivered beside her two eyes as she sprang to her feet.

Andrea opened her mouth to speak, but the woman cuffed her ear. She sprawled among the pine needles. The owl mask woman bound Andrea and Thomas wrist-to-wrist with a strap of cow's leather; she kicked and prodded them up over the windowsill, not without bruises and wrenching of joints, and dragged them out into the forest where she beat them until they submitted to her. She set them to work collecting fistfuls of pine needles.

*

—Come to the window and let me see.

The thorn man stands but does not open his eyes; the hard flat of the scissors against his back urges him forward, and a tap against his chest stops him. He stands in the starlight feeling her circle him. She has shorn him close, he feels; everywhere his skin is open to the night as the room is open to the night.

—I've gathered up all your hair.

A tap of the scissors behind each knee and he kneels on the rug.

BRIAN CONN

—I shall weave it again into a cord, the barber says, the softest hair I know and also the strongest, and again it will comfort me nighttimes. But have you anything else for me to take?

The scissors in the hollow in front of a shoulder push him back onto the rug, which shrouds him in a scentless enveloping softness. Steel brushes the hair of his genitals; the scissors are warm from so many snips and from long closeness to his body.

—Shall I take the hair here?

—I prefer to have it there, he says, for there is not much. But there is something else I would have you take from me.

—Some other hair?

—It is something within my body.

—Your breath?

—It is a subtle hair which grows within my body. Others do not call it hair, yet I think it hair for the way it tickles me: it tickles me within and its weight grows unbearable. I would have you extract this ticklish subtle hair from my body. Its fluid medium is my genetic material. For one year the mass of it has grown inside me, and now I would like it if you would take it from me.

—Then I will take it. There is a clay vessel under this bench. If you like we might contrive that you expel your genetic material in one way or another into the clay vessel, and then I will carry it away with me.

He feels her warmth along his length and knows that she is lying beside him. Her voice is above his ear, not far, and the puff of her breath is perceptible against his eyelids.

—Or else, she says, we might contrive that you expel your genetic material onto this rug, which is rich and soft as the intimate flesh of a person, and then I will carry away the genetic material in the rug. But that way is more cumbersome, perhaps. Shall I bring the clay vessel?

—Perhaps the clay vessel. Yet there is also the dry fountain; I might expel my genetic material there.

—And then I might collect it if I like, she says, or else leave it behind.

—As you like.

The scissors are playing over his chest, always the back of the blade, smooth and hard. Her skin smells of pears and ewe.

—After all I do not much want to take with me the clay vessel, she says.

—Nor the rug I should think.

—Then perhaps it would be most convenient for you to expel your genetic material into the fountain; but then should I desire to take away your genetic material I would have to employ the clay vessel regardless. But I think you will enjoy it best to expel your genetic material into the fountain, and then we will decide about whether I will carry it away.

—After all we might leave it in the fountain and allow the air to carry it away.

—But perhaps I desire to carry it with me, she says. Hold still.

Her breath moves to his throat as she crouches astride him. The scissors press his lips: quiet.

*

The sorter of the larder sensed the fury of the boarbristle woman even as she woke.

He reached for the soapdish with the thought of stunning her. But it was difficult to feel that it had not been he who had

5.4 Mercury

brought her to life, he with his lengthy ablutions: it had been his fingers that had moved her flesh when it had been still, and his limbs that had animated her limbs when she had not animated them herself. He was eager to watch her move without him, as though she were a homunculus of his. He resolved no longer to incapacitate her. Her feet were still wrapped in the towel by which he had dragged her up onto the slab, and he took it away.

Thus it was she who reached for the soapdish, recovering with wondrous speed, and swept it down toward his head to brain him; and she would have, for he was sluggish at the best of times, and more sluggish still under the enchantment of the summer night; but, sluggish or no, he started at her movement, and his start cost him his footing on soap-slick tile: he tumbled to the floor, and the soapdish smashed into fragments against the opposite wall.

He struggled to rise but became entangled in the towel. She sprang on him and straddled him as though to couple with him once more, as in the larder; finding it impossible, she pummeled him instead about the chest and face. He felt her nails sweep across his eyes and saw his vision blur. She snatched up the phosphor lamp and raised it over her head in preparation for crushing him. But tonight, hottest of all nights, the phosphor had softened into a liquid state; and, at the apex of the lamp's arc, the mass of it spilled out and splashed into the bathwater behind her. The light became a grimy aquatic effulgence. She swung the lamp blindly, and struck not his skull but the hand he had raised to ward her away; his wrist snapped. He cried out, setting off echoes in the tile.

She lurched out the doorway. He rolled onto his knees and one hand; the other hung from the wrist like a dead leaf. Fighting the towel and the soapy tile, he scrambled to his feet and out into the hall in pursuit. But the hall was already empty. He started out in one direction or else the other, and, encountering the door he had left there, found himself flying through the air.

*

—Claudia spoke of four stairs, said Deirdre, but here there are five.

—Moreover they are unlit.

It was a dark corridor. Farther on, past the staircase, the moon streaming through a skylight illuminated a columned gallery under a sloping roof. They were in a remote region of the bathhouse.

—Indeed it may be more than five, said Deirdre, for the top lies in darkness.

—We ought to return to Ulrika, said Seamus. Perhaps there is a door at the top of these stairs and perhaps not. But we ought to return, and search no more for the animal, which surely has gone away. Perhaps it too will return to Ulrika, or perhaps it will live alone henceforth; perhaps it will return in the winter and perhaps not. I feel as though I am being killed.

—There is something in the air.

—I have not seen these stairs before, nor that gallery. Though I trust well in you and in the decisions we make together, I fear we will never return to Ulrika, but will wander here forever on our own. We ought all to have bound ourselves together with rope.

Deirdre looked him over.

—Seamus, she said.

Afterwards they could not describe in detail the place where they had been.

—A dark corridor, they said, although farther on, past the staircase, the moon streaming...

—Dustmotes in the moonbeams? said Lemuel. Or did the moonlight stream purely?

It was never possible to establish a history of the dark corridor, but it was never left out of the history that Ute told.

*

Bound together by the strap of cow's leather in addition to or instead of the invisible bonds of love, Andrea and Thomas began to tug against each other.

—Needles, commanded the owl mask woman.

The moon shone on the pine needles as though it desired to drink them up but at such distance could do no more than lap at them with its light.

Andrea and Thomas watched as the owl mask woman squatted under a pine tree. Her body clenched and unclenched in a way that seemed painful to them. At length she coughed up a pellet, which she left in the boll of the tree.

They gathered pine needles, and time and time again

boosted each other up and tumbled over the windowsill into the bright empty room where the stone lay and the young tree stood. Soon all the floor was thickly carpeted with pine needles. The stone gleamed in the moonlight, as though shot with veins of quicksilver: shot with veins on the outside, it occurred to them, while the veins of the owl mask woman remained concealed on her inside. During the six spare days the sun thirsts for blood, but under the cold moon the owl mask woman kept her blood tight within.

They tumbled over and over the windowsill and into the moon-drenched pine-needle room. Soon they bled, and went bleeding.

They tugged at their bonds.

Again they watched the owl mask woman cough up a pellet and leave it in the boll of the tree. She deposited it there as though to come back for it another time. And if they climbed into the boll of the tree themselves, and looked out over the pine-needle snow because it was lovely? Then she dragged them out by the leather strap, scraping them against the bark, and flung them into a drift of stinging needles.

Though ankle-deep in snow, they were surrounded by the smell of pine. The needles they clutched pricked their palms. It was winter now. They had thoughts they had not had before concerning the owl mask woman.

*

The sorter of the larder woke prone on the cedarwood floor, a vulnerable position but restful. He tried to roll onto his back but discovered that his head was stuck to the floor with blood. He felt a hand between his shoulders, urging him to quiescence, and a cool something nosing round the bloody

BRIAN CONN

seal between head and floor. A pair of hands was working at the blood with a towel: moisture, the sound of dunking in a bucket of water, splash of wringing out, the cool cloth back again at his head.

—Too bad, the hands said, too bad about all this.

Putting aside their towel, they peeled him from the floor and rolled him onto his back, and soon took up again with the sponge around his eyes and face. Something smarted behind his nose and between his eyes, the sting of tears admixed with the pain of a wound: the pain of weeping blood.

—I shall not get up again I think.

—Then I suppose the matron will discover you in the morning; though which matron, I can't say.

The morning: should he remain he would have the misfortune of seeing the rays of the rising sun grope through the high windows in each of the bath-chambers, and thence into the hallway in parallelograms of various dimensions according to how far the doors had been left ajar. It was black everywhere; the sorter of the larder did not understand how the sponge found his head.

—My friend in the dark, said the sorter of the larder, allow me to advise you. If you love the larder then you ought never to care about any thing on the earth that is not a carrot or a cabbage or some other thing native to the larder. And when people come from far away on wagons, let them take their way and us take ours, and do not care for them: for by caring for strangers we care for fog and mist. That is my advice, or rather my conclusion; for you too are a stranger to me I think, and so I do not care for you and will not advise you; but because you are tending my health I share with you my conclusions.

Fingers intruded into his mouth; two of them pressed the soft flesh beneath his tongue. He began to vomit, but a hand clapped itself across his mouth and the urge left him.

—Laugh it off, my friend! the voice from the dark said; and, alarmingly, laughed.

The sorter of the larder shrank from the laughter. It occurred to him that the creature sponging his head was a species of laughing bat, which had located him via the echoes of its laughter.

—Blue pill! said the voice. For a kind of peace.

Even as he understood the words, the sorter of the larder had already swallowed the pill. He felt his tongue fondled once more, then started at a splintering close at hand. It was the nearby door being torn apart, he soon surmised. He felt wooden splints pressed against his wrist; then the hands retreated with an apologetic laugh, only to return at once to prod him.

—Do I remember right I ought to set it before I splint it?

A wrenching pain followed, and again his senses fled.

*

How did the boar-bristle woman climb the long staircase of the chimney? She climbed without recourse to the stairs themselves. This staircase was ceilinged by a low and cramped lancet vault, not of stone but of a dark-stained and greasy wood. Where the walls, rising vertically from the steps, first turned toward each other, there ran a molding to mark the transition between wall and ceiling: a rotten and irregular molding, on the top of which collected all the powders and excrescences that fell from above. It was on this molding that the boar-bristle woman supported herself. Her spine was not straight, but twisted; nor was it made of bone, that light and elegant stuff that forms the spines of people, but of a substance weightier and at the same time fitter for being wedged into nooks, like putty. She crept along the molding with her spine snug in the apex of the vault; and her elbows, bristly as bottle-brushes, she pressed out for stability against the convening walls. It is not known why she chose this position and not another. She progressed beetle-like and not rapidly.

The wood of the ceiling had been coated in a protectant, something gleaming and hard that began to melt under her heat, and to slough off under the onslaught of the bristles on her spine, and so to collect on her body and undo all the work the sorter of the larder had had to clean her. She thrust her head down, clear of the ceiling's scents, and sniffed the air. From above came the aroma of sexual arousal.

During the six days it was in the nature of living creatures to seek to rise into the air—to the highest point on the earth, and then, quitting that place, to a higher place still where no memory remained of anything.

*

—This stone fits well in my hand, said Andrea.

—As in mine, said Thomas, taking it.

There was this about the stone: it was a blunt object.

—All my life I have never picked up a stone in my hand to heft in this way.

—Every child ought to heft a stone in this way. We shall recommend it be included henceforth in the activities of the young.

—Many times I have feared the oxen, which are larger

than we and of alien disposition; yet never did I think to heft a stone in my hand for comfort against them.

—I would like it if you would advise me, said Thomas.

The owl mask woman was hunched over the boll of the tree. Andrea and Thomas stood on the forest floor under the operable window. Thomas set the stone gently on the ground, where it was taken up by the moon.

—We are bound together by this strap of cow's leather, he said, and we share the labor of collecting pine needles bathed in moonlight, and also of fearing the owl mask woman. Thus, although I feel this strap diminishing the bonds of love that exist between us, it seems to me that we are nevertheless bound together more closely than others. There is that within me that I desire to share with you, a girl well versed in history.

He lifted her up and through the window, and then she leaned out and drew him up too, and they stood together under the roof of the pine needle room.

—You may recall when a woman came from far away, said Thomas. She was a pallid woman with eyes as black as the mountain's deep caverns. She lay ill many days in quarantine, and grew paler every day until all the people came to stand on the quarantine boundary and peer at her through the curtain behind which she rested. Do you remember it?

—I remember it.

—She spat blood. But she grew beautiful as she grew paler, and everyone began to dream of her. Not we children, who have dreams different from the rest, but the grown people of the community began to dream of her, and spoke of nothing but their dreams. Her pallor was of a gentle brightness, the gentlest brightness to see at that time of year; the blood she spat was redder than any other thing, red as a rose you might say, or as the sun setting in the year's heat. Red as all that and redder. And her eyes black as the mountain's bowels. All the people clustered round the quarantine to look at her, and then one cried out was she not a woman? and was there not love? and went in to her, and thereafter was himself under quarantine. I was there watching from among the grown. They moved as though to stampede, and a wave of shuffling legs obscured my vision of the scene behind the curtain; but in the end every one of them stayed. When once again I caught a glimpse, I saw that the man's lips were stained with blood. Then the woman raised herself languidly onto her elbow and I fled. On the same day I pricked myself on a thorn and spilled my own blood on the trail. It vanished at once in the dry of the earth. Glass when it breaks

5.5 The Atrium

is sharper than steel. There is glass in this window, the operable window. And when people lived among glass they were surrounded at all times by the sharpest of objects, the shards of glass; yet the sharp edges were bound in among other shards of glass and so appeared smooth and transparent to them. I feel as though the moon would raise us up into a freer place, did we but acquiesce an instant to her light.

—You wonder whether it may be best for us to murder.

—On the day when the thorn spilled my blood on the trail, I saw what I never had before, the community as a confluence of currents; and I thought to myself under what circumstances to divert those currents, and how; and I was less at ease after that, feeling that I too might one day be among diverted currents, and the river flow on. But I did not murder that day.

—You did not.

—Nor ever, yet.

—In addition to stone and glass there is suffocation. I find it cold here; and the pine needles, though they are the dry needles of the days of long sun, have nevertheless the appearance of snow, and seem, even as we gather them up, to deepen under my feet. And so perhaps the conditions are best for suffocation.

—There is also this stake of wood, which I tore from a pine and have sharpened.

At that moment the owl mask woman finished her business in the boll of the tree. She looked around for them, and, when she spotted them peering at her from the window, flew at them with an inarticulate cry.

—Let us shut the window against her.

They did so. The window had no latch, but as the owl mask woman reached to raise it they jammed it shut at the top with the wooden stake. With a blow of her fist she shattered the glass.

Neither Andrea nor Thomas thought of fleeing. They discussed afterwards whether the movement in their thoughts that kept them from fleeing was a purity or an impurity, and decided it was both perhaps, a pure form of impurity that caused them, for reasons they could not afterwards articulate except to each other, to think only on the owl mask woman, or rather on the situation in which she held them. As she reached in through the hole she had made, endeavoring to work out the wooden stake without impaling herself on the remaining glass shards around the edge, they each took up one shard from the floor, both of them indeed sharper than shards of steel, and, together, cut themselves free of the leather strap.

The owl mask woman flung the stake away, raised the sash, and began to climb in through the window. The children together slammed the sash shut on her; but she withdrew her head in time, and they caught only her wrist under the bottom rail, knocking loose more glass as they did so. She sprang back, but the wrist was quite stuck now, and she only snapped forward again as though her arm were made of elastic. This oscillation persisted through several cycles; before it had entirely died, she thrust her other hand in through the window where the pane had been, careless now of the shards that cut her, took the sash in both hands, and tore it, the sash itself, the very operable portion of the window, away from the frame. There was a shower of splinters, inside the room as well as out. The owl mask woman shrieked, neither the sound of an owl nor yet the sound of people, and began to thrash her way, one-handed, her owl mask askew, up through the gap in the wall where the window had been. The sash cord, freed suddenly from the sash, swung to and fro above her head; and as she loomed in the window-frame she became tangled in it and could not disentangle herself. Thomas seized the end of the cord, wrapped it once around her feathered neck, and looped the end around a mullion, and Andrea gave her a shove out. The mullion shivered but held. The owl mask woman was hanged then; there was some quiet.

*

—Ought we to move the cask? asked Gabrielle.

—The beneficial animal came once to the cask, said Ulrika, but now it comes no more.

—I believe Gabrielle and I were nearly lost, said Boris.

All turned at a scuttling in the rafters.

—Is it there?

—It is a different creature, said Gabrielle, for example a bat.

—Nearly lost, said Boris.

—Few children have returned, yet the night deepens.

—We might move the cask among the other rooms, to tempt the animal near.

—Yet the others may return to this room, said Ulrika.

—We might go looking for the others, said Boris, taking the cask with us to tempt the animal near.

—And leave behind a trail of some kind.

The cask was heavy, but they made a lever of a broomstick and upended it. It rolled onto its side, across the curve of its fat belly, and seemed on the verge of standing up once again on its other end; but finally it rolled back, and pitched to and fro for some time like a wave of the sea, and then rested.

—What trail can we leave?

—Perhaps there is thread somewhere, said Boris, or rope.

*

The moon shone through the skylight and cast an inner disk of white on the darker disk of the floor. The children were in an atrium, like a funnel in shape, where the tall windows were trapezoidal in consequence, wider at top than at bottom, and the moon, directly above, shone through no windows but only the round skylight, leaving its milky pool in the center of the fleecy white rug. The walls were lined just under the windows with benches, and the benches piled with feather-ticklers and ewers of oil and velvet cushions, mainly red. The windows looked out onto a stretch of open slope adorned with long grasses, baked in the day and now chilled in the moonlight; and, beyond the slope, onto cedars.

—Never before was there glass in the windows, said Priscilla.

—Have we been in this atrium before?

—Never before has there been glass in any of the windows.

—But tonight there is glass, said Courtney.

—Let us knock it out, said Daniel.

They knocked all the glass out of the windows, not without cutting themselves and staining the pillows with blood.

Now that the glass was no longer in the window and the night could enter, they sat in a circle around the patch of moon. The skylight remained glazed: there was one remaining instance of glass in the room, the skylight, and it was precisely this that the moon penetrated.

—It is pleasant here, said Priscilla; let us bring Ulrika.

She and Oliver left the room in order to bring Ulrika where it was pleasant. A cool breeze blew from outside; the white of the moon seemed to blow in with it, and the grasses rippled under the moonwind like a dreaming mind.

—Milk, said Courtney, and left the room to fetch milk from the milk compartment beneath the bath-chambers.

They no longer thought of the beneficial animal, but only of sitting in the cool breeze of the evening in the atrium, in a circle on the white rug, and drinking their milk. The three children who remained in the room gathered around a window like a long cleft that admitted the night. When they turned away from the window there was a fourth among them, wearing a hawk mask. It was a young girl; they could not see who. She was looking down one of the corridors; and soon, as they watched her in surprise, she went off that way, and they did not see her again.

—Ought we to pursue her?

Nobody knew.

Footsteps approached from the same passage, but the child who entered was only Wallace.

—Did you see a girl there? said Margaret.

He had not seen her. They told him they were awaiting Ulrika and milk, and that after all it was better that he should join them in the atrium than that they should leave the atrium in pursuit of the hawk mask girl, and he agreed. A girl with the head of an ox came in. At first they mistook her head for a mask, but soon they saw that it was her head. She left down a different corridor.

—It seemed to be Berthe, said Caroline.

—Yet her head was the head of an ox.

—Indeed then it may happen to people, that their heads be the heads of oxen.

—Let us not think it strange, said Caroline, for nothing that does happen is strange. We are yet children and we know not the kind of thing that may happen in the world; but let us add this to the history of the crèche, so that we may grow in wisdom: it may happen that a girl has the head of an ox.

—Shall we pursue her?

—They have not yet returned with the milk, said Daniel, nor with Ulrika.

Gerta came in, and when they had told her about the ox-head girl, and how pleasant it was in the atrium, and that Priscilla and Oliver and Courtney had gone to fetch Ulrika and the milk but that none had yet returned, she said:

—If only we had numerous threads, or ropes: one end to hold in our hands as we go, the other fixed here to guide us back. In this way, though we wander separately seeking those who are absent, we might yet commune with one another, and also find our way back to the atrium.

Opening the benches that lined the wall, they discovered silk ropes.

—Let us untwist them, said Daniel: for we care not for the strength of twisted rope, but require the length of numerous threads, that we may wander far.

They gnawed off the cyclate-capped ends, untwisted the ropes, and tied the strands end-to-end into long cords, and the ends of the cords to their waists.

—Silk against flesh, said Gerta, twisting her belly against the binding rope: I think I have never been bound before. It is as warm as the hands of a person.

Then, independently of each other and without forethought, each twisted in the loop of rope to feel the motion of silk against flesh. Seeing each other, they laughed.

—Warm as the hands of each other.

—And to fasten the ends here in this room? said Daniel. I see no suitable prong.

—We might close the lid of the bench on the ends of the ropes, said Margaret, though I dislike it.

—It smacks of dilettantism.

—They will fall out.

—In the bench was a stake I think.

Wallace opened the bench. The stake was of white wood hard as stone. He pricked his finger on the tip.

—What is the floor here?

The floor under the rug was tile.

For the moment they threw the rug out the window onto the grass, and after it, liking the space, the pillows and the ewers and the feather ticklers, and all the other objects in the room; then they gathered around the pool of moonlight. Kevin, hanging halfway out the window, retrieved a single ewer for use in hammering the stake into the tile floor, which cracked.

*

The barber is poised to take her pleasure of the thorn man when a clamor from without arrests her. He raises his head and looks in the direction of the doorway.

—The gate, he says.

They passed through no gate coming here, yet the barber too has the impression that a gate has closed: a gate of yellow metal worked with lions and other beasts of antiquity.

—Some structure has given way on the stairwell, she says.

The thorn man shakes his head, invisibly in the dark, and the barber turns back to the window. The window was not glazed before, but now it is glazed. It occurs to her that she may smash the glass with her scissors should they require an escape. A silence persists in the room. Outside, there is nothing to see of the valley; just below the window, the tree-tops wave in a gale that has sprung up under the stars.

—Perhaps it was only cockcrow?

—Perhaps, he says. May I feel you now?

The room is filled suddenly with the scent of pepper-mint.

They hear the squeak of a bat, far off at first, then near-ing, coming up the stairs; and, though both are certain they had closed the door, they hear the bat pass freely into the room. For a moment they see its silhouette tumbling in front of the window, as though it desires, in the manner of bats, to stream out like smoke; then it flings itself back into the darkness of the room, squeaks once more, and falls silent. The barber and the thorn man remain poised, she on top of him. She dares not descend closer, lest they utter sounds of ecstasy; yet she dares not rise, because they will be apart.

A butterfly batters the window, white as a wisp in the starlight. Seeing it from the corner of her eye she thinks: the first flake of snow.

Suddenly she becomes aware of a face peering into her face. She can see only a short distance but it is certainly a face. She cannot tell how long it has been there before she picked it out of the dark. The scent of peppermint is close upon her, and beneath it an animal smell, like a cavern left unaired.

In a sudden panic she raises the scissors and slashes. They seem to meet flesh but there is no particular sound. Her hand is caught and she is thrown against the bench; the bench top-ples into the fountain and there is a crashing, then a howling. She finds herself among ceramic shards. The scissors are still in her hands. A wave of heat passes over her, a clammy heat quite like the heat of the day, then a wave of more intense heat as though an orifice of the earth had opened. There is a scuffling nearby. The barber feels her way among shards of ceramic on the rug. Framed as shadows against the window are the thorn man and a very large woman. She is atop him and he has arched his back. There is no sound from either of them. In an instant their joined silhouette plunges below the window-line and is lost. Again there are only butterflies, more of them now.

The ceramic shards clink against one another as the barber picks her way through them on hands and knees. As she nears the spot where the thorn man was, the ceramic gives way to damp and sticky rug. Her knees and shins are badly cut by the shards, and everything is warm. Finding a head under her hands, she identifies the scalp she has recently shorn; feeling further, she finds a ragged wound round the neck. It is wet, and as she makes her way around the body the rug makes wet sounds.

The glass of the window shatters. The large woman, in a wave of stench, passes wraithlike out the chimney and down into the treetops. Was there a sound earlier of lapping? There was the sound of lapping, as of the ocean's waves lapping at the shore.

*

—We ought to bury the body.

—Ought we to bury it with the mask? She seldom went without it.

—I think I would not like to be buried with a mask, said Andrea. But at the same time I do not like to take it off her. Would you like to take it off her?

—Not I, said Thomas.

The owl mask woman had wide sudden hips, squashed

a little from above, as though her torso had been thrust atop a spare pair of hips and had splayed them apart. There was a mole inside her left elbow.

—I do not love the owl mask woman, said Andrea.

—When we are buried by those who do not love us, then perhaps we prefer to remain masked.

—Unless there is one who loves her nearby.

—Who would love her?

They were both bleeding.

—Our duty is to love all creatures, said Andrea doubtfully, though we are yet children.

Thomas looked up at the owl mask woman, who still hung from the sash cord.

—Then we shall bury her with love, he said. Although I do not like to remove her mask I will summon love for her, like an alien organ within me, and then perhaps I will love her enough to bury her lovingly.

Andrea shuddered.

Thomas unbound the owl mask woman and she fell on the pine needles below.

—That unbinding was not lovingly done, said Andrea.

—It was lovingly done, said Thomas.

—And to think it will be you who buries me.

Thomas had been on the point of taking the owl mask, but now he stopped.

—Or someone like you, said Andrea; for sooner or later I shall certainly be buried.

*

They dragged the owl mask woman into the forest to bury her. The moon vanished behind clouds. The pine needles vanished too, and the forest dimmed. Thomas jumped at a noise from the direction of the bathhouse.

—The owl mask woman.

—She is here.

—Some other woman then.

The bathhouse was hidden behind trees.

—The window, perhaps, said Andrea; or its remains.

Neither of them moved, and the noise did not recur.

—There is no cause for fear, said Andrea.

Nevertheless they left the owl mask woman where she was and crept toward the window, which soon came into view, a deeper black in the black of the bathhouse. Andrea heard Thomas shuffling in the pine needles behind her, and felt him boost her up through the window; but the shuffling continued even as he lifted her, and even as she swung her legs over the edge of the ruined window-gap and dropped into the room—continued (it seemed her senses had swung round with her legs) from inside the room.

—Thomas? she said. She picked up a shard of glass from the pile near the wall, where Thomas had swept them; and, seeing a length of the leather strap there, picked it up too, and wound it around a corner of the glass. Holding it carefully in order not to cut herself, she peered into the dark.

Thomas also heard the shuffling of pine needles inside the room, and supposed it was Andrea. She disappeared without lifting him up, and he began to climb through by himself. As he sat in the window-gap, he heard

5.6 Mercury

a very short cry, perhaps only the creak of a board; and as he swung his legs around into the room, the shuffling of pine needles, which had seemed to come from within, seemed instead suddenly to come from without.

He looked out the window into the forest. There was a shape there, moving, and in its hands the gleam of silver.

—Andrea? he called. But it could not be Andrea, who was in the room behind him.

He took one step back. The moon was gone: the woman was no more than a shape in the darkness as she began to climb through the window. Thomas stepped forward again, thinking to push her out; but midway through the aperture she brandished the gleam in her hand and he retreated.

—Andrea?

The room erupted in sound: thumps, a flurry of pine needles; a cry, like the strangled cry of a woman in two voices. Thomas could not tell from which direction any of the sounds came. The small pine tree, which had no roots in the earth but had only been propped precariously by pine needles, fell on him; it was as though he had been attacked by a bushy prickly thing. Out of surprise he fell down under it—fell onto moving forms, and the source of the two-voiced strangled cry, and felt himself drawn into a grapple.

The moon came out. The barber was standing over him, waving her scissors; the pine pricked him from above; beneath him, and increasingly all around him, Andrea struggled with a woman covered in boar bristles. Thomas was certain that the barber intended to stab him, and found time to regret that he was not pure. But the barber lunged instead at the boar-bristle woman beyond him. The scissors struck something with a dull noise. One voice of the two-voiced cry escalated into a squeal.

Thomas extricated himself from the grapple and crawled out from under the tree. Behind him, a different gleaming thing gleamed in the hand of Andrea than had gleamed in the hand of the barber: not steel but glass. The grip of the boar-bristle woman had weakened after the blow of the barber; now Andrea brought her shard around, and soon there followed on the first dull noise a second dull noise, and a further squeal and flurry as the boar-bristle woman rose and staggered back.

The shard of glass had broken, and in breaking had cut Andrea's hand. Five drops of blood fell among the white wash of the pine needles. Thomas watched the blood. The barber watched the boar-bristle woman. The boar-bristle woman towered over Andrea and the barber both. She was cut in the flank and also in the other flank; blood streamed down, one side and also the other, smudged here and there, and black in the moonlight, as though she were coated left and right in ash. The wound in her head had opened once more, and her head too was as though covered in ash. All the perimeter of her, arms and flanks and head, all appeared covered in ash in the moonlight: old ash, cold now.

The barber lunged again with the scissors, the room was filled with cries, and nobody understood anything. The boar-bristle woman stumbled and the bathhouse shook with her fall; the scissors, pursuing her and missing, struck the stone.

A spark flew: steel on stone. For one instant in the room of white and black a tiny red eye winked.

A butterfly, Thomas thought: one of the orange ones; it is spring.

He seized Andrea's hand, careful to choose that which was whole and unbleeding, and dragged her toward the door. Behind them the voice of the barber joined the voice of the boar-bristle woman in renewed cries.

Thomas and Andrea stopped in the doorway to look back. This was the image that they would describe later to the circle of children: The boar-bristle woman had worked one hand around the nape of the barber's neck, thumb against the soft flesh under the chin; with the other hand she held the scissors-arm at bay; as the barber broke loose of her, and raised the scissors to strike once more, the moon vanished behind clouds.

The boar-bristle woman roared, steel clattered on stone, and a fountain of red sparks sprang up in the dark, just as though it had always been there and had only become visible with the extinguishing of the moon. The roaring went on, and a pounding now, and grinding, and still the roar of the boar-bristle woman; but the fountain of red sparks had engendered a red eye in the floor, soon a pool: the pine needles were burning. Thomas shut the doors.

*

—We must keep that woman from following.

—Or else slay her.

Although their phosphor-lamp was still here, the room adjoining the room of the operable window was in all other respects a different room from the room it had been when they arrived. It was a tiny hexagonal room with a floor of tiny hexagonal tiles, black and white. There was no visible ceiling, nor any door but the double door they had come through; the walls rose straight up, unchanging, even to the murky limit of the blue-green phosphor glow, and, as far up as Andrea and Thomas could see, they were set with deep shelves. The room was a complex of shelves extending up into shadow. Each course of shelves was inlaid with mosaic in yellow and black metal, and on each shelf lay a black wooden crate, sleekly varnished, its lid tied with red silk ties.

—The size for a child to lie in, said Thomas, did children lie in crates.

—We might blockade the doors with the crates.

The stairs ascended from the room to the doors, no longer descended as before, but ascended: six steps to a narrow landing where the two doors, heavy wood unpainted but deeply stained, filled one of the six walls.

Together they worked a crate out from a low shelf. It thudded to the floor. Andrea's hand was bleeding freely, and she pressed it against her chest as they shouldered and shoved the crate across the floor and rolled it end-over-end up the stairs to the landing and flush against the door. They repeated the procedure with a second crate.

There had been no noise from beyond the doors; now Thomas put his ear to the wood and listened.

—Lapping, he said, as of the sea.

*

The doors gleamed like metal in the phosphor-light. Two cleats stood out halfway up as though to receive a bar, but there was no bar. The architrave was decorated with further scenes in black and gold metal: on the left post, scenes of violence; on the right, scenes of love; the lintel above depicted the theft of the yellow and black metals from the vaults of a gnome king. The people in all the scenes wore the heads of goats and asps.

As Andrea and Thomas looked on, the scenes on the lintel wavered and dimmed. White smoke was trickling from the top of the door, up into the dark. A smell filled the room, as of pine but sharper, and their eyes began to water.

A blow fell on the door. Both crates shuddered and danced, and one of them skittered across the landing and down the stairs. When it struck the floor, its silk ties snapped and its lid jumped loose. Thomas pushed the remaining crate to block both doors and threw himself against it.

—You must bring another crate, he said.

—They are filled with earth, said Andrea.

Indeed, the lower steps were now strewn with a fine light earth that had spilled from the crate, earth gray under the angular shadows of the upper steps, but white as the sky where the phosphor light struck it.

—Also teeth, said Andrea. I cannot lift a crate alone up the stairs, for this hand of mine will do nothing.

She let fall a pair of dust-dead molars and climbed the stairs to lean with Thomas against the remaining crate.

—Perhaps in death we no longer labor side-by-side with one another, she said, but lie one atop the other in crates fastened with red silk; it is a thing to add to the history of the crèche, should we ever return there.

—Do you see the bit of metal, there among the earth of the crate?

—I examined it, said Andrea, and found it encrusted with filth and with blood. I dislike it.

—It gleams still.

A second and stronger blow knocked Andrea head-over-heels down the steps, and the second crate after her. The gap widened between the doors for an instant, and white smoke poured out, piney and choking; but before the boar-bristle woman could appear in the gap Thomas pushed the doors shut again. The crate smashed on the steps, and Andrea found herself covered in a rain of earth.

—We must have another crate, said Thomas. Should there come a third blow, she will emerge.

Andrea wrestled a crate from its bed with a crash, and, leaning against it with all her might, pushed it to the foot of the stairs.

—But I cannot bring it up the stairs, said Andrea.

—Then you must come up to the door, and we will hope that the third blow does not come, and if it does come then you must do all you can in regard to the door; and meanwhile I will try to bring the crate up the stairs.

—We might bar the door with the fragments of a crate.

She passed the planks of one of the smashed crates up to Thomas, and he barred the door with them as best he could. Another blow fell, the strongest yet; the makeshift bars snapped, the room trembled, smoke billowed from the doors, and a shadow moved in the smoke, but not quickly enough: once again Thomas slammed the doors shut.

Andrea climbed the stairs, leaving the third crate at the bottom, and pushed with him.

A thundering sound came up from below, the sound of a great cask rolling. A course of four shelves swung aside, and four children entered. Seamus and Deirdre rolled the cask of blue mass before them, Lemuel held the phosphor light, and Ulrika paid out rope behind.

—Crates, said Lemuel.

—Secret doors, said Andrea.

From the other side of the doors against which Thomas and Andrea pushed came the sweeping sound of pine branches dragged across the floor. With a blow which dwarfed all the others, the trunk of the small pine burst between the doors: the boar-bristle woman was battering the door with the pine.

Both Thomas and Andrea sprawled at the foot of the stairs. Andrea, being lighter, was knocked farther; she slid across the brief tiled floor and fetched up in a heap against the far wall. The five other children crowded to the door, coughing. The room was drowned in smoke. From where she lay, Andrea saw no more than shapes moving in the smoke. A child's hand emerged to snatch up a femur which had spilled from one of the crates, then withdrew back into the smoke; the shadow of the femur rose and fell.

At last the smoke cleared: they had beaten back the boar-bristle woman. But Seamus was no longer among them—or rather, his form was among them, but unmoving. The four of them remaining flung their small weights once more against the door. The stairs were strewn with earth and bones and splinters of crate and pine boughs and blood.

—The rope, said Thomas.

Deirdre leapt to pick up the spool of rope. She tossed it through the smoke to Thomas, who wrapped it around the two cleats, loop after loop of thin rope until the cleats were thick with loops. It was a compact light rope of strong silk. Thomas took one end and Deirdre the other; and, as Ulrika wrestled a fresh crate up the staircase and Lemuel held aloft the phosphor-lamp, they pulled the loops tight.

Stone ground on wood behind the door: the boar-bristle woman, Thomas understood, was pushing the boulder across the floor. A howl or wail of exertion from within, a final scrape of stone on wood as she lifted it, the pounding of feet as she charged; when the impact came it shivered and splintered the planks of the door, though they were thick as tree trunks. In the quaking of the room, five crates fell from on high and detonated on the floor in front of Andrea.

Thomas and Deirdre pulled tight the rope, which held yet, but threatened to snap.

*

The sorter of the larder, drawn on by the bellowing of the boar-bristle woman, stumbled through the secret doorway and into the room. Deirdre saw him first. In the smoke-shadows his head appeared to be the head of a crocodile; later the children would say among themselves that his head had indeed been the head of a crocodile, and that his maw had gaped. Deirdre, astonished, allowed the rope to slacken in her hands.

What were the thoughts of the sorter of the larder? Often he had held in his hand an avocado, perhaps ripe and perhaps not. In such a situation it dismayed him to place the avocado among the unripe. Let it be placed among the ripe avocados, he told himself; and let it be eaten, though it be not yet as ripe as it might be, for those things that are eaten are sorted in their final sorting; and sometimes it is ripe after all, for one never knows.

Those were the thoughts of the sorter of the larder.

He was enveloped in smoke. The phosphor light found him through the smoke, and he choked, either on the smoke or on the light; for both seemed to strike him at once. His head was wrapped in gauze bandages, the doing of his friend in the dark, so that the smoke smelled to him not entirely like smoke, but also like gauze; and the smoke burned his eyes, but they were already burning.

Ulrika, following the gaze of Deirdre, saw him too. She had worked the crate up to the landing, and had been on the verge of sliding it against the door; but now, with the strength of panic, she instead heaved it back down the stairs in the direction of the sorter of the larder. He fell under the onslaught of crate and earth, rose again, then crumpled at the foot of the stairs and lay shivering in a fit.

A blow struck the door: not the strongest blow yet, in fact perhaps weaker than most, as though the boar-bristle woman were succumbing to the smoke; but strong enough to cause the rope to snake away through the grip of Deirdre, for she had not yet recovered from the apparition of the sorter of the larder. She pulled her hands away with a cry; they had been abraded by the rope.

The door burst open and the boar-bristle woman stepped out.

—Lemuel, said Andrea. The boar-bristle was even then sweeping Thomas up in her hands; but it is certain that at that moment it was not Thomas that Andrea said, but Lemuel. She had taken up the bit of metal, black with earth and blood, from the floor; it happened to be a kind of sickle, and she held it awkwardly in her uninjured hand.

Lemuel helped her to roll the barrel of blue mass to the foot of the steps, near the sorter of the larder, and to stand up on it; and when she had stood he held her ankles.

The boar-bristle woman shook Thomas until they all heard the snap of his spine. Then, when she had cast him away, she descended toward rest of them, Deirdre and Ulrika and Lemuel quite still, and Andrea tottering atop the barrel. What were the thoughts of the boar-bristle woman? Andrea struck at her with the sickle: a thread of black appeared under her chin, widening quickly to a black bib which undulated rhythmically at its source. Her blood blanketed the sorter of the larder.

*

An odor wafted from the bathhouse. Nobody was sleeping; all were waiting for the heat to break. One by one they came to stand around the bathhouse in the dark and sniff at the odor, unlike the ordinary odors of the community. When the children began to come out, dazed and soot-stained, they too stood watching the bathhouse.

—Smoke, said one.

They murmured to one another. All had smelled the forest burning at one time or another. The night was overcast. The children would explain nothing, but said only that the bathhouse was filled with smoke and soot. The people sat from weariness.

Presently four more children emerged, sootier even than the rest, choking and bearing on their shoulders the sorter of the larder, whose head was wrapped in bandages and who was covered in black blood.

—Thomas? said one of them.

—I advise you to cling to the living, said another.

The flames never showed themselves. In the morning the bathhouse was unchanged in structure, and unharmed without, but covered in soot within, top to bottom, and filled with the odor that they afterward associated with that night, the night of smoke.

—And there was an additional odor at the time, said the binder of brooms, something brown that bloomed in my throat.

It soon became known that the brown odor that bloomed in one's throat was the odor of mercury: the fire had burned hot, the blue mass had boiled, and the air had stunk with its vapor. All had breathed it. How did it become known? It became known when the sorter of the larder presented himself to the medic: pink nose and pink cheeks in addition to his wounds, pink fingers and toes: as though the fire, burning still in a remote hallway and reaching through manifold membranes of distance and time, contrived to singe his extremities. His skin itched and peeled, his pulse raced, and the light burned him.

When the medic inquired at the crèche they distracted her at first with play. But they too were pink, and they too feared the light. Their fingernails and toenails littered the floor of the crèche.

—You have been poisoned by mercury, said the medic.

The cases of the children and the sorter of the larder were the first known; but all had breathed the mercury.

CHAPTER 6

MERCURY

6.1 Noctilucence

My hands are looking old. That happens whether or not you've done anything. It isn't at all dark. There is a dazzle to the air. It is fall or will be. We haven't enough daytime. It seems that we have but afterward we see that we haven't. Then a dazzle masks the dark.

The story of the man who milled applesauce. He was an old man. Shall I make his story public? It was I who helped him dig. All of that is well known. But some of it was known only to the man who milled applesauce and now is not known to anybody. That part will not be made public. What is the work the dead do? Anyway there is little public left here; I have not seen them on the paths, nor in the larder nor on the meadows, nor anywhere. Perhaps there will be a public again and they will have forgotten. Now there is nobody to mill applesauce and nobody to eat it. Though the story of this man is known it will please us to know it again. For we may forget it, I do not know how, and then when we know it again it will seem to us a new discovery and it will please us. Thus do we recycle wisdom even as all other things.

He was very old. I have said that already. He had no occupation but to mill applesauce. We found him most often near the large stone which overlooks the valley, up the hill from the creek. There he sat with his sieve and his scraper, and a cedar bowl beneath. And cedar pails into which to empty the bowl. That was during the bright months. The sauce apples grow higher on the mountain, those apples which ripen soft as mush; therefore if one warm day we did not find the old man sitting under the rock which overlooks the valley, we did not think of it, but only supposed that he was harvesting sauce apples higher up. Indeed we seldom saw him whether he was there or not, for his spot by the boulder was not visible from the path. More often we heard the ruck of his scraper against the bottom of the sieve. The rhythm of it did not vary. Those who approached on the path felt the influence of this rhythm even before they heard it, it seemed; by the time they said to themselves *there is that noise* their steps had accommodated themselves to it. Then they found themselves marching to a rhythm not their own. At times it did not sit well with them. They felt they had been tricked into the old man's rhythm. But he was an affable old man and if we did not want to march in step with his milling we had only to throw a pebble against the boulder as we approached. When he heard its tap he knew to desist. He did not mind. Because he sat under the boulder all day, his legs atrophied. Moreover he kept the sieve in his lap and sat bent over it and his back ached terribly. This was the substance of his conversation, when he met us walking at dusk: his legs not well and his back not well. But he had great strength in his forearms. I became grateful for the strength of his forearms when we did our digging.

That was under a sky without dazzle. That night the sky was dark. The contagion had affected us both and it caused our limbs and digits to tremble violently and to rebel against our will. Contagion made us its puppets as he with his scraping had made those walking the path his puppets. Unmaliciously. But the contagion had no power over his forearms, nor in my case over my fingers. Thus his forearms were yet strong and my fingers yet deft. And together in one way or another we dug. Now and then we people have a little bit of luck. It was easier for me I think. In any case I was not the one weeping.

That old man no longer accepted any sexual partners. He claimed he was too old. There were those who rejected the idea; the aged may take sexual partners as do the rest of us. Perhaps, it was argued, he set himself above the rest of us, or else below. In any case by refusing all partners he set himself apart. But it was true that none of us were as old as he. He had left the crèche very early, it was said, and gone to the road. There he had aged rapidly and accepted numerous sexual partners. So that when he came back to us his body had made great progress in its aging. Indeed, for some time he had had no teeth in his head. Whereas the rest of us had teeth; that is, before all of this. To those who inquired about the road he said that he had been some time there, a very long time—indeed, so long a time…and then he would describe the duration of the time without naming any activity that had occupied it.

That was the old man.

No, there is something else after all. It is that I enjoy

thinking of him when he sat behind the boulder. I did not like the scraping of his mill but I was never one of those who threw pebbles. Perhaps I liked it after all. I think I did not but perhaps there is some liking of it somewhere in me that disdains to be known by me or anyone. And it will end with the end of me and will not be made public. Nor will we recycle it, this liking that disdains to be known. It seems a very desirable thing now to march to the scraping of the old man's mill. Not because he is gone but because the scraping is gone. Were he yet with us and only the scraping gone it would yet seem a desirable thing. Now it is difficult to walk in any rhythm whatever. No, we stagger. There is not one of us can hold a steady pace. The season has broken and as though it had held us up we fall. On the paths and everywhere. By preference in the forest abutting the proscenium meadow, all together to facilitate our removal. As though the season had been a blanket in which we lay rolled up and which mimicked the world outside and sustained us in its midst. But after it the rain began, and the chill of the air, and our falling on the paths and everywhere; as though it had been raining all the time, but never before had the rain struck us, because the season wore the mask of blue sky. Among ourselves we called it burnt-brown rain owing to its scent in our lungs. Indeed there is a sensory apparatus in the lungs, not olfactory but not far from, more delicate than the sensory apparatus in the nose. It was not burnt brown in color. But at night it may have changed and become burnt brown in color. During the night it was invisible.

While the old man and I were digging we accustomed ourselves to seeing the landscape by scarcely any light at all. Rainclouds covered the moon as you might imagine. But

BRIAN CONN

nevertheless there was a light so very thin it hardly bears the name of light, a white light as it were sheathed in black, so that although it revealed nothing to our eyes we sensed with the more delicate sensory apparatus behind our eyes the white light beneath the black and found our way through the landscape which it revealed to us. But you will understand that this light did not illuminate the raindrops. Those were not illuminated. So that we heard the sound of rain, a wet muddy sound, and there was the sound of the frogs which love the rain and were abroad in great numbers. And we felt rain on our skin and thought it burnt brown in color. But after a time we no longer felt it on our skin though it continued to fall there. When my spade broke and I went to fetch another from the tool shelter, I thought the dry wood of the handle unnatural like the skin of an artificial life form. I mean a life form which does not exist. It frightened me. Yes, I confess it frightened me. I threw down the spade with a cry. Then I trod on it so as to submerge it in mud, and when I took it up again found its texture more acceptable. But still I did not like it until I had dug many strokes, enough that the mud and rain got into the wood. Blood too: in the morning I saw that my hands had blistered and that my body and all the things I had been near were smudged with blood. I took it for mine, but it may have been the blood of the old man.

Now what was the reason I was abroad that night? It was this: that earlier that day I had found the body of a child on the trail. In fact that was not such an unusual thing. He had all the marks of contagion. His extremities were red and he had lost his nails. I do not know what child it was. But he wore on his head a green hat, their welcoming hat. The child who had welcomed me to the community many seasons ago had worn the same hat. It was of special magnificence. On the head of the dead child it seemed smaller than it had seemed then. In the brim of it two beetles confronted each other.

This was on a small trail which few people trod; I had taken it to be away from those I might meet on the larger trails. Not in order to set myself apart but only because there is a limit to what one can endure. And for their part I felt that the others would be better pleased without the sight of my stagger.

I thought to bring the child to the crèche but I was incapable of it. Then I thought at least to bring the hat. There was no hatter any longer and they had I think only one hat. I drove the beetles away and at length persuaded my arms to seat the hat atop my own head, where it fit snugly. But when I knocked at the door of the crèche I received no reply. Neither cry nor commotion. The door was shut and I dared not open it. In back, in the croft, there stood the gallows. Whether they had had the pageant yet I do not know. They had got as far as erecting the gallows. Certainly I feel winter coming. I thought that all of them had died of contagion, leaving none to hang, but then I thought not, for there were very many of them. And often they did not answer at the door of the crèche even when all were alive and they were gay, for they were not obliged to. I left the hat on the doorstep. But I wondered who had come to be welcomed. A child had gone forth wearing the welcoming hat; so they had had word of a person coming into the community. But the flags were up and the messages sent: contagion. Though it was not contagious.

I wondered also: had the child died going or coming? That is, I wondered whether the new person had been guided into the community, or whether perhaps she wandered the road still. Without a guide it is difficult to come.

It was that and related questions that occupied my mind. In the evening when the rain increased I chose to walk outdoors. I became cold but hoped that I might meet the person who had come anew and who had not the contagion. I thought that I would like to meet such a person. And it would not matter what person it was or what things would be demanded of me. Only I did not want to lie among those who were dying. I loved them when they lived and I love them also when they are dead but there is only so much one can bear. But then as the rain increased and I continued to walk the trails I discovered that I no longer wished to meet anyone at all. Rather I wished to continue walking the trails. Not forever but for some time that need not end. It would not do to stop walking. The notion did not occur to me then; it occurs to me now because I fear it might occur to one who reads this to ask whether or not I wished to stop. I did not. Had it occurred to me I would have thought it repugnant. No, the only thing was to continue walking the trails. But I fretted a little to know that the sun would rise. It would have no choice. Then I might see farther and know that it was day. But it did not rise yet. Then when I did not wish to meet anybody I met the old man. He who milled applesauce I mean. I heard his spade first, and in its rhythm the same rhythm with which he milled applesauce. It was by this rhythm that I knew him: I discovered I had accommodated my pace to it unknowing, and I thought *that old man.* Although I did not wish to meet anybody I felt that I loved him above all other people. I allowed myself to love him above all other people because I only heard his rhythm and did not see him, and when I saw him it was by a hidden light which revealed nothing. Then I stumbled upon he or nearly so. That is, my body touched his. His skin was clammy with mud, also with age. It hung on him in an unhealthy way, I thought. I felt this with my hands. I did not like the feel of his skin but I loved him the more for that. I reached to steady him and found myself grasping him round the trunk. My forearms trembled with contagion and I shook him a little. But my fingers gripped him well. We stood comfortably for a time. Then he groped at my form, and I think he must have let the spade drop, though I did not hear it fall. He gave me to understand that he was digging in the earth. I knew that already but I liked to know it again. I had nothing to add. It did not interest me why. No, not then. Now it interests me, but only because all of this has happened already and it interests me to vary the ways in which I think about it. Now there is a dazzle in the night and the situation is quite different. That is, it has changed. Thinking it could do no harm I retrieved a spade from the tool shelter and assisted the old man in his digging. Though he had strength yet in his forearms, his digits betrayed him, and in the end it was necessary for me to take rope from the tool shelter and bind his fingers to the spade. As for me I gripped my spade well and the rhythm of the old man's digging quelled my spasms. All in all we worked well enough. And now and again I bumped against him. With my body that is. It bears repeating that during this time there was nothing to see except those things in the white light behind the black which we did not see with our eyes, but which illuminated objects as though from behind, so that the illuminated portions were those very portions which faced away from us. His body was cold, and I stopped knowing whether it was he or the mud that I pressed against with the parts of my body. Presently we unearthed a corpse. That was unforeseen I thought. Our digging was not in the forest beside the proscenium meadow where we preferred to die, nor on the path, nor in any other place that I recognized. It was a place I did not recognize. But perhaps it was after all a place I knew, but which, never before having seen any place illuminated by a light perceived not by my eyes, I took for some new place. We did not see the corpse, but rather began to strike something and then dropped to our knees and felt at it. We had struck it repeatedly with the spades and torn it up. It was the corpse of a man, either young or old. Perhaps I will call him young in order to avoid confusion with the old man who milled applesauce. But understand that he may have been old. I thought him old myself owing to the clamminess of his skin. But a young man might also have clammy skin. After all he had been buried. The old man thought him young and also gave me to understand that he thought this young man a stranger; he himself had buried this stranger earlier the same day. But now it seemed he regretted it. Then I wanted to help the old man bear the young man up from where he lay in the mud. The old man sat on the muddy lip we had dug and let himself slip down into the hole. Meanwhile I squatted on the same lip and reached down my arms in order to receive the burden. But the legs of the old man did not hold when he let himself down into the hole. He fell. He struck the young man and crowded him into the mud wall. I heard all of this and also saw in a manner of speaking. But it is not easy to know what I saw, the light being as it was. Or rather, it is not easy to know in what way the things I saw bore on the events that took place. The old man lay for a time beside the corpse. Finally I went down among them and felt them close together. One was neither warmer nor colder than the other and they lay in each other's arms. But the old man moved under my hands whereas the young man did not. I kept my hands on both of them in order to feel where they were. Then I did not know how to proceed. Moreover I did not know what person the corpse was, whether he was somebody I knew or a stranger to me as he was a stranger to the old man. I could not tell that. But I felt a silk banner tied around his waist and saw that its color was white, and that it was the banner that we people wear when we bear contagion yet nevertheless take to the road. Only in conditions of great urgency do we take to the road with this banner. Then those who would not risk contagion see it white against our skin from afar, and they wait in the forest for us to pass. Or I imagine that they do so: I have not worn the banner myself. Nor has anyone. But it was bound around the corpse which the old man held in his arms. I thought it must be a person come contagious from the road, perhaps he whom the child had gone to greet with the welcoming hat. Then I did not like it because it meant a second contagion would come among us. Or else, I thought, it may be one of us who had ventured out; but I could not see his face to tell whether I knew him. The old man thought him a stranger but also thought him young, whereas I myself thought him old, and because I doubted the old man in one particular I doubted him also in the other, and thought perhaps the corpse was not a stranger. A man of our community might have taken the banner to go onto the road. But it might have been any kind of man, young or old, coming or going. I thought to myself it might have been a man coming and then again I thought to myself it might have been a man going. As for the old man I felt him rocking to and fro under my hands. I heard him weeping. It was in frustration that he wept. He ground his teeth. That much I heard over the rain. He rocked to and fro. Again I wanted to help him because the two of us were together in the grave. And there was nobody else, but only the young man, that is to say the corpse. I squatted beside them and stroked the body of the old man in order to ease his frustration. His texture repelled me but I went on stroking in order to help him. Presently I felt that he was aroused. He sought to manipulate his sexual organ but his trembling prevented it. As for me, my arms trembled but my fingers did not. By steadying my forearm across the pelvic bone of the old man I helped him to move closer to the young man. Then he seemed easier in his mind. I felt that a piece of music now unexpectedly neared its conclusion. It was an unexpected conclusion. I thought how good it was that I should be there to know the way this music unfolded. I lay down with the old man, who still rocked to and fro but no longer wept. The young man rocked too and felt no less alive to my fingers than the old. It was a disjunction in time, I thought, and a music which became audible when we listened with a different quantity in place of time. When we listened in a different way it transpired that the old man loved the young man while the young man lived and the old man was young. They loved each other under the sun or atop the snow. And the light was not black but white, and the black was underneath. When we are very ill the dark sky admits a dazzle for us only. Those who come to bury us do not see it.

6.2 Simplicity

"The sandals made from rushes were the first sandals," Gretchen explained, "but afterwards, when nothing came of it, we began to wonder whether rushes were improper. Then we made sandals of clay instead."

"Clay!" said Dean.

"A frothy clay."

"Because we do not know what material they will prefer," Nash said. He spoke slowly: he had begun to think Dean simple. "They may prefer the most improbable of materials; but they have no means of telling us, and so we must try everything."

"When nothing came of the sandals made of clay," said Gretchen, "we returned to vegetable matter. Rinds and bark chiefly, but also leaves; those who will walk in the sandals being of but little weight, we thought leaves might suffice for them."

"Additionally, we asked ourselves what soles we might prefer to lift, were we in their place," said Nash, "and thought leaves."

"Not clay," said Dean.

Gretchen shrugged. "But perhaps those who will wear the sandals weigh less than nothing, and require clay to hold them near the earth."

"It is difficult to know," said Nash.

"Having no reports," said Gretchen.

The sandals lined the long room of the crèche three deep. In specifying the sandals made of rushes, clay, rind, bark, and leaves, Gretchen had only begun: there were also sandals made of cyclates, and of wicker, hemp, and roots; one pair was soled with cups filled with water, another with cups filled with juice; there were several pairs stitched delicately of blue-green molds, a long stretch soled in mushroom, and four soled in soap.

Gretchen and Nash had taken up all the sleeping mats, to devote the long room to sandals. The children slept in the larder now, between the water tub and the grinder.

"Are you simple?" said Nash.

Dean looked at him with wondering eyes.

"Because there is that in your bearing which bespeaks simplicity; and when we set out it would be auspicious, I think, to set out with a simple boy."

"It would cause us both to speak more slowly," said Gretchen, "and perhaps we might grow into workers who speak slowly, and then we might breed a community of workers who speak slowly, and that community will endure."

But Dean had eyes only for the sandals.

"How many?"

Gretchen and Nash exchanged a glance.

Dean left them for the late summer sunlight slanting in through the open windows. He turned round twice, each time peering over one shoulder and then the other, as though he had never seen any of it before; then he took a seat in the ocean of sandals, fondling them with his toes.

"Perhaps he meant," Gretchen murmured, "that those for whom we make the sandals will only depart when the sandals number as many as they, in order all to depart together."

"He may have meant it," said Nash, "and moreover it may be so. And if it is so, then we need only continue making sandals until they depart."

They observed Dean to nibble systematically at the soles

of the sandals, one after the other. He chewed a small sample of each, afterwards caching the chewed matter in the hollow of his elbow. The sandals had faced toward the center of the room, but as he tasted each, he turned it outward to face the windows.

"He makes sure which he has tasted and which not," said Gretchen.

"Will it please you to mature quickly?" said Nash. "I mean for the purposes of reproduction."

"It will please me enough, so long as the community be simple." As soon as she said it she regretted it. She turned from Dean to embrace Nash. "You know I value your genetic material as much as my own."

"I do know it."

"Only everything has been so complicated this season, the people coming and going, and all the speaking—I scarcely feel I've been here. I would have it simpler, always simpler. I know it is the simplest now that it has been for us, the simplest for some time; yet still I would have it simpler. And the genetic material of Dean is simple, I think. It is a helpless craving of mine."

They embraced again.

"Perhaps I will go as a girl," said Nash, "and see what comes of it; for I think it may be simpler so."

"Shall we all go as girls? In that way we will reproduce more quickly."

"In the simplest case we might all go as the same girl."

"All as the same girl," said Gretchen. "Indeed, it will be simpler so. Then what shall be our name?"

"Marmoreal or something like it, I think, that we might fit together as a single thing, whole and smooth as marble."

"Mirabiliary or something like it, I think," said Gretchen, "that we may work marvels."

6.3 Dermatoglyphics

I begin to grow hair on my head and wonder whether a person can rest unseen under her hair. It is a consequence of living under the earth perhaps. Many creatures under the earth go without hair, whereas on the surface of the earth all creatures but people grow hair. Therefore perhaps when a person retreats among hairless creatures she will grow hair on her head. The heads of the people who illuminate the cavern appear hairless, but I have not approached closely enough to know whether they be true people, or creatures like people but not.

When I first came here I found it dark, darker even than the night. I had brought with me all that I could muster: pots of nutritive broth, the blankets from the wagon, and as many seedwafers as the compacter of wafers had in her baskets. I had desired to bring the ox, but it would not pass the threshold of the cavern. A septic odor made me fear for my health, and when I uncovered a pot of phosphor I saw that all the volume of space here swarmed with vertical bars of matter. I supposed I had come into a structure of the late capitalists, long since sunk into the earth. I became afraid, but I asked myself, suppose I had come to deliver a crate to this place? It is my duty to deliver crates to all people to whom crates are to be delivered, even those who dwell in a structure of late capitalism. The vertical bars had gone long unpolished, for the late capitalists are no more. A coating of organic matter burdened them, white as milk; they had a texture like the interior of a creature, and when I touched them my hand came away wet with water and also grainy with fine silt. These bars rose up thickly in the cavern, and cast shadows over and across one another which stretched and curled as I picked my way through them, so that I became uncertain which direction was which. Before long I had come back, I thought, to the mouth of the cavern. But, though the forest and the night appeared the same, the ox was no longer there, nor the wagon, and when I turned back into the cavern I saw a large pool, black in the phosphor-light, which I did not recall. Three people were gathered around it, smaller than I. They appeared hairless, though they wore a radiance on their shoulders which may after all have been a species of hair. They did not greet me, but descended into the pool, and I thought perhaps their descent into the pool occupied their entire attention, and it was for this reason that they had failed to greet me. I greeted them, and when still they did not greet me I climbed down through the bars in order to approach them; but when I reached the pool, all three had submerged themselves. I did not see their forms any longer, but the pool shone with their radiance, as a pool of phosphor covered in oil, and cast mazy patterns on the ceiling.

It came to my mind then that these people who illuminated the cavern might be messengers of a kind. Although I had been eager to greet them before, I now retreated from the lip of the pool. I myself am a messenger, it is true, but the crates I bear are sealed so that I do not see what is in them, and it is for this reason that I love to bear them. For I perceive every deed of people as a lack, or deficiency, noting first and chiefly about it that it is not some other deed. And when it came time for me to leave the crèche, the eldest child recalled to me that my eyes when I was born were the eyes of a fish— that is, eyes which do not see in the air—and so the first thing I saw was a lack, and I only saw any positive thing some time later when the optic had sown a culture among some nerves in my brain. And the eldest child said that it is best for certain people to see in this way, for we all work together and it is no good our working together if we all see the same things, the things which are present, and none of us the things which lack. At that moment a crate was delivered to the crèche, in size like the bed of a child, for it was nearing Lammas; and as I watched from the aperture I saw the bearer of crates heave it onto her shoulder from the wagon, and I said that perhaps the thing I loved best was the thing in the crate, for I could not see it, and so did not perceive it as a lack. So she gave me her love and I went with the bearer of crates.

Perhaps it is because of all of this, and because I see in myself a lack rather than a presence, that I prefer not to be seen by messengers, and in particular by messengers who, passing freely between cavern and pool, might bear their messages not only over the surface of the earth but also through the subterranean waters.

Though I now kept back from the pool, and thought that the messengers had not seen me, I feared that they would climb up from the pool at some later time, while I slept or else while I labored unaware, and would formulate some message concerning me. Should they bear it only down into the pool I thought perhaps I might suffer them, for I included the interior of the pool in the interior of the cavern, and so in that case the message concerning me should not leave the cavern; but should they bear it onto the surface of the earth, or into other pools in different caverns, then it would not do.

As I thought these things I had been walking a circle around the pool, and now I saw a series of impressions on the shore. The ground was slick with an organic substance similar to that which coated the bars, and it held impressions only poorly; but nevertheless, though I had as much to imagine as to deduce their qualities, I became certain that these were impressions of feet, like the feet of people but smaller than my own. I soon picked out a deeper one, in a clotted ripple of organic matter which radiated from the pool out into darkness, and noted this peculiarity of it, above even its smallness: that, though it held a complete image of the foot's surface, like clay, it was filled, not with the curves and whorls which adorn the feet of people, but rather with a tangle of lines, knotted here and there, as though the foot which had made it had been covered in hair.

I spent some moments, the quality of which it was afterwards difficult to recall, in contemplation of this artifact, and wrestling with the meanings of hair and bare skin, heads and feet, the surface of the earth and its depths. When I looked up I realized that I had once more lost my place in the cavern: I had walked some distance around the circular pool but I knew not what distance; the bars and the floor rose similarly all around, and the pool's radiance, or rather the radiance of the small hair-footed creatures within the pool, pointed neither one direction nor the other. I knew not where the mouth of the cavern lay, nor the mouth like the mouth but not. Suddenly the radiance expired. I uncovered the pot of phosphor and retreated onto a notch in a palisade to eat a meal of seedwafer.

When I had eaten I began to ruminate. Often, I thought, I had disclosed the carryings-on of the messenger spores in my possession to the woman who makes seedwafers, yet she continued to speak of them without qualm. Perhaps she did not believe me. Or perhaps she made no move to believe me or not—perhaps the image which I communicated to her did not compel her to call it true or false. And yet this woman trusts my voice in all things: when I tell her what the road is she listens well, and when I tell her I hunger for seedwafer she treats it as a matter of importance. And if she treats it as a matter of no importance when I tell her of the deficiencies of people, and of the messages pertaining thereto that spread among inhuman creatures in the sky, perhaps that itself is a deficiency of people—I mean perhaps it is a deficiency of people that we see not the scope of our failure. But perhaps it is a deficiency of myself that I do see this.

I rose from the seat on the palisade. I had come only a short distance from the pool, and, having taken my seedwafer on the crest of a ridge, had only two directions in which I might descend, namely that from which I had come and the other: one leading to the pool near the cavern-mouth like the cavern-mouth but not, and the other leading deeper in, perhaps to the true mouth. But despite all this I once more failed to know which direction was which. The phosphor-light fell short of the foot of either slope, so that I could not see the pool anywhere. The septic odor assailed me once more. I looked toward the ceiling in hope that the radiance of the pool had returned, but the ceiling was dark, and I saw a movement in the darkness, as though of a creature, or else of fumes.

I descended the palisade in one direction or else the

other, into a region where the bars grew thickly, and formed themselves more often into further palisades, so that I scrambled over a landscape not unlike a hilly, thickly forested country in shape, yet hillier than any such country, and more thickly forested, and moreover coated, bars and floor alike, in the organic substance. But before long I found myself at a pool, one without radiance, and naturally I did not know whether it was the same pool again or a different pool; for all this cavern, though it had different parts to it, and though even a single part might look different at every moment as the shadows moved, nevertheless looked everywhere and at every moment quite the same. In this it was not unlike the communities of people, which seem to those who dwell in them to differ from one another, but which those of us who cleave to the road distinguish only with difficulty, for people are different everywhere in the same way.

As I descended to this pool I heard voices speaking the language of people. I covered my phosphor-pot and stood quietly, until it came to me that I was lurking in the dark in the way which does harm to peace. Then, in order to make a better account of myself, I again resolved to act as though I had a crate to deliver. But this time I resolved to act in particular as though I myself were the crate, to be delivered only to a place inaccessible to messengers; so that I, the bearer of myself, must ascertain whether I had brought myself to the right place, and so must make bold to learn whether or not this place was accessible to messengers. I uncovered the phosphor and saw on the shore of the pool three small people, either the same small people as before or different ones. Now once more I fell foul of my ignorance whether people in caverns grow hair on their heads or not. For if so, then these three, who were hairless as were the previous three, were likely the same as those three, for what chance of finding two different groups of three hairless persons in a place where most all persons had hair? And if not, then more likely they were different from the previous three, for they had not the radiance. They greeted me and said they did not come from anywhere. I asked them were they messengers or had they seen any, and as I asked it of them, two of the three circled round me, so that by the time I had finished asking I was in the midst of them. They did not answer. I looked toward their feet, in order to see whether they grew hair there, and so inform myself further concerning their similarity to the prior group of three, but it seemed, although the place where their legs met the floor lay at the edge of the phosphor-light and in the shadows of some bundles of rushes which they carried, and so I could no more than guess—it seemed that they had no feet at all, but that their legs joined the organic matter of the floor without hiatus, as though the organic matter had extruded and animated itself in the form of small hairless people. They asked me where I came from and I told them the road, and then they laughed and the smallest of them began to rummage within her bundle of rushes. I clapped my hands round her head, with the intention of hurling her into the pool, but her head crumbled dryly under my hands as though it had been made of a fungus. Then the three of them, one headless, fled chattering into the shadows, and I could not find them again. But I did not look far, lest I once again lose my place round the pool; for I had resolved, by that time, to take note of markings and directions within the cavern, and to devote more attention to navigation.

I inspected the floor of the cavern for footprints of these

people, again in order to know whether they were the same as the previous people or different; but I found, in place of the usual impressions of feet, clusters of tiny fissures in the organic matter, like dried-out mud-vents, having a sweet odor like the odor of nutritive powder.

Then a method occurred to me for learning whether that pool was the same pool as before. I trod many times to and fro between its perimeter and the place where the bars began to thicken, until I could not mistake the trail of my own footprints in the organic matter; this was so I might know that spot on the perimeter when I returned there. Then, having observed these impressions carefully in order to know them again, I set off on a circuit around the pool, searching over every spot of ground to see whether I might find another instance of my own tracks to tell me I had been this way before. I had gone not many paces, casting to the right and left in the light of the phosphor-pot, when I began to see numerous impressions leading in every possible direction. The first of these elated me, for I took them for my own, and supposed the cavern was not so bewildering a place as I had feared; but when I began to find so very many—far more, I thought, than I could claim for myself—I looked closer at one of them, and saw, vertically down its center, a pattern of sutures, as though the impression had been left by a person wearing her flesh knitted together at the bottom of her feet. I inspected the bottoms of my own feet to ensure that neither bore any mark of having been knitted, and, when I had satisfied myself that neither did, I turned to a different impression, which bore no suture-marks, but wherein I found, in each of the little wells of the toes (each clearly rendered, for it was soft ground there), a representation of an ox.

Then I despaired of identifying any impression as my own, for my feet bore no special feature that might allow me to recognize my own impression among so many others. And perhaps mine were the only featureless feet that had passed that way, but perhaps not. But, more than that—and I think now that perhaps I should have known it for a sign of something, that I despaired for this reason—more than that I despaired lest some other creature, a messenger perhaps, passing this way or some other way where I had passed, and inspecting the ground as I now inspected the ground, might discover my own footprints, and see them as I saw them, free of features, and think of me, the possessor perhaps of the only set of unfeatured feet in the vicinity or perhaps of only one of many sets of unfeatured feet, in a way which did injustice to the complexity of people; that is, lest such a messenger would think of me, and on my account of all the civilization of hairless and unfeatured feet, as a lack. Naturally the impression would spread quickly throughout the sea and sky. I tore strips from the blanket that I had carried this long way, and bound them round my feet, that I might preserve thereafter the true shape of my feet from the messengers that would follow. But this did not suffice. For although the strips of blanket might obscure my trail, they also caused me to occupy more of the space of the cavern, whereas in fact what I desired was to occupy less of it, or none. It is odd I think that to prevent my deficiency from becoming known I desired to perfect it—that is, rather than leave a marking with any lack, to leave no marking whatever. But perhaps it is in the nature of people to desire to perfect our deficiencies, for we love equally the perfect and the deficient. And even then this other matter did not yet occur to me, this matter of the hair which begins to obscure my head.

6.4 Epistle of Three Children to the Wearers of Sandals

For some days now we have been engaged in the manufacture of sandals. This has occupied every moment of our time. It is true that there have been moments, now in the afternoon, now at dawn, when we could no longer manufacture sandals, and then we have slept. Sometimes we have slept from the time the sun touched the tallest cedar until the time the sun touched the next-tallest cedar, and at other times we have slept from dawn until the next dawn. But in all cases, upon waking, we have recommenced manufacturing sandals.

We have had enough to eat from the larder, there being no one but us to eat it. By the time we have finished manufacturing sandals, the larder will be empty of food and the crèche will be full of sandals. In our discussions we have come to speak of ourselves as mechanisms for the transformation of food into sandals. Rarely, we think, have any people devoured what is in the larder with such recklessness as we, and rarely have any labored as we in the manufacture of sandals. But the need for sandals is now widespread in the community, whereas it is only we three who must eat from the larder—and that only until we go away, finally, by the road.

We have not yet seen the road, nor learned the use of this object, for we are children. But we have discussed it at length while manufacturing sandals, and the desire has emerged among us to set out, when we do set out, taking nothing with us and leaving nothing behind. This seems to us the way of entering most vigorously into a new state. Already we have submitted the sheds and canopies of the community to mycoids and the like, and sent away the animals which once labored in partnership with people, and planned our eating so that we might eat the last morsel from the larder on the day we leave. It is also for this reason that we manufacture sandals, to set loose those of you who require sandals to be set loose, so that you will neither come with us nor remain behind; and we hope that you will take with you every pair of sandals, leaving us nothing.

But this nothing to which we aspire is not only a material nothing. We hope also to cleanse ourselves of the intangible residues of this place that have accumulated in and on us like that gray powder that accumulates where the unspeakable phenomenon has excoriated the earth. That is, we hope to forget the things we have done here. It is for this reason that we write this epistle, to help in expunging the residues. In its way the production of this epistle is not unlike our production of sandals; for if the sandals will expunge you from the community, so, we hope, will this epistle expunge from our memories the residue of you and of your sandals. We will conceal this epistle in one sandal or another, perhaps in a sole, that you might take it away as well as yourselves and leave us free of it as well as of everything else, and it is of no concern to us whether you find it.

We desire most of all to expunge from our memories the sounds outside the crèche in the deep night. In our discussions we describe these sounds as keenings, and sometimes we have heard bumps. Moreover our dreams are filled with terrors. There is a simple boy among us; he said very little at first and he says less now, and his face, which had an open and wondering quality when he came, now hesitates, and appears forever ready to erupt in panic, as though he fears that something will come to get him. The thought that something will come to get us has disturbed us all during the deep night.

We believe that you make these noises yourselves in order to goad us to the quicker manufacture of sandals. And, indeed, at times when we might otherwise have slept, we have not slept, being afraid, but instead have manufactured sandals. But by day we manufacture sandals more slowly than we might, fatigued for want of sleep in part, and also distracted by the passage of the day on toward another deep night.

On a certain occasion we placed your sandals on our feet—for this, we understand, is the way they are meant to be used—and walked to and fro in the crèche, and then walked the pathways of the community as far as the creek, treading not on the earth but on the sole of the sandal. At once we found ourselves vying with the sandals for mastery. We veered into nettle patches and the nests of insects, and even when we regained control of our gait the sandals still strove to divert us, to fling us down gullies, and to sweep our feet from underneath us. But, in whatever direction they urged us, they strove always to separate us from each other; and we find the same thing as we manufacture them, side by side yet each committed to a solitary activity: we find their manufacture generative of a separation among us. Therefore we suppose that one object of these sandals is to separate people from one another. We suppose that there is some reason for this which we do not know, for we do not know what conditions pertain on the roads which you will walk. But we have introduced variation, as much as we could, into the quality of the soles, intending that, though you all set out at the same time, your sandals will fail, as finally they must, at different times, and will compel you to stop at different points along the road, and to found your communities at these different points, as many different communities at as many different points as there are individuals; for we suppose you will delight in this.

When we returned from our excursion we discovered that the sandals had opened wounds on our feet. These wounds became inflamed afterwards, and we fell ill; and we became grateful that there were yet vials of probiotic bacteria under the canopy of the healer of wounds, and that we were able to guess somewhat at the meaning of the marks thereon. Since that time we have made no further experiments with the sandals, but only manufactured them as rapidly as we might, and looked forward to the time of your taking them from us and departing. But we asked ourselves why it was that you should await these objects, and even keen and bump outside the crèche, in anxiety for them we suppose, and enter into our dreams. Perhaps, we thought, you have some reason for desiring to suffer. Or perhaps you desire to separate yourselves from the earth, but these sandals are not simpler than a rope for separating yourselves from the earth; but it may be a matter of nearness to the earth even in separation, or of reliance on the feet; but, in short, we supposed in the end that it was a matter of suffering. We have striven therefore to manufacture your sandals for the greatest possible discomfort. We have placed thorns in them, beyond those which were there already, and we have left rough clay unsanded; and those sandals which were delicate to walk in we have made more delicate still, to prevent you from walking easily.

Today we walked on our own six feet, without sandals, to the apiary, to encourage the bees to depart. We saw leaves on the path, one or two; and we thought, for an instant only:

soon there will be gatherers of leaves chosen to keep the paths clear. This thought both surprised and dismayed us. All things pass, not only leaves but also the gatherers of them, and even during the time when the community ate from the larder and did not require sandals we did not suppose that there would always be gatherers of leaves. But for an instant we deceived ourselves, and supposed that gatherers of leaves would soon begin their work—not that they would always come, but, what is equally foolish and what we have not yet learned not to think, that this particular time they would surely come. We became lazy, and desired to dwell in this image of the gatherers' of leaves imminent coming. But before we had time to apprehend it fully, it gave way in our minds to a different image, that of leaves ungathered accumulating on the path, as indeed they were and are. Then we found ourselves stricken in our bodies, as though from a blow to a part where the interior of the body lies near the surface. But at once the image presented itself to us once more, unbidden and quite untrue, of the gatherers of leaves soon chosen and the paths cleared. It was precisely the image which had just given way to the contrary image, but now we found that it had not given way, not really, but had persisted alongside the other, and had now returned, and even overcome the other, though it was false and the other true.

When we arrived at the apiary, we saw that a bear had been there. The bees had departed long since. All afternoon we could not think of the apiary in any other way than as having been upset by a bear. More precisely, we thought of the form and motion of the bear as he upset the apiary. Our expedition had exhausted our strength, and we fell asleep together. We woke lying very near to each other in the dark, having failed to uncover the phosphor lamps before we slept. You had not yet begun your noises. The images which had been foremost in our vision had been shuffled as we slept: once again we imagined the paths as they would be, choked with leaves ungathered, though we no longer beheld them with our eyes, nor anything but darkness; and, though we again imagined the scene of the bear upsetting the apiary, this time we thought no longer of the form and motion of the bear, but of the form and motion of the bees as they fled. A panic came over us. Because we had slept so near each other, our perspiration had mixed together on our three skins and also on the woolly cushion on which our three heads had lain. At that moment a bumping commenced outside the crèche. We took it momentarily for the bear, and thought that we should have to flee as bees flee, but never find our way back as bees find their way back.

In short, the deluge of images, true and untrue, accustomed and unaccustomed, has cast us into a state of confusion. The image of you as you were which prevails during the daytime paralyzes us, while the image of you which your keening summons at night cripples us; and all images compel our minds with a force apparently uncorrelated to their truth or their familiarity or anything else. After lengthy discussion we have come to consider this a fertile and promising state of affairs. For we prefer that all images consist side by side in our minds, none dominating any other, but each gathering to itself the singular strength that belongs to it, that we might enjoy them all equally and all at once. And if the state in which we find ourselves perplexes us, then it is only because of a great influx of images newly differentiated from the continuum of nonexistence from which images spring, and a great leveling of images hitherto suppressed in atavistic hierarchies; and in a word we have better hope now.

Nevertheless, this period is not easy for us. Even at the best of times a dread waits behind our thoughts. It has occurred to us to become scientists, in order to discipline our minds to dwell on images of all kinds with equanimity; for the scientist, so we are told, contemplates whatever images she likes, whatever the time of day: images of animals beyond the smallest smallness, and of fluxes both sustaining and menacing which surround us invisibly, and of obscure processes which must never be seen lest they transpire wrongly, and of processes which occur within the organs of our body even when they are bound inside our skin. And at times, particularly during the crepuscular hours when the sky is neither dark nor light, we do make a certain progress toward this art. But at other times the images we would master have the better of us. And we worry, too, lest this epistle fail to expunge every residue of you. Your noises have penetrated deeply. We worry lest after you have gone the residues of you continue to corrupt whatever scientific perspective has matured within us and turn our minds inexorably toward images of fear—perhaps, in the end, images of bloodshed. And our community, being a community of children, will have a name, and perhaps we will name it bloodshed. And later, when we are no longer children and the community has cast off the name of its childhood, perhaps the residues of you will yet remain with us, and we will devote ourselves not, as in days which we will have forgotten, to the manufacture of sandals, nor yet to a scientific exultation in diverse images, but to bloodshed, becoming known then as the community which sheds blood.

We have chosen, in order to bring ourselves closer to purity, to go forth in disguise. For the road sooner or later makes pure all who walk it, but it works more quickly, we are told, on those who walk it in disguise. Does it also make pure those who walk it in sandals? Perhaps it does; or perhaps there is a different road which does so.

There is one among us who is a boy, but he has taken the name and appearance of a girl in order to purify himself, and will soon mature into a woman. And there is another among us who is a girl, and she has taken strange drugs from under the canopies of scientists in order to afflict herself with a contagion that is unknown to us. She will walk separately from us, lest her contagion afflict us too; but we will call back and forth to each other. And as for the simple boy, he delights in the pain of the sandals, and before long he will steal a pair of sandals away from the crèche, and vanish into the forest, and go thereafter as a wearer of sandals; but when we go he will follow us. Thus we will take to the road as a girl almost a woman, followed at some distance by a stricken woman with symptoms of contagion, we know not what they will be, both of them haunted by a spirit of darkness who will be seen seldom and, being simple, seldom heard. In this way we will sooner or later fail to know ourselves. Meanwhile the autumn will pass and the winter will come. Perhaps we will further purify ourselves in the winter; perhaps by that time we will learn to sleep the winter long, like bears, and wake as different people during the thaw.

6.5 Angelophyta

An ox waited at the foot of the mountain. When Miriam saw it there she stepped off the path and stood in the ditch, behind a spray of birch leaves. The foot of the mountain was yet some distance away. She laughed at the memory of the ox's face. A butterfly alighted on the birch, reminding her that, although she was laughing as hard as ever she had laughed, she was not laughing aloud. Her feet were buried in leaves. She sprang out of the ditch and ran down the trail to greet the ox. A cool air rushed over her limbs. Still she forgot to make the sound of laughing. She wore neither hat nor sandals nor anything. The ox was chewing, but as she embraced it it opened its mouth and screamed. A shadow fell across her eyes. A man had come out from under the ox, carrying in one hand a pail of yellow foam and in the other hand a brush.

"Cleaning him," he said. "Are you clean?" He sniffed the air, and Miriam sniffed it with him. She smelled above all other smells the smell of the yellow foam, like the smell of sun-browned grass, rich and dead. The ox screamed once more, dwindlingly.

"I feel a purity," said Miriam, "if that is what you mean. No residue remains of the community which I have left; and, although I now make my way toward the community of the road, at the moment I am free of all communities and all structures and places and people. Yet I am not one of those who lurk alone, for I am on my way: as pure as a child which may even now lie dormant in one of the crates which you bear"—for a wagon stood behind the ox, under the shadow of the downstream cedar, and crates were visible within—"a child which belongs nowhere," she said, "but which is on its way."

"I mean are you clean in your body," said the yellow foam man. "For messengers will soon arrive which will interest themselves in the musk of people." Seizing her, he buried his nose under her arms, one after the other, inhaling deeply and looking far off at nothing; and when he was finished he pushed her away and pointed across the road at the river. "I advise you to bathe."

That was how it happened that Miriam did not set out on the road at once, but instead crossed it and stood on the riverbank, where brittle grasses scratched the soles of her feet. She peered down into the turbid waters of the river. Farther out, it flowed smooth and quick; but here, downstream of a mudbar, it swirled sluggishly. It was bordered with yellow foam, sticky to the touch.

"The water is not cool this time of year," the yellow foam man said, "and the current, flowing swiftly, has churned up solids of every description."

As he spoke, an expanse of slick black hide surfaced and sank again, and a stream of great greasy bubbles sputtered up from the deep.

"In all it resembles the fluids of the body; and for those who do lurk alone"—he gave her a hard look—"there is danger in it; for, should it overcome them, they have no companion to bring them out. But even they will desire cleanliness, lest the messengers bear away their musk." He set his pail on the foam-tainted grass beside her; its handle struck its side with a clunk. "Soap," he said. "I have compounded it myself of mosses and beneficial fluids. The skin hates it, for it mimics to the touch that phenomenon which we would forget; but, though it performs the function which we desire of that phenomenon, the function of purification, it omits those functions of destruction and the maddening of people, those which made an end to the civilization of the late capitalists."

Indeed, the yellow foam burned the soles of Miriam's feet where she trod on it, and made them itch; and, as she watched, it crept lifelike from the grass up her flesh, until it burned her ankles. The man fixed her with unblinking eyes and continued speaking:

"Should messengers bear away your musk, then all the messengers that even now form a celestial network beyond the ken of people, and all the messengers that may descend from those messengers in the future, or that may be bred in the future by people and later have intercourse with those messengers, all of them will know your musk; and then, for example, they will know how many of you there be, and your biological sex."

Then he told Miriam how a bat had come near him out of a twilight sky silver-blue in color, while he pored over the angelophyte colony in order to know his road. The bat had been mad, and he had driven it away by releasing an odor which bats detest, and which he carried for that purpose. But when he returned to his screen, the angelophytes there had news, borne by their cousins clinging to the bat's legs, of the far reaches of the continent, and other continents, and the sky, and places that were not on any continent or in the sky, and which he thought perhaps lay under the sea.

"For a new messenger has come into the sky," he said, "and established a network of watching creatures: I have heard a woman speak of it. And now tales will pass from earth to sky and back again, via bats, birds, balloons, and other creatures that move between sky and earth; and the messengers will keep their own civilization in the sky, vast in extent yet minuscule in figure, and misapprehend us in ways which I forbear to contemplate; and I tell you it will not surprise me if they soon interest themselves in our musk."

Then, though his skin was raw from scrubbing, he dove into the river and beckoned Miriam to join him; and when she stood still on the riverbank, for she felt dizzy, he beckoned her to douse him in the yellow foam, which she did, not without suds of it splashing up onto her hands and knees, where it burned her. After that he swam away and disported himself with his brush in the water.

"Are you of the community of the road?" she shouted. He had swum far from her. He ducked his head under the water and remained there so long that Miriam feared him swept away by an undercurrent; but in the end his head popped up, precisely where it had been, and she shouted again. He swam to her, and, climbing out of the water, trailing hands and dragging feet, and gazing reluctantly back, asked her to repeat herself a third time.

"Are you of the community of the road?" Miriam said. "For that is the community I hope to find, that community which is in motion."

His skin had suffered from this bath, which, she thought, must have followed many others. The air, drying him, brought out a layer of fine gray scale all over his surface, and a drop of blood welled from a crack in the skin at the angle of his neck.

"Messenger spores do love the road," he said, "and if we go without care we leave them our musk in innumerable places."

The road stretched to the right and to the left of the

place where they stood on the riverbank. They looked it over together, both to the right and to the left; but presently the yellow foam man began scratching himself with both hands, first chest and then legs and then everywhere, and Miriam looked over the road alone. In both directions it vanished, around a bend or behind the boughs of trees, but in one direction or else the other it became visible again, far away, ascending toward the pass at the head or foot of the valley: a streak of dust-brown, bordered by narrower streaks of white stone perceptible only as a dimming at its edges.

"Where does it go," she said, "this stretch of road?"

"All manner of places, the same as it always has." He carried on scratching, until she too began to itch.

"Then perhaps my way lies not on the road after all, but on the other side of the river."

At that the yellow foam man stopped scratching and leapt forward to seize her a second time. She shied away, but his arms elongated and would have overtaken her; but in the violence of his motion the skin under his arms cracked, painfully it seemed, for he shuddered and withdrew, swatting at the welling blood as at flies.

"That way lies the cairn of the androgyne," he said, "and perhaps other structures, and larger. Perhaps some go there who are not spirits of darkness"—here again he gave her a hard look—"as for example explorers, and those who harvest uncultivable herbs. But the region is not served by the road and not accessible by wheel, and is not a part of civilization. You might first walk some distance," he said, not resuming his scratching, but instead rubbing at his bleeding skin so that he was streaked with pink, "either upstream or downstream, to a place where the waters of the river are

BRIAN CONN

cold; and if you will not immerse yourself in the water here, which is too similar to the fluids of the body, then immerse yourself in that, which brings stillness, and ask yourself then whether you would seek community where there is no civilization. And if you would, then at least you will be clean in your body and filled with coolth, and not, as it were, in a fever." Dabbing soap on the blood which now trickled down his trunk, he took the bucket and stalked away toward the ox. It soon screamed; Miriam heard it from the mudbar in the shallows, where she had descended in order to gather rushes. When she had brought six armfuls of them up the bank to the dry grass beside the road, she sat on three of the white border-stones; and, finding the stones too hot, spread rushes over them for comfort, and gathered more. By the time the shadow of the yellow foam man fell on her again, she was weaving the rushes into a raft—weaving with practiced hands, for it was not unlike the sole of a shoe.

"And you will not reach the androgyne herself," said the yellow foam man, "for he lies within a structure of unimaginable complexity."

Miriam continued weaving and he soon went away again. When she looked up from her rushes, he was sniffing himself, and the air, and dabbing yellow foam on blood that welled in the corners of his eyes.

"They will interest themselves in blood as well as musk," he called when he saw Miriam watching him: "all the fluids which betray people."

He climbed into the back of the wagon, and Miriam saw him moving among the crates. When her raft had reached the size of a small mat, she carried it down to the water to test whether it would float. Sweeping the foam aside with her foot, she dropped it in. It did not sink, but neither did it float; and when she prodded it with her toe it bore up not at all, but retreated from her, down under the water. Its form faded in the murk and soon vanished.

A single waterfowl landed in a tumult of spray and white feather midway between that bank and the opposite bank. At once, without a sound, a current sucked it under, and it did not resurface.

"Anyway it will not be possible for you to cross," said the yellow foam man, who had come up behind her again, "for you are alone."

Miriam waded out into the river; her feet sank into the warm mire; foam, floating where water met air, burned her in rings below her knees. Soon she could see neither feet nor mire under the brown. A current tugged at her, and she stumbled and stopped. A butterfly came to play around her head. When she spoke to the yellow foam man again, she did not have to shout, because she had gone scarcely any distance from the shore.

"I might make a raft of the empty crates."

He did not answer, and she waded back to shore. Her feet reappeared, then the mire beneath them. A stray eddy, playing around her ankles, tightened suddenly; she fell, gripped the rushes, and pulled herself the last distance with her arms. She was covered in mud. The yellow foam man stepped away from her; but as she clambered past him and up the riverbank toward the wagon, brushing mud from her limbs, he called after her:

"Those crates which once bore children will float well I think, for they are of woodmatter cycled many times and rich with embedded air, to protect the children from the temperature. Perhaps one of them bore you yourself long ago."

The day grew hotter. Miriam dragged three empty crates from the wagon to the riverbank, and then the yellow foam man helped her, and dragged two more; and while she dragged one last, he brought out of the wagon a length of rope, not twisted rope, but a single thick strand of a kind manufactured by no spider she could name.

He gave her the rope and stood aside while she began to bind the crates together into a raft. She and he were silent together. She relished that time, and remembered it afterwards: the crates, resin-smooth and light as snow, came together as though they themselves willed it, and a strength in her fingers made the knots firm. The yellow foam man no longer scratched or rubbed, but studied her. Suddenly the creak of harness and the crunch of wheels disturbed the silence. The ox had set off on its own, drawing the wagon; behind the wagon walked a fat black wolf.

The yellow foam man cried out and stooped for a stone; but the wolf, far from pursuing the ox, favored it with a fond smile and turned aside to amble up the mountain path. His hindquarters swung to and fro in the sun. The yellow foam man forgot the ox and stood watching the wolf. Miriam tied the last knot. The raft was ready. There was a birch pole in the mud. She took it under her arm, shoved the raft into the river, and hopped aboard. The wolf paused to lick the earth. The yellow foam man tore his gaze from it, and, as the ox plodded up the road, and blood welled afresh from his own eyes and neck and shoulders and knees and all his other joints, seemed to take on for himself the fear the ox ought to have felt: he ran for the raft as though the wolf had frightened him out of his wits. He waded out into the current as Miriam poled away; fell, recovered, fell again; and finally Miriam planted the pole in the muck and allowed him to climb on board. The raft bore up easily even under his weight. He gripped its sides and looked back at the shore and up the path. The wolf had vanished round the bend.

"With his nails he will dig up all the fluids of people who are now dead," he said, "and soon the messengers will know how many there were, and their biological sexes." He had been seated on his knees, but now, even as Miriam poled farther into the river, he began shifting his limbs as though to sit otherwise; but as he shifted he could not leave off pinching the sides of the raft, nor refrain from flinging his head now one direction and now the other, in order to have a view of all the river at once; and such violent rocking of the raft ensued that some of the river came aboard, and they would have capsized had Miriam not stopped poling and sat very low and still in its center. Then they began to spin with the current.

"Should we find ourselves at the cairn of the androgyne," the yellow foam man went on, speaking, it seemed, not to Miriam but to himself, "I shall look on it merely as a crate, within which lie love and marvels I know not yet. And indeed I have often striven to see with the eyes of the new children who lie within the crates I carry, and to think what it is to have the world not with me on my side of the crate, but apart from me on the other. The moments ahead of us are but sealed crates whose contents we know not, and the moments behind us are but sealed crates whose contents we have forgotten; and perhaps this is only a new way for people to move together, this breaking open of unbidden and misdelivered future moments the contents of which we may never fathom; nevertheless—" and here he seemed suddenly to remember about the ox, because he gave a lurch and raised his head up to look that way, and a tendril of river reached up and flicked him overboard. Miriam held out the pole for him, but he could not get a grip on it, and the current swept him away.

6.6 The Cairn of the Androgyne

Miriam carried a bowl of white metal down from the cairn, down the winding trail and out under the clover-blue sky. At once she forgot all she had seen inside, as though it had been a dream that the sun had washed away. But it left her with a throbbing in her marrow.

She was surprised to hear the rattle of a viper. It came from a cloven stone, down where the trail fell away into a tangle of sticky summer brush. She listened for a period of time which she did not afterwards recall; and when she came to herself, although the sun had sunk low in the sky and she no longer heard the rattling or anything else, she had the impression that it had gone on unchanged for all of that time, until she had no longer heard it, but had heard instead its cessation a moment ago.

A woman came out of the cloven stone and waded through the brush, up toward the trail. She progressed slowly, at first on account of the brush, and after she had left the brush on account of her method of walking, which was, with each step, to sway toward that foot which she had just placed on the ground, until all the bulk of her body stood directly over it, and then, subsiding like a pendulum from that peak, to execute a small hop by way of switching feet, and sway back again toward the other side. On account of this gait her head oscillated to and fro with a wider range than is usual in the heads of walking persons, and her breasts, hanging heavily from her clavicle, swung in counterpoint. Miriam had ample time to observe her. With one hand this woman gripped a viper behind its head, and with the other stilled its rattle; the viper swung in time with her breasts.

Miriam set the metal bowl on the trail and sat beside it to watch the woman approach. The day was warm, but cooler than that which had come before, and among the trees, whose leaves were rimmed with gold, lay a darkness richer than that which had lain over the summer. The passage of the snake woman coaxed a sweet hypnotic odor from the fern on which she trod; perhaps that was why she walked in that way, that the herbs on which she trod might release their odor, and their oils coat her feet. The snake writhed angrily in her grasp. She stopped short of the trail, and instead of bowing, which would have exposed her to the bite of the snake, performed an upright squat and a bounce.

"My limbs throb fiercely," Miriam said, rubbing them.

"It is not uncommon."

"I have come a great distance," said Miriam, "and a man on my way suggested that you are not ordinary people here, but people of monstrous aspect; for you dwell, it seemed to him, in a lonely place."

Miriam felt suddenly precarious on the trail, and could not find her balance. The woman shook the snake at her in a not unfriendly way. Miriam remembered seeing a certain star on a certain day which had been the beginning of winter, long ago it must have been: a star between the planks of a crate, in the days before she was a child. She followed the snake woman down onto a steep slope. On one side stood the cloven stone and on the other side the land descended flatly, in a way that alarmed her for the steepness and also for the way the trees grew straight up despite the steepness and so made a sharp dizzying angle with the ground; but from its bottom there came the tinkling of a creek, or else a glimmer of it through the gloom. They descended deeper, but not as deep as the creek, and then turned to traverse the slope. That was difficult because the slope wanted to throw them down and into the creek and yet they must resist it and walk above. But soon Miriam found herself walking easily, and then they were descending in a different way, not down along the slope as before but down into the slope, for the shape of the hillside had been modified. They descended into a space like a bowl. Ever steeper the walls rose around them. All at once they found themselves in a twilight swale. There the snake took up writhing again and the woman was obliged to wrestle with it. But although she threw it and held it, nevertheless its rattle rattled in the gloaming, and then people came out from the trees and performed a dance. One played a wind instrument in conjunction with the rattling of the snake, and the one he faced performed a dance of standing quite still and beating his wrists one against the other with cocked-back hands, the dance of a handless man pounding maize. At the same time a humming waxed in the swale and the day dimmed. At last, in the cool of the evening, the snake subsided, and the snake woman was able to restrain it with only one hand. Then a number of them performed a dance of squatting and ris-ing, not unlike the squat and bounce the snake woman had performed. Miriam took it for a greeting, and asked aloud whether she would be at home among these people. But they did not answer because they were distracted by the humming, which waxed still louder. The snake woman performed a dance of planting the largest vertebra of her neck in the earth, and arching her back, and hopping in circles around the fixed point of her neck, as one running in a spiral toward the sky; and all of this she did without injury, for the ground there consisted of a gentle putty, which gleamed except where it was dark, not unlike the creek. Miriam, receiving no answer to the question whether she would find her home here, retired onto a bed of moss in the moonshadow of an oak, and curled around the metal bowl. Perhaps she slept or perhaps not; but, either waking or else coming to her senses from a stupor, she saw in front of her a very fat woman with cheekbones raised high and a chin red even in the dusk and cleft not once but twice, as though three cherries depended from her lower lip.

"A radiance from the center of things," she explained, seeing Miriam's eyes on her chin, "quite odorless and invisible, yet rich near here; it makes us different in our bodies than we were, sometimes better and sometimes worse. Will you dance?"

Suddenly Miriam began to weep, a thing she could not remember having done before. The radiance woman patted her shoulder, but it did not comfort her. She clutched the bowl, and when she heard the plunk of her tears in it commingling with the snake's rattle and the wind instrument and all the forest-crackling dancing racket, she sobbed deeply and said:

"I only wanted to know whether you were of monstrous aspect here and whether I should be at home."

BRIAN CONN

"It all depends on what is inside of you," said the radiance woman. "Here we live on ruins, and near a source of radiance, because it makes our bodies feel different, and thus plants the seeds of further differences inside us—I mean differences different even from the ordinary differences which distinguish people; and if you too desire to see all the substances of your person developed by radiance, and for new images to flourish in your thoughts which never flourished there before, nor ever flourished anywhere else, then perhaps you might remain in this and similar places, and be, as you call it, at home. What have you there?"

She meant the metal bowl, which, all over its surface but particularly in the pool of tears at its bottom, held the moon.

"A bowl," said Miriam, "silver I think. I found it in the cairn and thought I should use it for eating." She dumped the tears out and gave the bowl to the radiance woman. "It is of curious design."

"It is right that the cairn should feed us—I mean that the dead should feed the living, and not the other way around. Did you feel at home in the cairn?"

"There was a form within," said Miriam, "a person I suppose, or else a spirit of darkness. Even when I grasped her limbs he failed to stir. The chamber was dark because I had removed only a single stone from the wall in order to enter, and the beam of light that fell through the gap did not happen to fall on the form; and so I do not know whether she was indeed a person, or a spirit of darkness, or a construct of clay or web or some substance rarer still; but I think that, though his form was that of a person, her flesh was not the flesh of a person, because my fingers told me so. I felt this object in his hands, and a cloth too, which she had pressed to it as though for polishing; or again it may have been a clump of webbing, or another substance. I took the object but left the cloth, if it was a cloth."

"It was not always a bowl, I think, but long ago a helmet," said the radiance woman, putting it on her head and taking it off again; "he polished it long in the dark: see how she made it gleam."

And indeed a certain light, more than moon and stars, hung in the air around them; but even as Miriam bent her head to inspect the mysterious artifact and the radiance which she imagined it to have absorbed from the woman's head, a nearby dancer flung the viper into it. It curled up peacefully there and seemed to sleep.

"It was a thing the late capitalists wore," said the radiance woman, "in order to avert catastrophes obscure to us. But certain it is that it made another bar of their prison and another barb in the maw of the monster which gnawed their guts: another means of placing one person above and another below, and of keeping out those who were without, and in those who were within. And so not unlike a bowl in its way." She gave it back to Miriam, who poured the sleeping viper onto the ground and placed the helmet carefully beside it. "Here we eat only the food which it is convenient to carry in our hands, as the philosopher suggests. But all of that has nothing to do with what is inside you, and whether you shall be at home here."

Miriam yawned, unexpectedly sleepy. "Fever at times," she said; "I confess it has been inside me before, and I suppose it will be again. And at times when I am lost I feel as though I were filled with a mist."

BRIAN CONN

"And at times do you feel as though you were a wolf?"

"Yes," Miriam nodded, "at times like a wolf; and at times like I am falling, and yet with a frantic and scarcely reliable motion keeping myself aloft from innumerable catastrophes which I sense all around me with subtle senses—which is to say, like a bat."

"Yes," the radiance woman said, "like a bat."

"But at all times," said Miriam thoughtfully, "I suppose I am filled inside with blood; and I desire to remain so as long as I may."

"Strange that he should polish it so," said the radiance woman, kicking the helmet away, "as a scientist might polish a mirror—for did you not say it was dark in the cairn? And so she could never have seen her reflection."